More Praise for Leann Sweeney's Yellow Rose Mysteries

"I adore this series."   —Roundtable Reviews

"A welcome new voice in mystery fiction."
          —Jeff Abbott, bestselling author of *Cut and Run*

"Will leave mystery fans eager to read more about Abby Rose."   —Bill Crider, author of *Dead Soldiers*

"*Pick Your Poison* goes down sweet."
          —Rick Riordan, Edgar® Award–winning
          author of *The Lightning Thief*

"A witty, down-home Texas mystery . . . [a] fine tale."
          —*Midwest Book Review*

DEAD GIVEAWAY

A YELLOW ROSE MYSTERY

Leann Sweeney

A SIGNET BOOK

SIGNET
Published by New American Library, a division of
Penguin Group (USA) Inc., 375 Hudson Street,
New York, New York 10014, USA
Penguin Group (Canada), 90 Eglinton Avenue East, Suite 700, Toronto,
Ontario M4P 2Y3, Canada (a division of Pearson Penguin Canada Inc.)
Penguin Books Ltd., 80 Strand, London WC2R 0RL, England
Penguin Ireland, 25 St. Stephen's Green, Dublin 2,
Ireland (a division of Penguin Books Ltd.)
Penguin Group (Australia), 250 Camberwell Road, Camberwell, Victoria 3124,
Australia (a division of Pearson Australia Group Pty. Ltd.)
Penguin Books India Pvt. Ltd., 11 Community Centre, Panchsheel Park,
New Delhi - 110 017, India
Penguin Group (NZ), cnr Airborne and Rosedale Roads, Albany,
Auckland 1310, New Zealand (a division of Pearson New Zealand Ltd.)
Penguin Books (South Africa) (Pty.) Ltd., 24 Sturdee Avenue,
Rosebank, Johannesburg 2196, South Africa

Penguin Books Ltd., Registered Offices:
80 Strand, London WC2R 0RL, England

First published by Signet, an imprint of New American Library,
a division of Penguin Group (USA) Inc.

First Printing, November 2005
10 9 8 7 6 5 4 3 2 1

Copyright © Leann Sweeney, 2005
All rights reserved

The Edgar® name is a registered service mark of the Mystery Writers of
America, Inc.

 REGISTERED TRADEMARK—MARCA REGISTRADA

Printed in the United States of America

For Mike. I love you.

ACKNOWLEDGMENTS

A writer needs the support of so many, and I have been blessed with the best writer's group on the planet: Kay, Amy, Laura, Linda, Charlie, Bob and Mary, your support and insights make me work hard every week to write the best book I can. I thank you from the bottom of my heart. Susie, Isabella and Spicey, you are like family. Thanks for sharing your home. Jeffrey Cranor, my webmaster and publicity man, you do a fantastic job. A special thanks to Tim Carter, retired death row guard, who answered my endless questions with enthusiasm. To all the readers who have e-mailed saying they love Abby, you have no idea what joy I feel knowing I brought someone the treasured escape of a book. Thank you, Carole Mann, for your help and commitment. I love you, Mike, Shawn, Jillian, Jeffrey and Allison. Lastly, Claire, you are the best advocate I could have ever imagined, my dream-come-true editor. Thank you.

1

If Daddy were alive and standing beside me tonight, he'd say we've got a skunk down the well. A situation. I was in a parking lot on Houston's south side, leaning against the driver's-side door of my Camry and sipping on a Diet Coke. I wouldn't be getting near the espresso bar to meet with a witness in my new case. Not with crime scene tape strung in front of the building and red, white, and blue police cruiser lights electrifying the night sky like a patriotic carnival.

Folks from the sports bar farther down in the strip mall had wandered out to see what was going on, too. From the number of cars in the lot, the bar must have been packed for the Friday night NBA play-off game. Then a TV station news van pulled into the lot just as the faint mist dampening my hair and bare shoulders turned into a warm June drizzle.

Patches of fluorescent oil from departed cars slicked the blacktop separating me from Verna Mae Olsen, my witness. That's assuming she was inside the coffee joint and trapped by whatever event brought the police here. Maybe someone strung out on a caffeine high had foam in their mouth rather than in their coffee. Those five-dollar brews *will* piss you off some days. I sure hoped nothing serious had happened in there.

I'd interviewed Verna Mae several days ago in Bottlebrush—a town about an hour from here and as different from Houston as a toy poodle is from a coyote. My newest client, Will Knight, hired me to do what the police couldn't accomplish nineteen years ago—learn who had abandoned him on Verna Mae's doorstep. He and his adoptive parents hoped I'd uncover information about his birth family, and since I'm a PI who specializes in adoption issues, I took on Will's case.

Verna Mae seemed the logical starting point, and I thought I'd heard all she had to tell the other day, but she surprised me by calling tonight. I invited her to my house in the West University section of the city, but she insisted we meet here. Why at this coffee bar, I had no idea, but I'd agreed, and we'd exchanged cell phone numbers in case we missed each other.

Missed each other? Isn't that what just happened? If she were inside the café or sitting in her car watching this police show like I was, I'd feel a whole lot better if I heard her voice. I opened the car door, put the soda can in the cup holder and reached across the seat for my phone. Then I dug in my shorts pocket for her number. When I punched in the digits, it only rang once.

"Why are *you* calling this phone?" said a familiar male voice.

I opened my mouth but nothing came out. It was Jeff, Sergeant Jeff Kline of Houston PD Homicide. My Jeff. The guy I love. He'd recognized my caller ID.

"Talk to me, Abby," he said.

"You-you have her phone," I said. "That's not good."

"Whose phone?"

"Verna Mae Olsen. A witness I was supposed to meet. From what I'm seeing in this parking lot, I'm guessing that might not happen."

"Where are you?" he asked.

"Look out the window and you'll see me."

"I'll do better than that," he said.

The line went dead, and a second later he pushed open the glass door, ducked under the crime scene tape and strode in my direction. He held something in one latex-gloved hand and the badge clipped to his belt glinted in the halogen lights that had been set up to better illuminate the lot and storefront.

My heart was hammering now. Jeff's presence, plus his possession of that phone, equaled more than skunk trouble. By the time he reached me, my mouth was so dry I wasn't sure I had enough spit to talk.

Jeff wore his cop face—tired and all business. I'd seen that look when we first met, the awful day when my yardman was murdered and he drew the case. He held up a small black cell phone enclosed in a Baggie. "Who is this Olsen woman?"

"I-I interviewed her a couple days ago and she asked me to meet her here."

"You can ID her?" he said.

"ID her? You mean . . ."

"I need you to look at a body," he said, his tone less brittle, tinged with genuine regret.

"Oh, no. What happened, Jeff?"

"I'm guessing a robbery got out of hand. *Guessing.* That theory could change." He gestured for me to follow and led me toward the coffee bar, a.k.a. the Last Drop. As we walked, he put the cell phone in his pants pocket, removed his gloves and balled them up. Those went in his other pocket.

The rain had picked up by the time we passed the crew of cops on the sidewalk outside the shop. Several nodded at me in greeting. I'd met them when I went with Jeff to one of Houston PD's favorite watering holes. DeShay, his new partner, was talking to a tall young woman with grape hair, low-riding capris and a nose ring. I knew DeShay better than the others, and he looked my way, saying, "Hey, Abby. What's up?" like it was no big deal I'd show up at a crime scene.

We did not enter the Last Drop as I expected. Instead, Jeff led me around back to a wide alley that ran behind the shopping center, probably for delivery truck access. More halogens had been set up, and jumpsuited crime scene workers were canvassing the area around the back door of the coffeehouse. On the other side of the alley, a huge grassy ditch for flood-water collection was illuminated, too. Down in that ditch I saw a figure kneeling beside a dark mound I assumed was the body.

Telling me to follow exactly behind him so as not to disturb any uncollected evidence, Jeff walked carefully down the bank, taking a path where the grass had already been flattened by footsteps.

"How could you find *anyone* back here?" I asked.

"Pure luck. Guy tied up his dog outside while he went in for coffee. Black Lab with a helluva nose. Dog got loose, and here we are."

The crouching figure was in a blue oxford shirt, the fabric on her shoulders splattered with rain. As we drew closer, I could see the victim's feet. The once white tennis shoes were stained brown, and the wide small feet certainly could have belonged to Verna Mae, a short, plump woman around five feet tall. The day we met, I was struck how round and small she seemed in contrast to my client, who checks in at a lanky six-foot ten. Will's a college basketball player and went with me to Bottlebrush to meet with Verna Mae.

The woman in the oxford shirt stood and turned to face us. She had a round face, stringy gray hair, and held up her gloved hands like she was ready to do surgery. "What do you want, Sergeant?" she asked, not acknowledging my presence.

Her gruff manner and the fact she was standing over a dead person made my shoulders tighten.

"Dr. Post, this is Abby Rose. She can possibly ID the victim," Jeff said.

The woman smiled at me. Her teeth were yellowed and her eyes were sharp with interest. She refocused on Jeff. "You found family without having any ID? You have skills I didn't know you possessed, Sergeant."

"She's not family," he answered.

"Oh." The detached, cold expression returned.

"Well then, have a gander. I've cleaned off her face."
She waved a hand at the body.

At first I thought the body was covered with fire
ant hills, but the smell told me different. They were
coffee grounds. *Jeez*.

I recognized Verna Mae, mostly because of her dis-
tinctive gray eyes. They were glassy and wide now,
and her chubby face looked like she'd been hammered
with a meat mallet. Her broken nose lay against one
bruised and swollen cheek, and her bottom lip was
split. Blood covered her teeth and chin.

I stepped back. Tried to swallow the hot, sour Diet
Coke that rocketed into my mouth.

Jeff grabbed my elbow and pulled me back away
from the body. Good thing, because I bent over and
vomited everything but my toenails.

He rested a hand on my back as I rid myself of the
last ounce of bile, then he put his mouth to my ear
and whispered, "You okay?"

I nodded, wiped my lips with the back of my hand.

When I was upright again, Jeff said, "If you're not
able to continue, Ms. Rose, we understand." This formal attitude was apparently for the benefit of the doctor, who was again kneeling by the body.

I made myself take another good look, willing my
stomach to behave. "That's her. Verna Mae Olsen."

Dr. Post looked over her shoulder at me. From her
expression, pukers were obviously a pain in the ass.
She dug into the pile of coffee grounds and lifted one
of the dead woman's pudgy arms. Wet coffee clung to
Verna Mae's skin like dirt. "No rigor or lividity. This
corpse is fresher than the grounds they dumped on top
of her. Why do you think they did that, Sergeant?"

"Great way to hide a corpse," Jeff said.

"Made a helluva mess," she muttered. "Murderer
probably has the stuff all over their shoes. Forensics
can probably even match coffee brands these days."

"Yeah," Jeff said. "We bagged grounds already."

"Good, Sergeant. Now, could you take your witness
somewhere else? I've called the van to remove the

body, and she'll be in the way. And get one of your police friends to clean up her vomit. I don't want me or my people to step in it."

"I'm really sorry about getting sick," I told Jeff as he guided me back up the incline and across the alley.

"No problem." He used the walkie-talkie feature on his phone and said, "Hey, Rick. There's vomit by the body."

"You need me to collect it?" Rick responded.

"Don't bother. Not evidence. A witness lost it. Just wanted you to be aware if you happened to wander up that way again."

"Gotcha," the man answered.

Seems there was a little animosity between the ME and HPD, just as the press liked to speculate. As we arrived at the back entrance to the Last Drop, Jeff clipped his phone on his belt and held open the door for me. I went into a narrow hallway. By now, my shorts and white blouse were soaked, along with my sandaled feet, so the blast of air-conditioning had me shivering from bottom to top.

I noticed a restroom on the right and a storage area filled with huge, clear bags of coffee beans on our left. The aroma was unbelievably strong, and the room might as well have been a goat pasture—that's how pleasant the smell was to me at the moment. With gritty grounds between my toes and the churning in my gut, I wasn't sure I'd ever love coffee as much as I used to anymore.

Jeff rested his hands on my cold shoulders. "You did good. Sorry you had to go through that, but you've really helped us out."

"I feel so bad for her, Jeff. She must have been terrified before . . . before she died. What could she have possibly done to deserve that beating? She was just this oddball, small-town woman obsessed with a baby she found years ago."

"Let's sit, talk a little more about what you know about her," he said.

"Can I rinse my mouth first?"

"Sure. Want some gum, too?" He patted his shirt pocket where he kept his ever-present pack of Big Red.

"No. I don't want anything even marginally connected to the food pyramid."

"Okay. I'll meet you up front."

I stepped inside the lavatory, closed the door and leaned back, my hand on the knob. I closed my eyes, but that only made me see Verna Mae's battered face again, the face that had been so happy when I'd brought Will to see her.

I caught my reflection in the smudged oval mirror across from me and saw that my skin was the color of concrete and my hair so wet it looked black rather than auburn. I stepped over to a sink that resembled the bottom of a dirty coffeepot, turned on the faucet and splashed my face. After I rinsed away the taste of bile, I stared again in the mirror, ran my fingers through my hair and pushed back my bangs. I looked like I'd been through a car wash without a car, but this was as good as it was gonna get. I went back out into the hallway and walked the short distance into the coffee shop to give my statement, thinking about Verna Mae lying dead so close by and wondering if her death had some sad connection to my client.

I counted five cops besides Jeff, both uniformed and plainclothes. Three of them had taken advantage of the crime scene location and held steaming cups of coffee. Not the smallest size, either. Two others were interviewing a tattooed, fair-skinned Hispanic kid who couldn't have been more than twenty. His canvas apron bore the Last Drop's logo.

Jeff was seated at one of the half dozen small round tables lining the wall opposite the espresso bar. I took the bentwood kelly green chair across from him. He repositioned himself so his knee fit between both of mine and I mouthed a thank-you for the comfort he must have known this would provide.

"No coffee, I take it?" he asked.

"No," I said emphatically.

"Can you give me the victim's address so I can get someone on this notification?"

I did, and he wrote this in his notebook.

"She was a widow," I said. "Lived alone. I'm not sure· who they'll notify."

"We'll contact the local cops for help. I've never heard of this town. What county are we talking about?"

"Liberty," I said.

Jeff waved over a patrolman, tore off the address I'd given him and said, "Get on this notification. Liberty County address."

"Sure, Sarge," he answered, and left for a more quiet corner of the café to make the call.

Jeff refocused on me. His short blond hair glittered with rain, and the stubble on his chin looked more copper than golden in this light. He took two sticks of Big Red gum from his rain-dampened shirt, unwrapped them and folded them into his mouth. After he'd chewed a few seconds, he said, "As I mentioned, this looks like assault and robbery. Do you know anything about the victim that would make me see this differently?"

"Not really, considering I only met her once. But I can tell you she was alive two hours ago."

Jeff looked at his watch. "Seven?"

I nodded, and he jotted this down. "I take it you couldn't ID her because her purse was missing." I said this more to myself than to him, feeling calm enough to think logically now. "Where'd you find her phone?"

"In the alley. She must have dropped it."

"You couldn't find out who she was from that?"

"Prepaid. Never been used. Didn't even know it was hers for sure until you called. And yes, her purse is missing. So far we have no witnesses to an assault, but we have her name, so maybe we can match her with one of the cars in the lot—although the asshole might have stolen that, too."

"She drives a Cadillac," I said. "Late model, cream

colored. I saw it in the driveway when I went to her house."

Jeff rolled his eyes. "She probably had one of those damn Gucci purses slung on her arm and a three-carat diamond on her finger."

"More like one carat," I said quietly. "And a gold Rolex."

"I didn't see those. Christ. Why didn't she plaster a sign on her back that said ROB ME?"

"She struck me as someone who wouldn't have known any better," I said. "Lady wasn't hooked up right, Jeff. Very odd person, and I'm being respectful of the dead when I say *odd*."

"I'm interested in your take on her, but hang on." He again used his phone to walkie-talkie with Rick. "Look for a cream-colored Cadillac in the lot. Might belong to the victim." He closed the phone and looked at me again. "You say the Olsen woman was obsessed with an abandoned baby case?"

"Yes. Gosh, where do I begin? The interview with her was . . . strange."

"Strange. Okay. Keep talking."

"My client's a young man named Will Knight."

"Will Knight?" Jeff said, sounding surprised. "How old is he?"

"Young. Nineteen."

"Does he play basketball at the University of Texas?"

"You've heard of him?"

"Heard of him? Why didn't you tell me when you took his case? He's the best product to come out of a Houston high school since Okafor."

"Who's Okafor?"

"Never mind. You say, Knight hired you because he's adopted?"

"Yes. His adoptive parents encouraged him to look for his birth family. Will was abandoned on Verna Mae's doorstep as an infant, something Will has known since he was old enough to understand. Apparently abandoned babies draw a little press coverage, so Verna Mae's name was in the news. Anyway, Will says he's ready to put some closure on his past."

Jeff grinned. "*Closure on his past?* Those were a nineteen-year-old kid's words?"

I smiled. "Okay. It's a direct quote from Kate's psych evaluation." My twin sister, Kate, is a psychologist and does workups on all my clients. Adoption reunions can be emotional, and I don't proceed unless I feel reasonably sure the client is mentally prepared.

"Sounded like Kate's lingo," Jeff said. "What's the kid's story?"

"Will is biracial," I answered. "Raised by white middle-class parents. He's thought of himself as white his whole life. Then he goes to UT, and things changed. The team and his new friends consider him black. He wants to understand that better. He's okay with it, but it really got him thinking. Smart, insightful kid, if you haven't guessed."

"Hope he doesn't get all stupid when he lands his hundred-million-dollar NBA contract. Sometimes green is the only color that matters with these young superstars."

"You're being judgmental. Will is not your typical, cocky jock. He seems pretty damn normal to me—and to Kate."

"He *is* an amazing athlete, which means reporters are gonna be on this case like fleas if they find out he's even remotely involved."

"They won't hear it from me," I said.

"Someone in the Department's always taking a leak in the general direction of the press, but let's hope we can keep Will's name out of this. You both went to Olsen's house. When was that again?" He poised his pen for my answer.

"Two days ago. Then she calls me tonight. Says she needs to talk to me. I figured her more as the High-Tea-at-the-Warwick-Hotel type than a coffeehouse patron."

"Why couldn't she talk to you over the phone?" he asked.

"Believe me, I asked that question. She said she was in a rush, but would stop here on her way back to Bottlebrush. Said she had more to tell me about Will."

"That was all?" Jeff asked.

I closed my eyes, thought hard about every word Verna Mae and I had exchanged earlier. "That's all I remember, Jeff. Sounds to me like she was here in Houston, but that she didn't come to town just to chat with me."

"Maybe. Or she could have been passing through. Anything unusual about the tone of her voice? Was she nervous? Upset?"

"She seemed the same as when we met in person—someone whose roof wasn't nailed on tight."

He looked up from the notebook, his blue eyes narrow. "Explain."

"First off, the woman was as happy as a hog in a peach orchard when I brought Will to meet her. She may have been surprised to hear from us, but she was prepared. Verna Mae knew *everything* about Will, had followed his every move since the day he was left on her porch."

"How did that happen? Adoption files in this state are welded shut," Jeff said.

"With the cases I've worked so far, don't you think I know that? First thing I did after talking with Verna Mae was track down the caseworker who picked up baby Will from the local police. She owns a private nanny service now. I'm meeting with her Monday, and sure hope she can shed some light on how Verna Mae learned so much about my client."

"Could the Olsen woman have contacted Will Knight tonight? If she was as obsessed as you say, maybe she came to town to meet with him."

"Will would have called me, especially after how strange she seemed the other day," I said. "She made us both feel about as comfortable as Baptists in Las

Vegas. No, I'm thinking Verna Mae had business in the city. Anyone with as much money as she seemed to have has *business*."

"You should know," Jeff answered with a grin.

"Smart-ass." I used my knee to bump his.

Kate and I inherited buckets of money along with a still-profitable computer company when our daddy died, money that I use to help unwed mothers like my own biological mother had been. The money also helps support my PI business—a business I started to help adoptees locate their birth families. Bottom lines aren't important to me; reunions are.

"Business would be a logical explanation for Verna Mae showing up," I said. "The CompuCan CEO is always calling Kate or me to approve or sign stuff."

"Okay, she may have been in Houston for reasons unrelated to your case," he said. "But from what you've told me, seeing Will Knight the other day might have brought her here, too. Does he live in town?"

"He does. Bellaire. You want me to call him? See if he saw her today?"

Jeff didn't get a chance to answer.

A man wearing a dark suit came in with a uniformed cop trailing on his heels.

"Who's in charge here?" the man said.

Jeff pushed back his chair and slowly rose. "That would be me, sir. How can I help you?"

"What the hell happened?" The man was red-faced, and his bulbous nose bore evidence of more than coffee drinking.

Jeff walked the short distance separating us from the newcomer and stopped within inches of the guy's face. "Who's asking?"

"Jack Brown. I own this place," the man said.

"Sergeant Kline. HPD Homicide. A woman was murdered out back, Mr. Brown, then buried in a pile of coffee grounds. Those grounds your own special gift to the environment, maybe?"

Brown's bluster disappeared. "Wet grounds are heavy. Expensive to have hauled off."

"Yeah. That's what I figured. You cooperate, and maybe the city won't be too pissed off about how you handled your garbage problem." Jeff turned to the cop standing next to the clearly agitated owner. "Show Mr. Brown to a table, and I'll be with him in a minute. Maybe he'd like some coffee."

Jeff came back over and bent close to my ear. "I need to interview this one now that I have his complete attention."

I whispered, "Okay, I can wait."

"Please go home. I'll call you."

"But—"

"And do me a favor? Let me talk to Will Knight first."

He said this nice enough, but he wasn't asking for a favor: Jeff was warning me not to contact my client.

"If you say so," I answered.

Now, sometimes you gotta dance to the tune the band plays, especially when one of the fiddlers is your cop boyfriend. But as I drove home, I had to think long and hard whether this was one of those times.

2

I arrived home around ten, grabbed a Coke from the fridge and headed for the living room, unable to stop thinking about Verna Mae's call to me today and the horrible way she died. The sheer brutality had me as mad as a bull in red dye factory. I needed to find out what had happened. I mean, why beat a woman to death for jewelry and the contents of a handbag that could have been snatched without much effort? But maybe she had some fight in her and pissed off her assailant. If the bad guy was on drugs, it wouldn't take much to set him off.

Then there was Will. He would soon learn about this, and I sure wanted to be the one to tell him. I did have his number on speed-dial. One press of a button and I could see if he was home, walk that tightrope Jeff had placed between me and my client by asking Will if he'd had any surprises today—like a visit or call from Verna Mae.

Don't be an idiot, I told myself. I needed to respect Jeff's request, and I sure didn't want to get on the wrong side of HPD. I was still a new PI and under the supervision of Jeff's good friend Angel Molina of the Molina Detective Agency. Though I *am* a registered investigator, I only stay that way if I don't get into trouble. Getting into trouble with Jeff would affect not only my ability to work as a PI but also our relationship . . . which could affect Jeff's friendship with Angel . . . and maybe then affect the prospect of getting my little subsidiary of the Molina Agency, Yellow Rose Investigations, licensed by Texas in a few years. That damn domino effect will get you every time.

No call to Will. Period. But I had to do *something*.

With my calico cat, Diva, watching from the arm of one of the overstuffed chairs, I practically wore a hole in the Oriental rug in front of the sofa while sorting through all this, thinking about what I'd seen tonight and trying to remember every detail of my conversation with Verna Mae the other day. Could there be a clue from our meeting, a clue to explain why she contacted me today, a clue connected to her death?

Sipping intermittently on my soda, I recalled the woman's enthusiastic greeting when we'd arrived at her house, an encounter that immediately made Will and me uncomfortable. It would have made any sane person uncomfortable. I mean, what was Will supposed to do when a stranger hugged him like the human equivalent of Saran Wrap? Verna Mae's nose only came to his navel, and she pressed her plump face into his abdomen, wrapped her fleshy arms around him and held on for dear life. He reacted by raising his own arms as if he were being fitted for a tuxedo, all the while staring at me bug-eyed.

After she finally let go, she gave me one of those pat-you-on-the-back type hugs, thanked me for bringing her boy back home and walked us through her *I Lust for Waverly* house to the dining room. There we found a meal fit for a July Fourth picnic. Fried chicken, potato salad, a slab of ribs, baked beans and a gallon of sweet iced tea were laid out on a massive table—enough food to serve the state legislature.

We filled our plates—she'd even brought out the good china—and went out to the front porch. I chose the wicker chair right next to a planter filled with baby's breath, and Will sat to my right. Verna Mae flanked him on the other side. Thank goodness the round glass-covered table was high enough that he could fit his unbelievably long legs underneath.

I no sooner took my first bite of beans when I dropped my napkin. I bent to retrieve it and saw it had blown under the planter, the one I hadn't paid much attention to when we walked inside despite its presence near the front door. The one I now realized used to be a bassinet.

A white wicker bassinet on wheels.

I felt like ten caterpillars were crawling up my neck. "Um, unusual use of a baby bed," I said. "Did it belong to one of your children?" About then I was praying that was the explanation, but my gut told me otherwise.

"I have no other children, Ms. Rose." She rested a hand on Will's arm. "I placed the bassinet where I found my boy that night."

A brief, tense silence followed before Will said, "Cool," and continued eating.

I believe that's how teenage boys cope with everything—by eating.

Verna Mae raised the thin eyebrows over her gray eyes—the only thin thing on her body. "You may have the planter if you like, Will."

He gave me this pleading sideways glance that shouted, *Please help me.*

"A baby bed in a men's dorm might make for some interesting jokes," I said, trying to sound lighthearted rather than critical.

"Of course," she replied. "I was just . . . kidding." Her tone was terse enough that I knew the lighthearted approach had failed.

So much for my acting skills. "Why don't you tell us about the night Will arrived."

Her face relaxed and her eyes glazed over in dreamy remembrance. "I heard him crying. Jasper—he was my husband—said a cat was in heat. But I knew better. Thank goodness Will came to us in October, because the weather was perfect. No danger of him freezing or dying from the heat." She turned to Will. "When I picked you up, you quit crying right away. You knew we belonged together."

More hairy little feet on the nape of my neck. More painful glances from Will.

"But that's not how things worked out," I said.

"Thanks to *Jasper*." She practically spat his name. "Will was sent to *me*. God knew how much I wanted a baby, but Jasper called the police—even after I told him it was downright blasphemous to go against God's will. We should have kept our baby."

"But . . . your husband did what he was supposed to," I said, trying to sound apologetic for pointing this out.

She looked at me like I'd tracked horse manure onto her plush white carpet. "The *right* thing to do, my dear young woman, is to accept what God gives you. And He gave me a perfect baby boy."

Will subdued a "Yeah, she's definitely crazy" smile by scooping up one last giant forkful of potato salad and shoving it into his mouth.

"If you'd kept him," I said, "wouldn't people have wondered where this baby came from?"

"They might have had questions," conceded Verna Mae. "But folks in town knew we wanted to adopt. It's not like I didn't talk to everyone and their step-cousin about our desire for children."

"Did you apply to be Will's foster parent after he was taken from you?" I asked.

"That's not something I wish to discuss." From her brusque attitude and the little twitch near her eye, I figured I'd better leave the subject alone.

According to my amateur psychological analysis, this woman was angry at her dead husband and mad at the system that took Will away—grudges she'd held for nineteen years. Focusing on her old wounds wouldn't help Will find his birth parents. I needed to know what had *not* appeared in the newspaper articles, anything that would give me a place to start looking for clues. I said, "The articles Will's parents kept about the abandonment were pretty sketchy. Did Will come with a note? Or a special formula or baby bottle? Anything?"

"Nothing but the little T-shirt and diaper he arrived in," she said.

"No blanket?" I asked.

"Maybe a flannel receiving blanket. I don't really recall."

"Did he arrive in a box or a car seat or . . . what?" I asked.

"One of those plastic infant seats that you could buy anywhere back then. Officer Rollins took everything with him that night. Said he needed them for evidence. *Evidence.* Like it was a crime God left Will here with me." Her eyes filled and she blinked hard to fight back the tears.

Explaining to this woman that child abandonment was indeed a crime back then, and still is if you don't drop the baby off at a hospital or other safe haven, would have done no good. I chose another direction. "Did you hear anything about the baby in the days that followed?"

"Only that CPS got custody. Ridiculous arrangement. He already had someone to love him. But look at him," she said, beaming at Will. "He's turned out beautifully despite all those mistakes."

She put her hand on Will's forearm and kept talking, rattling off stories about championship games he'd played in, starting with Little Dribblers. Little Dribblers, I learned, was not a team of bib-wearing toddlers but rather a youth basketball league.

Will and I may have been squirming before, but this was the *Twilight Zone* moment—when we realized she'd followed Will around, maybe even with a camera. "And . . . how did you learn all these things about Will?" I asked. Because she shouldn't have known anything, not even his name.

She stared at me, color rising in her cheeks. "Why does that matter?"

"Probably doesn't," I answered quickly. Getting her more agitated than she already was did not seem like a good plan, so I decided to keep my thoughts to myself about how Will's adoption information should have been better protected.

"It's been very difficult since he went away to college, though," Verna Mae went on. "That drive to the university in Austin is simply awful."

The drive to the university? She was still stalking him today, and right there I should have quit worrying about the woman's mainspring popping and pressed harder for how she got her information. But did I? No. Stupid me changed the subject, asked about how the town reacted to the excitement of an abandoned child. And that's where I failed as an investigator. She was practically admitting to stalking the kid, but the idea made my stomach do little flip flops, made my skin prickle. I moved on, asking questions that didn't provide us with anything new.

The Coke I'd been sipping had made my hand cold. I quit pacing and set the can on my coffee table. How I wish I'd probed further the other day, gotten past my own discomfort at Verna Mae's obvious obsession with a kid who, by law, was supposed to have remained anonymous to her. The only other thing I learned of value was the name of the policeman who took Will away—Burl Rollins—currently chief of police in Bottlebrush. My calls to him yesterday and today had not been returned, but maybe, with Verna Mae dead and a county deputy sent to hunt up her relatives, he might talk to me tonight.

Yes. That's what I could do now. Jeff didn't say anything about my contacting the police in Bottlebrush.

Diva followed me into my office—a converted study right off the front foyer. Once the cat was settled in my lap, I powered up my computer and within two minutes had Burl Rollins's home phone number. An unlisted number would have taken a little longer, but his was right there in the white pages.

A sleepy woman answered on the fifth ring.

"Is this Mrs. Rollins?" I asked.

"Yes, ma'am. And who might you be?"

"My name is Abby Rose, and I'm an investigator calling about a local woman named Verna Mae Olsen. Could I speak to Chief Rollins, please?"

"What kind of investigator?" she asked warily.

"Private. Unfortunately, Mrs. Olsen passed away this evening and—"

"Oh, I know she's dead, and so does the Chief," Mrs. Rollins said.

"Terrible thing," I said. "I identified her body and . . . it was very . . . upsetting. I'm hoping to find out what happened to her, and maybe your husband can—"

"You identified the body and now you're asking *me* what happened? Somehow that doesn't compute. Had she hired you for some reason?" Mrs. Rollins asked.

"No. She was simply a person of interest in a case I'm working."

"Person of interest? Aren't you slick with your cop lingo? Listen, Ms. Rose, you want to talk to Burl, you better be straight with me."

"I would, except I'm not sure the Houston police would want me discussing what I saw tonight."

"Burl tells me everything and the reporters will be saying plenty tomorrow, so why don't you just tell me what the hell happened?"

If I'd learned one thing in my short career as a PI, it's that you have to give to get. So I gave. "Mrs. Olsen was severely beaten. That's all I know."

"Beaten? My heavens, that is *not* a nice way to go. Who'd be mad enough at a middle-aged country woman to beat her up? And I'm not just asking to be nosey. Burl would be asking you the same question."

"The police think she was robbed. I take it Mrs. Olsen was well-off?" I made it a question. It was her turn to give now.

"Listen, Ms. Rose. You're not getting another thing out of me until you tell me what's going on. What kind of case are you working on?"

I explained about Will, how he was the baby found on the doorstep so long ago.

"The *baby*? You don't say?" She sounded genuinely

surprised and a whole lot friendlier all of a sudden. "Now that's pretty interesting. I'm certain Burl *would* like to talk to you. Give me your number and I'll have him call you in the morning."

"I-I'd kind of like to speak with him tonight."

"You're out of luck. He's picking up the warrant to get inside Verna Mae's house. Deputy Sheriff called for his help about thirty minutes ago."

"He's at her place?"

"He will be, I expect. Said he'd get the warrant and meet the deputy there."

"From what Verna Mae said the other day, I assumed she lived alone. Why would he need a warrant?" I asked.

She yawned. "Because Burl does things by the book. Now give me your number. When he gets home, I'll tell him you want to talk to him."

I gave her my cell number and said, "Sorry to have disturbed you" before I hung up.

My brain was swirling with questions, and I knew I wouldn't be getting any sleep tonight. Stroking the purring Diva, I wondered if I could reach Bottlebrush before Burl Rollins was finished at Verna Mae's house.

The drive took far less time than when Will and I had made the trip, partly due to a deserted interstate—though a speedometer hovering at eighty helped, too. I arrived before midnight and found a county sheriff's patrol unit parked in Verna Mae's curving front drive along with a dark-colored Land Rover.

I pulled up behind the Rover, killed the engine and slid from behind the wheel of my Camry. The air was rich with country smells—the sweetness of honeysuckle in the night breeze layered over the scent of new-mown grass. When I climbed the porch steps and passed the wicker furniture where we'd sat and chatted, I looked away. I didn't care to see that bassinet again.

The front door stood ajar, the entire lock removed and lying on the porch slats. I pushed the door wider with my toe and heard male voices in a far-off room.

"Hello?" I called.

No reply, so I stepped inside. The same overpowering gardenia smell I remembered from the other day about slapped me in the face. Verna Mae must have a punch bowl full of potpourri somewhere. I slipped off my still gritty sandals, suddenly feeling the need to respect her white carpet. Whoever had just come in had not done the same. I easily followed two sets of dirty shoe prints that led to two men standing in a study. I noticed a gigantic rolltop desk and wall-to-wall mahogany bookshelves. The men's backs were to me, looking in desk drawers. One wore a black police uniform.

I cleared my throat.

They both turned in surprise, the deputy's hand on his weapon.

"Good evening, ma'am. Are you looking for Verna Mae?" the older cop said, apparently nonplussed by my arrival. His uncombed, gray-streaked hair tufted out over his ears, reading glasses sat low on his nose and he had brown eyes that sagged like a basset hound's.

"I'm not looking for her," I said. "I know she was murdered."

"Is that so? How did you find out?" asked the man. I noted a Bottlebrush gold police shield pinned to his shirt pocket.

"What's your business here?" the deputy piped in. He looked about twenty, with chiseled cheeks, a military haircut and biceps the size of world globes.

The older man put a hand on the deputy's arm. "Now, Glen, this is a friendly town and I'd like to maintain that reputation, if you don't mind. I doubt this little lady came here in the dead of night to cause us any trouble. Are you a reporter, miss?"

"No, sir. My name is Abby Rose and I'm a private

investigator." I started to unzip my bag. "I can show you my license if—"

"We'll get to that later. I'm Burl Rollins. Chief of Police in town," he said. "Your name sounds mighty familiar. Why is that?"

"I left you several messages over the last few days. I wanted to interview you for a case I'm working, one that involved Mrs. Olsen."

"Hmmm. And now she's departed this life. There's only one case I can think of that involves her *and* me, and that was a long time ago."

I nodded. "Abandoned child."

"How does that explain what you're doing here?" Muscleman Glen asked. I could tell he was making an effort to be "friendly" this time, but he didn't quite pull it off.

"Son," the chief said, addressing the deputy with a stern look. "You never mind about that. I think your job is to help find Mrs. Olsen's kin. Keep looking through the desk for any contacts while Ms. Rose and I get better acquainted."

"Yes, sir," the deputy said. He turned and went back to work.

Despite the attitude, I had to admire Glen's physical attributes. He had the nicest butt I'd seen since . . . well, since Jeff and I had that long hot shower together the other morning.

Chief Rollins and I went to the kitchen, a room I had not visited the other day. I felt smothered by the overabundance of ornate Victorian furniture in the rest of the house, but the kitchen seemed to calm me, despite the clutter of spice racks, hanging pots and new appliances made to look like antiques. Maybe it was my imagination, but the room still smelled like the blueberry cobbler Verna Mae lovingly watched Will consume.

We sat at a small oblong table draped with a crocheted cloth and I said, "Could I ask you something that may sound dumb, Chief?"

"Sure." He smiled. The guy had the small-town charm act perfected, but there was a wariness in his sad eyes. No, sir, Chief Rollins did not fall off the stupid truck. He was sizing me up good.

"Why would you need a search warrant to come in here? I mean, Mrs. Olsen is dead. She can't object."

He folded his hands on the table, and I noted knuckles thick and twisted with arthritis. Bet he'd have a hard time firing a weapon these days.

"Who said we had a search warrant?" he asked.

"Your wife. I called your house before I came here."

He grinned. "Ah. How'd you enjoy talking to the Missus?"

"She's . . . very straightforward," I said.

"Aren't you tactful? Good quality for an investigator. As for the warrant, what do you think would have happened if we came barging in here without one and whoever killed Verna Mae was sitting in her parlor enjoying her satellite TV?"

"Oh, I get it," I said. "Since the killer stole her purse and keys, maybe even her car, he could have come here to get more stuff. Should have figured that out myself."

He nodded. "The police don't ever want to be SOL in court. I've answered your question and now you need to return the favor. Tell me why you're here, Miss Rose."

"Call me Abby," I said.

"Okay, Abby. And I prefer Burl as long as we stay friendly. See, friends are honest with each other, isn't that so?"

"We're friends?"

"For now. Why are you here?"

"To talk to you. I suspect you're a busy man and that's why you didn't return my calls."

He pulled a small tape recorder from his pocket. "You wanted to discuss the baby case, huh?"

"Yup."

"If we're gonna go there, first tell me about your interview with Verna Mae the other day—and you don't mind if we save this conversation for posterity, do you?"

He was smiling, but obviously he was working this case, despite the fact that Verna Mae died in Houston. I wondered how Jeff would feel about this small territorial issue.

"I don't mind at all if you tape me."

He turned on the recorder, and I explained about my visit to Verna Mae and how my client had come with me.

When I finished he said, "You're telling me your client is that baby I took away from this very house?"

I nodded. "That *baby* is now six-foot-ten and plays college ball. His name is Will Knight."

Burl smiled broadly. "*That* Will Knight? Plays for UT?"

"None other." I needed to get up to snuff on my college hoops. Everyone seemed to know the kid.

"I'll be jiggered," Burl said. "You brought him here? To see Verna Mae?"

"Not sure I should have, but yes."

"You regret it, huh? Guess you figured out what most of us in Bottlebrush know. Verna Mae Olsen never forgot about the kid. Can't say I have either."

"That's exactly what I wanted to talk to you about. Can you—"

"Chief Rollins?" The deputy was standing in the entry to the kitchen.

"Yes, son?" Burl said.

"I think I found a place to start." He was holding a thick business-size envelope. "It's her last will and testament, sir."

"I assume you've had a look?" Burl said.

"Yes, sir," he answered.

"Well? Who gets what? Is it someone we can contact right away?"

"She left everything to a man named William Knight," he answered.

Burl Rollins blinked then leveled his wise eyes on me. He was not smiling when he said, "Is that so?"

3

"Don't look at *me*, Burl," I said, scrambling to answer while trying to gulp down my surprise. "I didn't know anything about Mrs. Olsen's will. My client didn't either."

"You know for sure, do you?" he said.

"What's going on?" the deputy asked.

"Nothing. I'll handle things from here," Burl said. "You've been a big help, but you can get back to your regular watch."

"You'll call HPD with this?" Glen held up the envelope.

"That's right," came Burl's smiling response. But his gleaming charm was tarnished by a hardness in his voice.

Before the deputy left, the chief got the name of the HPD officer who had made the original request to the Liberty County Sheriff's Department.

Thank goodness Jeff gave that chore to someone else, I thought, remembering his request to one of the policemen at the coffee place. I watched the chief flip open a cell phone and punch in the number.

After a few seconds he said, "This is Chief Rollins of the Bottlebrush Police Department. I understand you need information for a notification on a victim named Verna Mae Olsen?" Another short pause as Burl listened, then he said, "I'd be happy to discuss what we've learned with whoever's in charge of the investigation."

I sat back in my chair, stomach in my throat. *Damn. He wanted to talk to Jeff. I might be up a creek in a wire boat after all.*

"Hold on." Burl looked at me. "Got something to write on?"

I took a deep breath and pulled the crumpled paper with Verna Mae's phone number from my pocket.

The chief smoothed it out, pulled a pen from his shirt pocket and said, "Go ahead."

Meanwhile, I marveled at how cooperative I was being at assisting in my own demise. Even upside down I recognized every digit he wrote. Jeff's cell number.

Burl thanked the officer, disconnected and started to dial again. I reached across and grabbed his thick wrist. "Could we talk before you make that call?"

He closed the phone. "About what?"

"The detective who's in charge is . . . a friend of mine. Got me my PI job, as a matter of fact. I don't think he'd be too happy if he knew I'd driven here tonight."

Burl sat back, arms folded, that stupid, evil phone tucked under one armpit. "Bet he won't be happy. So?"

"Is there some compelling reason he needs to know?" I asked.

"How would you answer that question if you were in my position, Abby?"

I hung my head. Bit my lower lip. "I'd say I had to give the investigators everything I knew. This is a murder case, after all." I stared him in the eyes. "But I could tell Sergeant Kline myself when I see him. It's not like my trip here has anything to do with the murder. I just had questions for you, questions about a woman who wanted to talk to me tonight and never got the chance."

Burl placed the cell phone on the table between us. "Tell your friend *now* that you're here at Verna Mae's, and then we'll continue our conversation."

"Now?" I stared at the phone, the little palm-size

instrument of torture seeming to grow larger the longer I looked at it.

"If this pisses your friend off, work it out later. Right now we owe Verna Mae Olsen our best effort before more time passes."

I sighed. He was right. I was being totally selfish. Still, my hand trembled when I picked up the phone. The chief pushed the paper toward me, but I shook my head. "Don't need that."

Jeff answered on the second ring with "Sergeant Kline."

"Um, hi again," I said.

"Abby?" He sounded even more stunned than when he got the last weird call from me.

"As you can probably tell from the caller ID, this is not my phone," I said quickly.

"You're full of surprises tonight. Whose number *is* on my screen?"

"Burl Rollins. He's the Chief of Police in Bottlebrush."

A few seconds passed before he said, "Okay. What have you got for me?"

I couldn't tell from his tone if he was pissed, or glad to hear from me, or just totally confused.

"Some surprising information," I said.

"Great. I love surprises in a murder investigation. Especially when they involve you." He might as well have added, "Because about now, you've got more problems than a mailman at a rottweiler show."

"I'm at Verna Mae's house, and the police have discovered Will is her sole beneficiary," I said.

A long silence followed before he said, "Please tell me you just found out, that you didn't know this when we talked earlier."

"Of course I didn't know," I snapped. "I'm sure Will didn't know either."

"Why? Because he would have told you?" His tone was ripe with sarcasm.

"That's right," I answered.

"Maybe there's a few things you don't know about

your client aside from who is birth parents are. If the chief is there, let me talk to him."

I handed the phone to Burl, and while he reported to Jeff in more detail, I wiped my sweaty palms on my shorts and wondered how I would clean up this little mess I'd just made.

When Burl flipped his phone shut, he said, "The sergeant said you should meet him at HPD headquarters at ten a.m. tomorrow."

I checked my watch. It was after one already.

"Sharp," Burl said as he stood. "Which means you better get yourself back to the city if you want to sleep tonight."

"But you said we could talk about the baby case after I called Jeff . . . I mean Sergeant Kline."

He pushed his wire-frames up on his nose and sighed heavily. "You sure you want to do that now?"

"I've got a client who needs answers."

"Sounds like your client needs to provide a few of those himself."

"Yes, and he'll do that. But could you tell me more about your investigation into Will's abandonment?"

Burl lowered himself into the chair. "Not much to tell. About wore me out hunting for clues."

"What happened after you took Will from Verna Mae?"

"Turned the kid over to CPS the following day. Couldn't get a caseworker out that Sunday night. Me and my wife, Lucinda, kept the baby overnight. It's not like we didn't have two cribs going already—a nine-month-old and a two-year-old. That kid sure had a set o' lungs on him. And he was big. The wife put him into one of the little snap-up pajamas our youngest had outgrown. I remember her saying she had to use the three-month size. She figured he wasn't newborn, but now that I know he turned out to be a giant, maybe he was."

"Maybe. You asked questions around town, I presume?"

"Sure. Thought it would be easy to find the parents,

since the kid looked to be mixed-race or black. The Missus is a retired nurse and said another reason she didn't think he was newborn was because she could tell he had some African-American in him. Seems black newborns look white at first, so she thought the boy had to be at least a couple weeks old. Jasper mentioned the baby was black, too. All I saw was a great-looking, healthy kid with curly dark hair. Real shiny. Handsome as he was loud."

"Did you hear any rumors about mixed-race couples at, say, the high school?"

He shook his head no. "We only had about five hundred kids total in the schools here. A mixed-race couple would have been noticed, there or anywhere. Would have been talk around town, too. There wasn't."

"You think someone came a ways to drop off the baby, then?"

"I guess, but Verna Mae's house isn't exactly right off the highway. That bothered me. Made me put some credence in her going on and on about how God brought the baby to her for a reason. Hell, maybe she was right."

"She told me the same thing. The clothes, the infant seat? No leads there?"

"I checked, but they weren't bought in this town. We didn't have the Wal-Mart back then, only a grocery store. Couldn't plug brand names into a computer and trace the purchases, either."

"Did those personal items go with him when CPS took over?"

"I suppose. Can't say as I remember." I read discomfort in Burl's tired eyes.

"Frustrating case, huh?" I said.

"You betcha. Verna Mae hounded me for information about the baby for days afterward. Then she quit calling after the family court hearing that placed the child in state custody." He shut his eyes, seemed to be thinking hard. "But we know now she found out about him somehow, considering she left him everything."

Burl rose suddenly, saying, "Wait a minute." He shot out of the kitchen, his fatigue apparently gone.

I followed, jogging to keep him in sight as he ran down the hall and took the stairs.

I caught up to him in Verna Mae's bedroom. He was on his knees, pulling a lidded cardboard box from under a four-poster bed decorated with enough ruffles and tassels to supply a fabric store for a year.

"What's going on?" I asked, hurrying to his side.

FOR W.K. was printed in black marker on the lid he now removed.

Inside were stacks of scrapbooks and photo albums.

"Glen told me he'd found books under her bed filled with a bunch of old newspaper articles about basketball. Said he thought it was peculiar Verna Mae was interested in sports, what with the frilly house and all. I told him she *was* peculiar and said he should keep looking for what we came for."

He opened one album. On the first page was a year-old *Houston Chronicle* article about the state high school basketball championship. The next pages contained clippings from other newspapers around the state covering the championship from two years ago. Several had photos of Will—not shaved bald like he was now, but with plenty of wild dark hair—a basketball in one huge hand, and jumping high for a layup.

"I'm betting those books go back even to his elementary school days from the way she talked the other day," I said.

Burl looked up. "You're sure your client didn't know about her interest in him before then? Or about her will?"

I knelt and picked up a different album. "If he did, he's a damn good actor." I flipped open the page and saw a photo of Will in a stroller, recognized his adoptive mother, Annabelle Wright, wheeling him in the park. Telephoto lens? Probably. There were more articles, these from the smaller paper that served the community where Will grew up, stories from the days when he played in Little League baseball and the youth basketball program Verna Mae had mentioned. Seems Will had been an all-star no matter what sport he played. Made the honor roll and had been inducted into the National Honor Society, too. It was all there. Page after page chronicling his young life.

I felt a chill. Hearing such things from her lips had been creepy enough, but holding the proof of her fixation was even more disturbing.

"I'm not sure if her being so stuck on a kid she knew only for a few hours has anything to do with her death, but something's not right," Burl said.

"You mean with these albums?" I asked, not understanding.

"That boy wasn't a stranger to her. It's obvious she loved him."

"No kidding." But then it dawned on me where he was headed. "You don't think he was *her* baby?"

His smile was back. "You may be green, but you're a thinker. If Jasper Olsen's wife bore another man's child, a black man's child, then Verna Mae was lucky to escape with her life. Knowing that nasty SOB, he mighta killed her."

"You think she made up the story about finding Will? That she was forced to give away her own child?"

"I never explored that possibility. Not once. She was so . . . well, *hefty*, she could have hidden a pregnancy. What a stupid, greenhorn fool I was." He banged his forehead with the heel of his hand.

I put the album back in the box and noticed something beneath the stack of scrapbooks—the corner of a brown paper sack. "What's this?" I said, lifting out the albums and setting them on the carpet.

I pulled out the sack and started to peek inside.

"Let me do that." Burl took the bag and stood.

Carefully he slid the contents onto the bed. Baby clothes. Tiny white shirts and one-piece sleepers. And a blanket of creamy, soft wool. I rose and fingered the blanket, turned a satin corner over to check the label.

"HANDMADE FOR POSH PRAMS," I said.

"About nineteen years old, I'd say." He stared at it, his lips tight with anger. "She lied to me, withheld evidence, and I never once questioned her about the kid possibly being hers. Sloppy police work, is all I can say."

"Is the blanket really evidence?" I asked. "She could have bought it herself."

"Right. When? You won't see a fancy blanket like this in Bottlebrush. She probably had to go to Houston to buy it. Did she rush there on that Sunday evening, buy the blanket, then keep it when Jasper called me to pick up the baby? Doesn't make sense, Abby." He carefully placed the blanket back in the sack, his shoulders slumped, his expression haggard. "You or HPD need any assistance, call me. Meanwhile, I'll just hang on to this."

"Giving me that blanket would help," I said.

"I'm thinking I'll ask around. Someone in town might know where Verna Mae got it."

"But—"

"This is evidence collected during the execution of a warrant," he said. "The blanket stays with me. Time you went home, Abby. Get some sleep. We'll talk again."

4

I arrived home from Bottlebrush about three a.m. Although I was so tired I could have slept in a barrel, I had one irritated cat to deal with. Diva had been without a warm body to cuddle up to, and she wanted a Fancy Feast bribe before she'd make up with me. She made this very clear by hissing when I picked her up, jumping from my arms and racing through my small living room to the kitchen beyond.

The answering machine was bleeping, too. She wasn't the only one who wanted my attention. While I pried open a can of Seafood Dinner, I punched the PLAY button and heard Will's voice.

"Hey, Abby. It's Will," he said in his slow, soft voice. "Me and the parents had a call from some police guy. He told us Mrs. Olsen passed on. Give me a call right away, 'cause my parents are kinda bent. You got my cell number."

I didn't blame his parents for being upset. Murder is not what they signed up for. Since Jeff had already made his contact, I decided I was free to call my client—but not in the middle of the night. After dumping the cat food in Diva's dish, I trudged upstairs, stripped and fell into bed. I did set the alarm for seven a.m. If I wanted to speak to Will and his parents before my appointment with Jeff at headquarters, I needed an early start.

It seemed like only seconds later that I was hitting the snooze button. I punched it twice more before I grabbed my phone off the nightstand and called Will. He answered after a few rings, obviously roused from sleep.

True to the Will I was getting to know, he was far more polite than I would have been. "Uh, hi, Abby."

"Sorry I woke you." I sat cross-legged, my back against the headboard.

"No big deal. What's going on with this murder? I mean, that cop who called was stone serious, so it must be true."

"Oh, it's true." I gave him a condensed version of what happened to Verna Mae, though I omitted my visit to Bottlebrush.

"The officer wanted to know where I was last night. Here with my friends and my parents is what I told him. Then he talked to Dad. They don't think I'd hurt her, do they? I mean—"

"Listen, Will, your parents would probably like to be around when we talk this over. How about I drop by in, say, thirty minutes?"

"Sure, okay. I'll let Mom know you're coming so she won't think you're some reporter knocking on the door. She is super-stressed about reporters, anyway. They're always hanging around during the season, and this sounds like something they'd love to dig into."

"I'm sure they would. See you at eight." I disconnected.

Eight . . . jeez, I thought as I closed my phone and set it on the nightstand. I got up, headed for the bathroom and stumbled over Jeff's running shoes. I couldn't complain: Mine were a few steps beyond his. I picked up both pairs and tossed them into a corner, saying, "Cold water, work some magic. I need to get my brain in gear fast."

I realized the coffee aversion that had surfaced last night after seeing Verna Mae buried in wet grounds was persisting, this enlightenment coming after I made an optimistic stop at a Starbucks drive-through on my way to the Knight home. The strong coffee smell wafting out the window made me want to puke, so I ordered chai tea. Never had it before, but Kate swears by the stuff—not that I'd ever tell her I'd voluntarily ventured to the fringe of her organic, all-natural, soy-filled world. I needed caffeine if I planned to have a coherent conversation with anyone, and the girl at the window said the tea worked as well as a tall latte.

Will's parents lived in an older, redbrick house on a wooded street in Bellaire, a city that blended with Houston on the southwest side near the Galleria shopping mall. Since it was Saturday morning, a few joggers manned the sidewalks, but most of Bellaire was still waking up. The air was thick with humidity after last night's rain, despite the early morning hour. So much for my refreshing shower. My skin felt sticky when I pressed the doorbell at the Knight home, and I wished I'd worn shorts and a tank top rather than jeans and a stretchy green shirt. This spandex fashion fixation was not created with Houston weather in mind.

Mrs. Knight answered the door, and the cheery face I recalled from the last time we'd met was darkened by concern. "Good morning, Ms. Rose. Will told us you were coming." She widened the door for me to enter.

"Like I said the other day, please call me Abby," I said.

"Sorry. I forgot. We're having breakfast and I made plenty. Can I fix you a plate?"

"Uh, sure. Sounds good." Hungry or not, I knew better than to refuse a meal. I didn't know Will's mom well enough yet to determine how hardcore Texan she was.

She led me through a home eerily similar to my own with its small foyer and living area, but an overstuffed sectional sofa and a floor-to-ceiling stone fireplace offered the homey touch that my place lacked. I definitely needed a house makeover.

The kitchen was larger than mine and obviously the center of family life. An additional fireplace with a love seat in front filled one corner. A curving breakfast bar separated the kitchen area from an alcove with built-in seating bordering the bay window. Will was sitting on the farthest edge of the cushioned bench so that his legs could stretch out unhindered by the pedestal base. His sandy-haired father sat across from him with the metro section of the *Houston Chronicle* spread out on the table. Probably reading about last night's murder.

"Sam, fetch Abby a chair from the dining room, would you?" Annabelle Knight said.

Sam Knight stood and smiled, as did his son. Weird seeing them together. Mr. Knight couldn't be more than two inches taller than me, which put him at about five-six or -seven. Then there was monster Will. He was so muscular and tall, he could have picked up his dad under one arm and his little bit of a mom under the other and jogged a couple miles.

"Morning, ma'am," Mr. Knight said before leaving to get the chair.

"Hey, Abby," Will said, his voice sleepy, his lids heavy with fatigue, though not heavy enough to mask his pale amber eyes. Bet the UT girls liked having this guy on campus.

"William Knight, is that how you address a young woman?" his mother said.

"I told him to call me Abby, so it's fine," I said quickly.

"Then it's 'Good morning, Abby.' Not 'hey.' " But she smiled a loving smile in her son's direction when he offered his sheepish "Yes, ma'am" reply.

Mr. Knight arrived with a maple dining chair and placed it facing the window and next to Will.

"Thanks," I said.

"My pleasure." Mr. Knight sat back down. I saw that his scrambled eggs and sausage were untouched, and the paper did indeed have a headline atop the metro section that blared WOMAN FOUND MURDERED BEHIND ESPRESSO BAR.

Mr. Knight tapped the paper. "Terrible thing. When he was in high school, Will and I used to catch college hoops on cable at a sports bar right near this place."

So that's why Verna Mae chose the Last Drop for our meeting. She'd probably been there watching for a glimpse of Will more than once, if I had her figured right.

"Abby," Mr. Wright went on, "do you know anything more than what the newspaper says? The policeman who called last night mentioned you were at the scene."

"I was. Verna Mae phoned me to meet her, but unfortunately I never found out what she wanted to talk about," I said.

Mrs. Knight moved a plate with eggs, toast and two sausage patties in front of me. "This is awful. That poor woman."

Her husband slid over so she could sit beside him.

Mrs. Knight said, "Will and several of his old high school friends were watching the NBA play-off game when the officer called. I have to say, I was a little upset when the sergeant asked if Will had been out during the early evening. He hadn't, of course. He'd been looking forward to this get-together with his friends all week." The doorbell rang, and Mrs. Knight squeezed her eyes shut. "It's those awful reporters. I know it."

"Let me handle this," Mr. Knight said.

Will's mother let her husband out. As he jogged from the kitchen, his small potbelly jiggling under his warm-up jacket, she called, "Tell them to leave us alone."

"Mom, chill, okay?" Will said. "They're just doing their job."

"Tough living with a celebrity, huh?" I said.

"The reporters don't bother me all that much," Will said. "Since we didn't win the Big Dance, they've pretty much left me alone."

"Big Dance?" I said.

"The NCAA tournament," Will answered.

Mrs. Knight said, "Didn't win it *this* year. Will's heading for UT for basketball camp in a couple days. He'll do weight training and meet with a nutritionist, so he'll be a force to reckon with on the court. Then they'll go all the way next season."

"Mom, we're a team. It's not only about me," said Will.

Mr. Wright returned, but not with a reporter on his heels. It was Jeff.

My chair made an awful scraping sound when I pushed away from the table and stood.

"Uh, hi," I said.

Jeff looked me square in the eyes for what seemed like a long time but was probably no more than a second.

"I got an invite for breakfast," I said.

"I see." His expression told me he was sure they hadn't called me on a whim at this hour. He looked back and forth between Will's parents. "Just wanted to meet you folks face-to-face and apologize for upsetting you last night."

"You're Sergeant Kline? The one who phoned?" asked Mrs. Knight.

"Yes, ma'am." His tie was loosened, his sports jacket wrinkled, and he looked so damn tired I felt guilty for my four hours of sleep.

"You have nothing to apologize for," she said. "You didn't murder that poor woman. God knows, I've been praying for her soul. If not for her, Will might never have come into our lives." Her eyes filled with tears.

"Mom," Will said. "I was supposed to end up with you no matter what."

She smiled sadly and nodded.

Jeff reached out a hand to Will. "Jeff Kline."

I noted that despite his exhaustion Jeff had enough energy for a huge smile and a vigorous handshake. Plus he'd introduced himself with his first name. *Hmmm. I think the man is smitten.*

"Fantastic last game in March despite the loss," Jeff said.

Oh, yes. This was a love story in the making.

"Thanks, but we've got an awesome point guard. 'Course you know that."

"You had thirty-four points, right?" Jeff went on. "And how many blocked shots?"

I cleared my throat. "Um, my breakfast is getting cold."

Mrs. Knight held out another loaded plate for Jeff, and Mr. Knight had snuck off for an additional chair.

We crowded around the table and ate and talked about basketball. It was sort of like the first day of my immersion Spanish class at the University of Houston, the one I dropped after a week. I didn't understand a word of what Jeff and the Knights were saying. I only knew they all spoke the language but me.

When we were through eating and Mrs. Knight refused my offer to help her clean up the dishes, Jeff addressed Will and his dad. "As you probably know, Ms. Rose identified Verna Mae Olsen's body last night. I assume she informed you that Mrs. Olsen left her property to you, Will."

"I did no such thing," I said. How I wanted to punch Jeff about now. I'd hoped to ease into that particular revelation.

Meanwhile, Mr. Knight's jaw had dropped, and I heard utensils crashing behind me in the kitchen.

Will said it all with his astonished, *"What?"*

Jeff looked genuinely surprised, and maybe even a tad embarrassed now that he realized I hadn't already spilled these particular beans. Beans. Yuck. I'd never before considered that expression might be a reference to coffee beans.

Mrs. Knight came rushing back to join us, wiping her reddened hands on a checkered dish towel. "That's why you're here? To recheck our son's alibi because you think he expected to inherit money from a stranger? Money he knew nothing about until this minute?"

"Ma'am, I have to contact or interview everyone who spoke with the victim recently," Jeff said. His throat was all blotchy above his collar. "A phone call isn't enough."

"Will would never harm anyone," a red-faced Mrs. Knight said.

Jeff had regrouped and returned to his calm cop mode. "I never said he did."

He had slipped up by not talking to me first, though. Maybe it was the lack of sleep, but I suspected his mistake had more to do with Will the Sports Hero. Seems I had plenty to learn about this aspect of the man in my life.

Mrs. Wright said, "I think you should apologize to—"

"Annabelle," Mr. Knight cut in with an admirable take-charge tone. "You're jumping to conclusions. Let the officer talk."

Jeff nodded at Mr. Wright. "No problem, sir. I do apologize. Your son obviously was with you and his friends last night. We'll speak with the other young men present, but I'm sure they'll confirm what you've told me. My main purpose in coming was to ask a few questions about the meeting Miss Rose and Will had with the victim the other day."

"Oh. That makes sense," Mrs. Knight said. By her embarrassed expression, you'd have thought I'd just told her that her dress was tucked into her panty hose.

"I believe I told you all about our meeting with Mrs. Olsen, Sergeant Kline," I said, trying to sound as patient and composed as Jeff.

Will squinted and cocked his head. "I get the feeling you two know each—I mean, aside from what went down last night."

"How could you ever guess?" I said. "We know each other quite well, as a matter of fact."

"From other cases?" His eyes were bright with curiosity.

Smart, intuitive kid. No wonder I liked him so much.

"We're colleagues," Jeff said. He offered out his gum, and getting no takers, unwrapped a few sticks and folded them in his mouth. "Back to why I'm here. Did Mrs. Olsen contact you after you met with her the other day?"

"No, sir," said Will.

Jeff looked back and forth between the Knights. "Either of you speak to her?"

They both shook their heads, and Mr. Knight said, "Never."

"Please be honest, Sergeant," Mrs. Knight said. "Do you think her death is somehow connected to our son?"

"We don't have evidence aside from her bequest to support that theory right now," Jeff answered.

"Very strange to leave everything to Will," Mrs. Knight said, half to herself. "And you knew about this, Abby?"

"I only heard late last night—one reason I came here this morning. I drove to Mrs. Olsen's house after I left the crime scene. Since she'd called me to meet with her at the espresso bar, I felt—"

"Could we save that discussion for later?" Jeff said. "Right now I'd like to hear Will's take on the victim. Did anything in particular stand out about her?"

"Ask me, she'd been smoking weed or taken some major head pill," Will said.

"William," his mother said. "The woman is dead, for heaven's sake."

Jeff held up a hand, chewing hard on his gum. "It's okay. This is exactly the kind of thing I need to know. What made you come to that conclusion?"

"She knew everything about me, from the time I was a kid. It freaked me out. She never said anything about leaving me her stuff or anything, though. That is *so* crazy." He looked at his mother. "Not *crazy* crazy. Sad crazy, Mom. She may have been weird, but—"

"She didn't deserve to die," his mother finished. "Why didn't you tell me she knew things about your childhood?"

"I'm the one who should have told you," I said. "That's why you hired me. I was concerned about her obvious knowledge of Will, especially since she shouldn't have even known his name. That's why I've made an appointment with the social worker who handled the original CPS case—to find out how Verna Mae got so much information."

"Molly Roth? Our old caseworker?" asked Mr. Knight.

Jeff stood abruptly before I could answer yes. He

said, "I think I have all I need for now. We'll be in touch."

Mr. Knight stood, too. "I'm concerned, Sergeant Kline. What if there's a connection between our son inheriting this woman's property and her murder? Would that put Will in danger?"

"We're doing everything we can to find answers," Jeff said. "If we find a connection and we think he needs protection, he'll get it. Right now, this crime appears to be a robbery-homicide."

The Knights nodded solemnly, and then Jeff turned and started walking out of the kitchen.

Something was wrong. Why did he decide to split all of a sudden? Was he still angry about my trip to Bottlebrush? No . . . my gut told me that wasn't it. "You still want me at the station by ten?" I called after him.

"Yes, ma'am," he answered over his shoulder.

While Mr. Knight followed Jeff out, Mrs. Knight asked if I'd like coffee.

"No, thanks," I said. "I'm trying to get off the java. Then maybe I won't have to get my teeth bleached as often." Still troubled by Jeff's attitude, I checked my watch. I had an hour to wait until I could talk to him alone and find out what was up.

When Mr. Knight returned, it was time to explain the theory Chief Rollins and I had come up with. More of what I'd wanted to *ease* into with the family.

I said, "Though I haven't discussed this with Sergeant Kline yet, I have a theory why Verna Mae Olsen left her home and property to Will."

"You do?" Will leaned forward, elbows on knees.

I nodded. "By the way, Chief Rollins is the officer who came out and took you from Verna Mae the night you were abandoned. Or maybe I should say *supposedly* abandoned."

Mrs. Knight's face paled. "Supposedly?"

I looked at Will. "You may have already met your birth mother, Will. We'll need your DNA to find out for sure."

"Are you saying that's why Mrs. Olsen left me her

stuff?" He checked his parents' faces for their reaction.

"And now she's been murdered?" Mr. Knight said. "This is unbelievable . . . horrible."

"We have no proof yet," I said, "but since she left everything to Will and kept close tabs on him for nineteen years, her being your biological mother might explain her behavior."

"I-I'm stunned," Mrs. Knight said. "We only wanted Will to know the truth about his past. To know who he was and where he came from. Know about his African-American heritage. But to have all this happen? I'm thinking we should leave well enough alone."

"Wait a minute, Mom," Will said. "You weren't there the day I met with Dr. Rose. She told me this wouldn't be easy. That I might learn things I wished I hadn't."

"*Dr.* Rose?" Mr. Knight looked at me. "I'm confused. Are you a doctor?"

"No, no," Mrs. Knight said. "Remember Abby told us Will would be interviewed by a psychologist, to make sure he could handle a reunion?"

Her husband nodded. "I remember." He looked at Will. "You had the interview while I was out of town. You said it went well."

"That psychologist is Abby's sister, Dr. Kate Rose. Very sweet lady." Mrs. Knight smiled at me.

"Dr. Rose knows what she's talking about," Will said. "She said I needed to be committed a hundred percent, just like I am to the game. Said I needed to be strong if I planned to go after this. I'm not dropping the ball because Mrs. Olsen died. We keep going. Okay, Abby?"

I nodded, lips tight. This kid was a winner in my book, even if he'd never played basketball a day in his life.

5

I left the Knight home after telling Will I'd make arrangements for him to have his blood drawn and the sample sent to the genetics lab I'd dealt with on a paternity case a few months ago. After checking in on the first floor at HPD, I rode the elevator to the homicide offices and made my way down the busy aisle to Jeff's cubicle. You've never seen paper-shuffling like what goes on at HPD. Fax machines rattled, phones rang and there was enough cursing to provide a script for hell. The place made me as nervous as a cockroach on a griddle.

But if I thought I'd get some time alone to find out what was bugging Jeff, I was wrong. Angel Molina was sitting across from him in the cluttered cubicle. Angel is my supervising PI and Jeff's good friend.

"Hey, guys," I said, taking the empty molded chair alongside my boss.

Angel gripped my neck, pulled me close and kissed me on the cheek. The strength of his Polo cologne nearly knocked me off my chair.

"How's my best detective?" He tugged at the cuffs of his pristine starched shirt.

I smiled. "Was that cheek swipe you gave me a metaphor for another kind of kiss?"

"Me? Kissing butt?" Angel said with a laugh.

"I almost believe you're sincere, except I also know you could sell sand to an Arab. What's this meeting about?" I looked at Jeff.

"It's about working this case," Jeff said.

"Oh, I get it. That's why you left the Knights' house. You're pissed off because—"

"Hold on, Abby," Angel said. "From my conversation with Jeff, I did not get the impression he is upset with you."

"Why do we need you as a mediator then?" Jeff might not be mad, but I was getting fired up and I wasn't sure why.

Angel patted my knee. "I'm here as a friend to you both. From what Jeff's told me, your adoption investigation and his murder case seem to be trains on parallel tracks."

"Maybe." I looked at Jeff, trying to read him. No such luck. His expression only revealed what had been there before. Fatigue. "Is that your take, Jeff?"

He took out his pack of Big Red and offered us some. I refused, but Angel took a stick and after unwrapping the gum, carefully folded the paper into a tiny rectangle before putting it in the wastebasket behind us.

"Here's what I know, Abby," Jeff said. "You're as competitive as I am when it comes to cases. That could cause us some serious problems on this one, personally and professionally. I don't want that."

"You think I do?" I snapped.

"Stop with the defensiveness," Angel said. "What I told Jeff, what I'm telling you, is that these two trains, they're not in a race. Do you see that, my *amiga*?"

"Okay. So how—"

"These trains, they might come to a crossing and one might have to slow up and let the other pass. You see this, too?" His dark eyes had softened, like Daddy's used to when he tried to calm me down.

I said, "What you're saying is that if Verna Mae's death is connected to Will, I have to back off?"

Jeff shook his head. "No, that's not it."

"Then quit dancing around and tell me what you want from me." What was it with these guys? Did they think I might explode or, worse, start crying when

I got the whole scoop on this little deal they'd cooked up before I arrived?

"Sorry," Jeff said. "I have a hard time thinking anyone but me 'can solve a case. Ask all my former partners. Anyway, since I've worked with Angel's agency in the past, I don't see why I can't again."

I paused, realizing this wasn't at all what I'd expected. "Since technically I work for Angel, we can . . . collaborate?" I could feel my defenses melting away, feel my stomach unknot. Jeff was behaving in a mature, thoughtful way, something my ex-husband never would have done in a trillion years. Funny how past pain had me reading this as a hostile encounter before I had all the facts.

"You're in," Jeff said, smiling for the first time. "I can't waste time chasing down a connection to Will Knight that might be a total dead end unrelated to this murder, old information that might only have to do with *your* investigation."

I grinned so wide it hurt. Jeff and I on the same case? Very cool.

"You'll be under Angel's supervision, like you're supposed to be," Jeff said quickly. "That's gotta be in my paperwork or I'm in deep shit. You haven't been doing this job long enough yet."

"Please keep reminding me of that," I said.

Angel tousled my already scary hair. It's not like I had any time to do anything with it this morning, since I'd jumped straight from the shower into my car.

"You make me laugh, Abby girl. She's something, no, Jeff?"

"She's something, *yes*," he answered. He said this with such obvious sincerity, he won back all the points he'd lost by reminding me I still had to be supervised.

"Now that we have an arrangement," Angel said, "I have to leave. New detective to train. He's not a fast study like you, Abby. He thinks investigating is like working in some Hollywood film. Wait until he's done ten divorce surveillances, then we'll see what movie he thinks he's playing in."

I rose and stepped aside so Angel could leave. He shook Jeff's hand before flashing a white smile as impeccable as his shirt.

Once he was gone, I moved over to the chair Angel had vacated to be farther from the busy aisle that ran between the cubicles. Good thing, because a greasy-haired guy in cuffs was being "helped" out of the office and might have landed right in my lap had I not moved.

Jeff leaned back, his chair resting against the modular desk behind him. "I think this will work, don't you?"

"As long as I remember which train I'm engineering. There is something I didn't get a chance to tell you." I explained my theory about Verna Mae possibly being Will's biological parent, how her obesity might have concealed a pregnancy. "I want to compare his DNA to Verna Mae's."

"You got a sample of her DNA last night?"

"Oops. I'll need that, won't I? Maybe Burl will let me grab her toothbrush or something."

"Since we have her body, we've got more than enough to spare. Tell me where to send a sample."

"Thanks. I think I'll like working with you." I gave him the name of the lab, and he jotted it on his calendar blotter. He always has about a hundred notes and numbers scribbled all over the place, and I wondered how he kept them straight.

"We probably won't see much of each other in the near future, Abby. I'm following a gang angle on this murder, and getting a gang lead is about as tedious as it gets."

"Gang angle?"

"We found the Olsen woman's car in the lot—thanks for the tip on that. The bad guy probably climbed right in while she was waiting for you, made her drive around behind the coffee place. Drove back after he killed her, got in his own car and took off. Crime scene people are processing it now, looking for a trace that could lead us to the killer."

"What does that have to do with gangs?"

"We've had some carjackings in the past few months, elderly women beaten and robbed. Previous tips indicate a gang connection in those cases. Doesn't exactly fit the M.O., since the Olsen woman was younger than the other victims and her car wasn't stolen, but it's close enough to follow up on."

"Why *not* take her car? It was expensive."

"Maybe too expensive, too flashy. The bad guy figured we'd find him easily. The thing had GPS, the whole nine yards."

"Any witnesses?" I asked.

"Crowded busy place, that lot. Believe it or not, the busier the place, the less likely people are to notice a snatch. We'll be interviewing plenty of people anyway, and that's not something you need to be involved in. If you don't know about witnesses, you won't have much to tell reporters should they come calling."

"Oh. Because of Will's being a collegiate star athlete?"

"Yup."

"Are you hedging? Do you have a witness who says Verna Mae was carjacked in the lot and driven around back?"

Jeff sighed. "You don't quit, do you?"

"Never. Is that what happened?"

He sighed. "No witnesses so far. We can only hope we find something the killer might have left behind besides coffee grounds on the floorboard. Fingerprints would be a bonus."

"I don't know, Jeff. Don't you think a struggle, even in a busy lot, would have been noticed? He must have had a gun or—"

"Or she knew him. Anyway, solving the murder is my job. You have plenty to do on your end."

"Yeah, but think about this. What if someone knew Verna Mae planned to meet me? What if that person didn't want the meeting to happen? Could that be why she ended up dead?"

Jeff grinned. "I think your daddy would say you

have a total lack of ignorance. If you find out anything supporting your theory, come see me. Meanwhile, I have to look in more obvious places. Like gangland. But only after I slog through paperwork hell. Time for you to go."

"I'm out of here." I came around his desk and took his face in my hands before he could protest. I planted one on him and found his mouth sticky-sweet with gum, just how I liked it.

"Go before one of the nosy jerks I work with sees us. We now have a professional relationship, remember?"

"No sleepovers?"

"Well . . . we will have to discuss the case," he replied, his eyes glinting.

"Glad we're on the same page." I smiled and left.

Unlike Jeff, who seemed to go days without sleep, I went home and crashed. I awoke hours later to find my sister, Kate, standing over me.

"Are you okay?" she whispered.

"I'm fine. Unless there's a reason you're whispering." I sat up and rubbed at my eyes. Diva stuck her head out from under the quilt and blinked a few times, then ran out of the bedroom. She was ticked. Her visit to cat heaven had ended too soon.

"I was whispering so I wouldn't startle you," Kate said.

"What are you doing here?" I asked. "Don't you have patients to see?"

"It's Saturday, Abby."

"Is it?"

"Yes. I saw your car in the driveway and you weren't downstairs. Since it's after two o'clock, I was wondering if you were sick."

"You've been spending too much time with Aunt Caroline. I'd expect her to come in and check on a break in my routine, not you." Aunt Caroline is Daddy's sister and she's always on the look out for ways to meddle in my business. I swear she drives down my street twice a day to see what's going on.

"Please don't compare me to her," Kate said.

"Sorry," I said quickly. "I just don't want you to run home for your homeopathic playbook, okay?" Kate loves to take care of me with the most god-awful herbal concoctions on the planet.

"You haven't napped since you were three. What's going on? And what happened to your hair?"

You'd think twins, even fraternal like us, would have plenty of similar traits, but Kate got the good hair, hands down, her dark brown hair so shiny and bouncy she could have done shampoo commercials.

"I was up late on a case and wasn't exactly concerned about my personal grooming. It's sad, though, isn't it? You could probably shave my head and make a hay bale."

Kate laughed. "I'm with you there. Is the Knight case making you lose sleep?"

I nodded. "That woman who found baby Will on her porch was murdered."

Kate sat next to me on the edge of the bed. "Oh, my God. That's awful. Did you ever get to talk to her?"

"Yes. Finding her was easy. The Knights had all the newspaper articles about the abandonment. But the way she died wasn't at all easy. I feel so terrible about the whole thing, Kate."

"Is her death connected to Will's case?"

"It's kind of a long story. While I take my second shower of the day to wake me up, would you mind running home for some green tea? Then we can talk."

She looked at me like I'd asked her to go on a safari. "You're serious?"

"Just plain green. None of that chai stuff."

"Sure, but—"

"I promise, the tea is all part of the long story."

While she went home—eagerly, I might add—I showered, used about half a bottle of conditioner on

my hair and dressed. The hair did show some improvement, but now I smelled like a peppermint.

Hot green tea for us both was waiting when I came
downstairs, and we sat at the kitchen table while I
filled Kate in on the events of the last few days.

When I finished, she said, "You went to Verna Mae
Olsen's house in the middle of the night? By
yourself?"

"You have to leap on an opportunity when it pre-
sents itself." I drank the last of my plum/berry green
tea, deciding it was pretty good even without much
sugar.

"What's your next move?" Kate asked.

"The social worker. Maybe she knows how Verna
Mae found out about Will. Then there's that blanket.
The brand name is POSH PRAMS. I'm hoping I can
trace it."

"From nineteen years ago? How?"

"Don't know yet. Got any ideas?"

"Hey, you're the investigator. My concern is Will.
How's he handling this emotionally?"

"Very maturely. He's an awesome kid."

Kate smiled. "I think so, too. Sensitive, but tough.
If you think Verna Mae was his mother, who was the
father? Obviously not Jasper Olsen."

I rested my elbows on the table and supported my
chin with my fists. "That's another challenge. Maybe
we can get back inside the house, look for clues to
lead us in the right direction."

"We?"

"I could use your help. That woman had a lot of
crap."

"Don't we all," Kate said.

6

Though I'd hoped Kate and I could get inside Verna Mae's house Sunday—Kate didn't see patients on Sunday—Burl Rollins said it would be another day or so before the property would be turned over to Will. After this disappointment, my sister convinced me to take a day off, and we spent Sunday shopping on the Kemah Boardwalk, then overdosed on shrimp and crab at Pappas Seafood Restaurant. It was a good distraction, one I needed.

My appointment with Molly Roth, the social worker who had worked Will's abandonment case, was for nine a.m. Monday, so I was on the Southwest Freeway heading toward Roth's office in Sugarland by eight-thirty. Houston freeways at that time of day? Basically a cuss-off with hand signals.

I'd researched Roth and discovered she'd left Children's Protective Services many years ago and currently ran a private agency that supplied parents with certified nannies—that according to the sales pitch Roth had insisted on delivering over the phone when I called her for an appointment. I wasn't even sure I'd convinced her I had no interest in hiring anyone from her agency unless they wanted to babysit a spoiled cat:

Her tenth-floor office was housed in a smoked-glass high-rise right off the freeway. When I entered suite 1012, a woman in her late fifties wearing glasses and a vintage navy suit with pale blue piping on the lapels flew into the waiting area the minute I arrived. She nearly tripped over a child-size table and chairs piled with books and puzzles.

"Hi," I said, extending my hand. "I'm—"

"You're late. You must never be late in this business. Now get in here." She grabbed my wrist and pulled me through the waiting area into an office populated by enough stuffed animals, cartoon posters, dolls and toys to rival a Disney World gift shop.

The woman squinted at me through lenses so thick they magnified her dark eyes and made her look like a koala bear.

"What's happened to you?" she said. Her voice sounded like the Molly Roth I'd spoken with the other day but with the frantic button turned on. "You did something different to your hair. And we talked about clothes. No clingy T-shirts like this." She pulled at my pink V-neck and appraised the rest of me. "The khakis are okay, but—"

"Ms. Roth, I think you've mistaken me for someone else. I'm Abby Rose. Remember, we spoke on the phone and—"

"You're not Julie?" She craned her neck and moved in so close we were practically nose to nose. "God, you're *not*. Okay, you're new. Do you have a criminal background? And don't lie to me, because if I get you this job and find out later you lied, I'll—"

"We have an appointment, Ms. Roth," I cut in. "About a case you worked for CPS."

Roth blinked, her jaw slack. Then came the dawn of realization. "Oh. That's *today*?"

"Yes, ma'am," I said.

"I really don't have time for you. A nanny hasn't shown and—"

A cell phone twirped from its resting place on Roth's cluttered desk. Papers went flying everywhere when she swooped down on the phone. She flipped it open and said, "Julie? Where in heaven are you?"

I saw color rise up the woman's pale neck and

scorch her cheeks. "Oh. Yes. Of course. That's right. Thank you for checking in."

Roth closed her phone and then her body went slack, her arms limp at her sides. "Today is *Monday*. Did you know that?"

"Um, yes. That's when you told me to be here."

"And Monday is *not* Tuesday."

"Not last time I checked." Why did I have the feeling I'd be getting absolutely nowhere with this interview?

Roth smiled, adjusted her glasses. "But that's a good thing, Ms. Rose. No child is without their nanny because today is Monday. Now. How can I help you?"

"Um, could we sit down?"

"Yes, certainly. Absolutely." She glanced around in what I assumed was her usual agitated fashion and scooped up a pile of folders and neon stuffed fish off the chair that faced her desk. Then she opened a closet to my left and tossed them inside, quickly shutting the door before the other thousand things inside fell out.

She gestured at the empty chair. "There. Sit. Coffee?"

"No," I said quickly. Besides the fact that I'd sworn off coffee, she might need a year to find the pot.

She took a seat behind her desk and started stacking papers, her nervous fingers less than effective at organizing them into piles. She finally shoved everything to one side and rested folded hands on the desk in front of her. "Now, what are we here for today?"

"Do you remember our conversation last week when I called?" I asked.

"It's been so hectic, Ms. Rose. You sell yellow roses or something, right? I suppose if one of my nannies showed up with roses her first day on the job that *would* be a nice touch, so I'm listening." She blinked and smiled and blinked those big eyes a few more times.

Definitely no one home in there. Funny how phone conversations just don't give you the full picture. "Actually, I work for Yellow Rose Investigations. I'm a private detective who specializes in adoption cases. You once worked for CPS in Liberty County. My client, Will Knight, was in your care for—"

"The Knights! Yes! Sweet people. Good foster parents."

"They ended up adopting a baby you placed with them. But you knew that, right?"

"Certainly I knew that." But Roth looked more confused than a mosquito in a nudist colony. "Why didn't we do this over the phone? I mean, it's not like I know much more than you seem to know."

"You were busy when I called the other day and said you'd rather speak in person. Said you'd be able to recall the case better if I gave you some time."

"That's right. Well . . . hmmm. Let me think." She bit her lower lip.

"Did you happen to save any old notes?" I asked, so full of hope and *so* kidding myself.

She pointed at me and smiled. "Yes. Old notes. I could have done that. Where would they be?"

Obviously this woman couldn't pour pee out of a boot if the instructions were printed on the heel. "Maybe I could ask you a few questions and the memories will begin to flow." I said this sweetly, rather like a nanny telling a bedtime story.

"Yes. That might work." More blinking.

"A baby was left on a doorstep. A mixed-race child."

"Right. The police called me, but I couldn't get out that night. My car wouldn't start. To this day I have a problem with the whole gas, oil change, maintenance thing. But I'm learning."

"Burl Rollins, the officer you spoke to, took care of the baby overnight."

"Yes. Nice man. His wife was a doll, too. We played bunko together. Did you know that?"

"Interesting," I said. And irrelevant. "Did you ever meet the Olsens, the people who discovered the child on their porch?"

She thought for a second. "I *did* meet her. She came to my office, but, what was that about?"

"I'm hoping you can tell me," I prompted.

Molly Roth squeezed her eyes shut, her expression pained. "Recalling conversations from years ago is very difficult. Maybe you could tell me what Mrs. Olsen has to do with any of this, because she was never a part of that child's life aside from calling out the authorities. The baby was placed in foster care, adopted and gone from Bottlebrush quickly."

"I hate to tell you this, but Verna Mae Olsen was murdered Friday night, right after she met with that now grown-up abandoned baby. She knew all about him—had for years, as matter of fact."

Roth leaned back in her chair, her face blanching with shock. "My heavens. What a way to start the week."

"I'm working with the police on this case, and we really need your help. Please think hard, tell me everything you can recall."

"Okay. Help me out. What year was the child abandoned again?"

"Late in 1987."

She rubbed her index finger under her bright red lips. "Hmm. What did Mrs. Olsen want with me that day she came to the office?"

"Did she want to talk about Will? Maybe learn where he would be placed?"

"No. Besides, I wouldn't have told her. Not that I was the best caseworker on the planet, but there were things I could and couldn't say to people."

"If she did ask about his foster care placement perhaps you told her that was confidential information?"

Roth's face brightened with realization. "Foster care! That's it. She asked about becoming a foster parent."

"Because she wanted to be *Will's* foster parent?" I recalled how Verna Mae had bristled when I brought up the subject.

"No . . . it was after he'd been placed, and if I

recall, she never mentioned him. I don't think we ever put a child in her home, though."

"Why was that?"

"Could be we lost her information during the break-in, along with the other things those vandals destroyed. Yes. In fact, I'm sure that's what happened. Funny she never reapplied . . ."

"Break-in?"

"I kept cash in the office—to help families buy diapers or groceries or pay rent. Emergency fund. Couple hundred dollars. CPS really does do good work trying to keep families together. Anyway, someone, or maybe more than one someone, broke in and stole the money. It wasn't a big secret I had petty cash, considering I handed out quite a bit throughout the county. Had to be young people responsible, because they trashed the place. Burned things, wrote graffiti on the wall. Adolescent acting-out, we presumed."

"Must have been upsetting," I said.

"Yes. What a mess they made. Even delayed that abandoned child's permanent placement. Everything was nearly finalized. His file went missing along with several others—probably burned, since we found a pile of ashes to go along with the spray-painted walls and overturned file cabinets."

Now *this* was important. "This happened after your visit from Verna Mae?"

"After. Like I said, her paperwork probably was destroyed, too."

Destroyed because Verna Mae applied to be a foster parent to size up the place? Though I couldn't see her breaking and entering, she could have paid someone to steal Will's information. "The police believed juveniles were the culprits? You don't think Verna Mae could have had anything to do with it?"

"She couldn't have knocked over those heavy cabinets. And those curse words on the wall? Had to be adolescents."

"Other paperwork went missing, you say?"

"Yes. What a nightmare. Delayed several placements. I wasn't very good with all the paper I generated, anyway. Then to have files crumpled, destroyed, burned. Well, it set me back awhile. It's not like they give caseworkers a secretary."

I asked a few more questions, but concluded I'd squeezed everything I could out of her. Besides, when she asked if I might like a job caring for children, I got out of there as quick as chained lightning with a snapped link. After I got behind the wheel of my car, I hunted in my bag for Burl's business card. I wanted to ask him if he had any knowledge of this so-called vandalism in the CPS office.

A dull throb had begun at the back of my skull, and I had a feeling the coffee withdrawal was beginning despite the green tea fixes. The thought of drinking even one sip of java still made my stomach flip over. Once I got back on the road, my first stop would be for a Diet Coke.

I found Burl's number, dialed his cell and said "Hi" when he answered on the second ring. "I could use a little help."

"Shoot," he answered, "but make it quick. Got a court date in thirty minutes."

"Do you remember a break-in at the CPS office sometime after Will was placed with the Knights?"

"No, but the CPS office isn't in Bottlebrush. I wouldn't have been involved. I can try to find out, though. When was this?"

I told him about my conversation with Molly Roth.

"Come by later today and I might have something on it."

"Come by?"

"Yes, ma'am. And bring Will. I have the keys to the house."

"Already?"

"There's still a few legalities, but Verna Mae used the lawyer as the executor and that sped things up. He says Will can take possession."

"Okay. We'll be there."

7

About four Monday afternoon, after Will and I stopped at the lab to get his blood drawn for the DNA comparison, we arrived at the Bottlebrush police station. Green-gray mold crept along the walls under the gutter of the beige brick flat-roofed building. From the style, the station must have dated back to the sixties, and obviously the sun did not shine on the front door of Bottlebrush PD.

A white patrol car sat parked in front alongside Burl's Land Rover. The Rover's navy blue paint glittered in the late-afternoon sun like it had been washed and waxed this morning.

"Nice ride," Will said, nodding in appreciation as we walked by.

"Burl Rollins is obviously a man who's proud of his horse," I answered.

Will held the door for me, and we entered the station. Burl was sitting behind a waist-high counter and stood to greet us.

"This can't be that ten-pound baby that spent the night with me." Burl, who wore a short-sleeved blue shirt and purple necktie circa 1970, grinned like he'd eaten a banana sideways. He came around the counter and shook Will's hand, gripping the kid's shoulder with his other.

I wasn't even acknowledged until their happy reunion ended about thirty seconds later.

Finally Burl looked at me. "Thanks for coming,

Abby. I'll get Mary to cover the phone so we can talk. She's on break." He disappeared down a short hall behind the counter and returned a few seconds later with a young black woman in a brown uniform. She held half a sandwich in her hand and nodded at us before taking the seat Burl had been occupying when we arrived. Only two cops. Big change from my visit to HPD on Saturday, where officers were as thick as bats under a San Antonio bridge.

The gun belt strapped around Burl's waist seemed to dance with his steps as he led us to his office, a room about twice the size of my closet, though far neater. One entire wall was lined with filing cabinets, and labeled boxes were stacked to the ceiling. He had made room for pictures of his family on the table behind him, right next to the computer. The woman that I assume I'd spoken to on the phone the other night was flanked by three teenage boys. The youngest had a smile crammed with braces.

We all sat, Burl behind his desk and Will and I in folding chairs across from him.

"Three boys?" I said. "Bet that's a challenge."

"Smells pretty bad at our house some days. Sorta like a locker room, huh, Will?"

They both laughed while I inwardly winced in sympathy for Mrs. Rollins.

"Let's get down to business," Burl said, looking at me. "Did you mention our, uh, theory about Verna Mae to Will?"

"He's aware she might have been his mother," I said.

Will folded his huge hands in his lap and stared at them.

"How do you feel about that, son?" Burl asked.

"It is what it is," he answered softly.

"I'm sure Abby's told you it may not be true. For proof, we'll need your DNA. I can grab something of Verna Mae's for hers."

"Actually," I said, "HPD is already on that."

"Oh," Burl said.

I sensed his disappointment, affirmation of my earlier guess that he wanted a part in this investigation. I could see why. This was his town, his unsolved case.

"Sergeant Kline isn't even sure Will's abandonment has anything to do with Verna Mae's murder," I said, "but in case it does, he wants to know if she was Will's biological mother."

"I understand." Burl looked at Will. "The probate lawyer been in touch yet?"

"Um, no." Will seemed a little confused by the question.

"He said I can turn the keys over to you." Burl pulled open the middle desk drawer and took out an envelope, which he slid toward Will.

"She had a spare set of keys?" I said.

"Yup. Hanging right there on a hook in the kitchen. So unless some relatives appear out of nowhere to contest the will, the place is yours, son. She owned about two acres. Lots of renovations done, I noticed. 'Course, my last visit before this week was a long time ago. The place probably needed them. I'm guessing that house and land are worth a pretty penny."

Will turned and stared at me. "What do I with a house, Abby? The only thing I know about houses is that the trim needs painting every five years, and when you're as tall as I am, it's your job. The only other thing I know how to do is cut the lawn."

"You can hire someone for those chores," Burl said with a laugh. "See, that's another reason I asked you to come. She had money, too."

"Money? No one said anything about money." Will looked at me. "This is so frickin' weird. I didn't even *know* that lady."

"She thought she knew you well enough to give you about two hundred grand," Burl said.

Will looked stunned, and maybe I did, too, since I became aware of a beautiful mahogany clock on top of the bookcase. I only noticed because the room grew so quiet you could hear it tick-tick-ticking above us.

Will finally broke the silence. "This isn't like winning the lottery. You know what I'm saying? The lottery makes you think about cars and vacations and stuff like that. This? This I don't like."

I patted Will's shoulder. "Don't stress until we know more. We'll figure it out, okay?"

Will blinked several times, lips tight, then said, "Okay. Sure." He didn't look all that sure, though.

I faced Burl. "Does Sergeant Kline know about this money?"

"Yes, ma'am. I just finished talking to him before you two got here. I mean, that's enough cash to kill for. And I'm not talkin' about you, son," Burl said to Will. "Someone might have thought they were due an inheritance and hurried Verna Mae to her grave to get their hands on it."

"Friends or relatives or what?" I asked.

"Far as I can tell she had nobody, but maybe Jasper had relatives and those folks thought they'd be Verna Mae's logical choice to inherit."

"Jasper? Why does that name sound familiar?" Will asked.

"Verna Mae's late husband," I answered.

"Oh. Right. She talked about him the other day." Will was trying to maintain his calm, but his flushed cheeks and clenched fists told me different.

"Jasper was a mean one," Burl said, shaking his head. "My wife would have my hide if she heard me speaking ill of the dead, but he's gone and his ornery spirit is gone with him. What matters is the man was a plumber. Self-employed and by no means rich. Where the heck did Verna Mae get all that money? Far as I know, she never worked outside the home."

"Maybe all her relatives died and left everything to her," I said.

"Possible," Burl said. "Anyway, your guy Kline is on it. Said he'd be checking her bank records."

"My guy?" I said, failing to filter my thoughts before they spilled from my mouth.

This brought a smile from Will for the first time since he'd shaken hands with Burl. "How'd you figure out they're into each other, Chief?"

"You think I came in on a load of turnips, son?" He laughed, and so did Will.

"Could we move on?" I was definitely feeling uncomfortable.

"Sure. What else do you need?" Burl asked.

"That break-in at the CPS office?" I'd filled Will in on Molly Roth on the drive here, so he was aware of the lost paperwork.

"Oh, yeah," Burl said. "County's sheriff's office people are digging through their old cases. They were the investigating agency on that one. Lucky I got friends over there, 'cause even with connections, it might take awhile for them to come up with anything."

"Thanks. Did you want to ask Burl any questions, Will?" I know I would have if I was him, considering Will once spent the night in the man's house.

Will hesitated, pursed his lips a few times before speaking. "What happened that night, Chief? I mean, when you came and got me?"

Burl leaned back, his hands clasping his silver belt buckle. "It was Jasper who called. Pissed as hell. But then, he stayed that way. When I got to the house, you were sound asleep in that little plastic infant seat. Too big for it, but I had to make do when I carried you over to my place in my truck. Strapped the seat belt around you. My wife was thrilled I brought you home, even if for just one night."

Will smiled briefly, then said, "But what about them? The Olsens? You said Mr. Olsen was mad."

"Like I said. He stayed that way."

"What was *she* like?" Will asked.

"You want to know everything, huh?"

"I *need* to know. Especially if she was my birth mother."

"Okay. I won't lie. Verna Mae wasn't quite right in the head, and that particular night she was crying so bad, Jasper sent her to the bedroom. Practically pushed her down the hallway. He told me she'd been saying how they could keep you, pretend you were theirs. Jasper had a good laugh about that." Burl cast his gaze downward, obviously embarrassed.

"He laughed?" I said.

Burl looked at Will. "We should just skip the rest, son. You don't need to hear what some ignorant redneck had to say. Everything worked out great for you. The way you carry yourself, the way you play ball, everything about you says you've been raised right."

"Tell me why he laughed." Will's tone had gone hard, out of character for him. "Tell me now."

Burl shifted in his chair, avoiding eye contact with both of us. "Okay, he said Verna Mae was stupid to think she could pass you off as theirs. Said he wasn't having any black baby in his house for one more second."

Will stared at his hands, his long fingers intertwined and white-knuckled with tension. "That's what I figured. Thanks for being honest."

A tense silence followed before I said, "Guess we're done here." I started to get up, then remembered the blanket. "You really don't need that blanket now, right?"

"I collected the blanket as evidence during an executed search warrant, so yes I do," Burl said evenly.

"But it probably has nothing to do with Verna Mae's death."

"*Probably* is your key word, Abby. If I give it up and the blanket turns out to be even remotely connected to the murder, the thing's worthless as evidence."

"How could an old blanket be connected to her murder?" Damn, I hate to hear no. Made me want the stupid thing even more.

"Don't know, but the blanket stays with me, and when I have proof it's not important, then it's yours with Will's permission. I learned long ago, you collect evidence, you keep evidence until you're sure it's worthless. I'm a careful man, Abby Rose, a trait that's served me well in the police business." The country charm had been turned off. He meant business.

"A few pictures wouldn't break your chain of evidence, would it?" I had to leave with something, because that DNA test might turn out far different than what we expected. Besides, that blanket was linked to Will's past, if not to his birth parents. I was learning to be careful myself.

Burl sighed. "Guess pictures wouldn't hurt."

While Burl unfolded a step stool and climbed up to reach one of the stacked file boxes, Will looked at me.

"I'm glad she didn't keep me," he said. "I'm telling my mom and dad how much I love them the minute I get home."

I patted his knee. "Good idea." I took my camera phone from my purse.

After cleaning off his desk, Burl laid out several sheets of blank white paper and placed the cream-colored blanket on these.

I snapped off a few shots.

Will leaned forward for a better look. "You think this was mine? It doesn't look all that old."

"The blanket itself is well-preserved, but check out the label." Burl turned over one corner so I could photograph the label.

The small rectangular piece of satin had yellowed with age, and the stitching on the edges was frayed. Underneath the embroidered words HANDMADE FOR POSH PRAMS I now saw something else—100% HAND-SPUN NEW WOOL. I'd had little chance to notice this the first time, seeing as how Burl had commandeered the thing almost immediately. If the word "posh" didn't make it sound expensive, "hand-spun wool" certainly did.

"You sure I can't have this?" I said.

Burl smiled. "Your cop friend wants it, all he has to do is ask and I'll turn it over properly to preserve the chain of evidence."

"Okay." I held up my phone. "The pictures will do for now, and we do appreciate your help."

"My pleasure. Great to meet Will all grown up." He carefully folded the blanket and returned it to the box. On paper taped to the box lid he wrote down the date and time he'd accessed the contents.

"You want to take your keys, Will?" I nodded at the envelope still lying on the desk.

Will shook his head. From the look on his face, you'd have thought he was eight years old and I'd asked him to open up the closet where the boogeyman lived. "No. Could you, like . . . deal with them for now?"

I picked up the envelope. "Sure. But your parents might want to get a lawyer on this."

Will released an audible sigh of relief. "Yeah. Sure. Whatever."

We said good-bye to Burl and left.

I'd had a notion to stop at Verna Mae's house, but I decided Will had been given plenty to chew on today. The house could wait.

8

By the time I dropped Will off at his home early Monday evening and explained about the money part of the inheritance to his mother, my stomach was complaining about missed meals. I'd eaten nothing since breakfast. I called Jeff's cell, hoping we could grab a bite together, but he said he wouldn't be leaving work for several more hours. He was chasing Verna Mae's money trail.

I decided to stop by Kate's house for the company, but only after picking up a Chick-Fil-A sandwich and a Diet Coke. Who knows what might be on the menu at her place. Probably yellow gooey vegetables or enough bulgur wheat to feed a barn full of chickens for a month.

When I arrived, I discovered that vegetables would have been glorious in comparison to what was truly on the menu. Our Aunt Caroline's baby-blue Lincoln Town Car sat in the driveway. If not for Terry Armstrong, Kate's significant other, I would have floored the Camry and hightailed it home, but Terry was returning from a walk with Webster, their border collie. A very slow walk, no doubt, since Webster is so lazy he wouldn't wake up from a nap even if a herd of sheep got into the living room.

Terry spotted me, waved and smiled. Yup, I had to stop. Either that, or be ratted out to Kate and Aunt Caroline that I'd been in the neighborhood and split.

When I climbed out of the car, Terry released Webster's leash, and the dog came running to greet me. "What's with him?" I asked. "He hasn't run anywhere since he found a body in my greenhouse last summer."

Terry is about six-four with an easy smile, lean frame and a spirit as kind as my sister's. "Didn't Kate tell you?"

"Tell me what?" Webster planted his feet on my waist and sniffed at my Chick-Fil-A bag.

"Our boy is hypothyroid. He's been on medicine for a week, and we can already tell the difference."

We started walking down the driveway toward the back door. "I always said something was wrong with him."

"You know Kate. She wouldn't trust any ordinary vet, but she found this woman who uses natural medicine and chiropractic. Webster's now beginning to act like a real border collie."

I stopped. "You're kidding. Webster's seeing a chiropractor?"

"Hey, between that, the medicine and the acupuncture, he's improving every day," he said.

"Acupuncture, too?" Still, I had to admit Webster was a new dog. He beat us to the back gate, and once we came in through the kitchen, he hurried to his water dish and began lapping like he'd done a marathon in the desert.

As Terry led me into the living room, I took a deep breath to help prepare me mentally for an encounter with my aunt. Kate was curled up in a corner of the leather sofa, and Aunt Caroline sat across from her on the love seat. Since learning last year that my aunt had lied to Kate and me all our lives about our illegal adoption, Kate had generously forgiven her, but I hadn't. Didn't know if I ever would.

"Hey, Abby," Kate said, her dark eyes lighting up.

Aunt Caroline smiled. I believe she'd be a perfect candidate for some talk show centered around people addicted to plastic surgery, because she'd had plenty and then some.

"Abigail. What a nice surprise," she said.

"Hi, Aunt Caroline. You're looking . . . bright."
She was floral today. Flowered silk shirt in pink and
fuchsia, matching skirt. Heck, she even had a fake
poppy in her white hair. She looked like *The Secret
Garden* gone bad.

Terry cleared his throat. "Ladies, if you'll excuse
me, I have work to do." He strode through the room,
Webster on his heels. I heard them climb the stairs
and wished I was going with them.

Instead I sat on the couch, set my drink on the glass
coffee table and started in on my sandwich. Nothing
like deep-fried chicken on a buttered bun to make the
company more tolerable.

"How many fat grams are you consuming this evening, Abigail? You won't keep that handsome policeman interested long if you . . . Well, you know what
I mean. Or has that little infatuation ended?"

"They're very much in love," Kate said quickly,
probably knowing I was ready to spit a pickle in Aunt
Caroline's direction.

"In love? As in cohabiting?" Aunt Caroline asked,
her carefully penciled brows rising.

"That's not really your business," I answered as
sweetly as I'm capable of. How I wished we *were* living
together, but Jeff still kept his apartment despite
spending seventy-five percent of his time at my place.

Aunt Caroline held up her hands in surrender.
"Sorry. I just don't want to see you hurt again. You
have an ex-husband in jail, if you've forgotten. . . .
But, wait. What an idiot I've been. That's why you've
taken up with someone the exact opposite of Steven."

"That *someone* is the most honest, sensitive man
I've ever met, and to repeat, this is none of your business." Though I wanted to tell her to burn her tongue
on her own potpie, I managed to stay calm.

"Aunt Caroline, is something bothering you?" Kate
asked. "Because I think you're trying to press Abby's
buttons tonight." My sister, always the shrink, was at-
tempting to analyze Aunt Caroline. Like it would do
any good.

Maybe Kate's insight had an impact, however, because I noticed tears in Aunt Caroline's eyes. Made me wish my give-a-damner was broke, but it wasn't. She was sad, and for some foolish reason, that bothered me.

"You're right, Kate. I am upset. Hans has left me." She blinked hard, not letting the tears escape.

"I am so sorry," Kate said. "You really cared for him."

Yeah, I thought. *Because he was about forty years younger than you and allowed you to live in fantasyland.* "That's too bad," I heard myself saying. He *had* kept her busy and, well, yes, happy.

"I apologize, Abigail. I didn't mean to 'press your buttons,' as Kate so aptly put it. I suppose I am a little jealous. Sergeant Kline is . . . Well, let's put it this way: I wouldn't mind if he ate crackers in *my* bed." She smiled.

I laughed, mostly because the image was absurd. Then she and Kate joined me in a good guffaw. Tension broken.

"Maybe I should start over," Aunt Caroline said. "Kate tells me her practice is thriving. What about your job, Abigail? Any new cases?"

"As a matter of fact, yes. And since you bring it up, maybe you can help me with something." I put my half-eaten sandwich in the bag. "There's this blanket that might be a clue to the parents in an abandoned-baby case I'm working. The label says the blanket was made for Posh Prams. Could Posh Prams have been a local business or a store, say about twenty years ago? Because I found nothing even close to that name in the yellow pages."

Aunt Caroline sat back and picked up her glass of white wine from the end table beside the love seat. She sipped, obviously thinking. "Sounds British. Never having had children of my own, it's not a store I would have visited, though I do like the name. Have you been to the Village? That British import shop that's been there forever? They might know."

"Aunt Caroline might be onto something, Abby," Kate said. "It's a place to start."

They were right. I should have thought of this myself. The store they were talking about was in Rice Village, which wasn't actually a village, but several streets near the university lined with expensive specialty stores and yuppie hangouts like the Gap and Banana Republic.

"Okay, I'll check it out. Thanks," I said.

Aunt Caroline seemed pleased I'd actually accepted her suggestion without an argument, but who better to ask about a store that included the word "posh" than her?

We small-talked for a few more minutes, and then Aunt Caroline had to leave for some charity organizing committee meeting.

Once she was gone, Kate said, "How is the case going? Will holding up okay?"

I explained what I had learned about the money since we last talked about the case yesterday. "I'm wondering where her money came from, Kate. Burl Rollins didn't seem to have a clue, but . . . wait a minute."

Kate leaned forward. "What?"

"Perhaps Verna Mae was receiving child support from the father of her baby."

"I don't get it. Even if she was Will's biological mother, she didn't keep him," Kate said.

"True, but what if the father didn't know she'd given Will up? Or what if this man, whoever he was, paid Verna Mae off to keep her quiet about having his child?"

Kate sat back and considered this. "That would mean he had a giant reason to keep the baby a secret."

"A wife, maybe? Could be Verna Mae came to Houston the night she was murdered to meet with this man, prepared to ask him for more money now that Will had visited her? After all, she could easily tell

Will plenty of things about his biological family. Rather than pay up, the guy killed her."

"I guess that's possible," said Kate.

"Those DNA results can't come back soon enough," I said. "The lab usually gets me results within a few days, but HPD may not get Verna Mae's sample there for comparison right away. Damn, I hate waiting."

"Tell me something I don't know," Kate replied with a smile.

"In the meantime, I want to take another look inside Verna Mae's house. She could have hidden away more information about Will. You said you'd help, remember?"

"Yes, but how—"

"I have the keys. The house belongs to Will now. Tomorrow night after work okay for you? Or do you have group therapy this Tuesday evening?"

"I'm free. You're sure this is okay? We're not doing something the police won't like?"

"Burl handed over the keys, Kate."

"Then I'm game."

When I arrived home an hour later, hyped up on the half dozen Diet Cokes I'd consumed, I played with Diva for awhile. She loved chasing the feather-on-a-stick, and I loved watching her do cartwheels and flip-flops.

When she finally gave up and dragged her toy into the other room, I went up to my bedroom and was just finishing the whole wash, exfoliate, moisturize routine when I heard Jeff's key in the lock downstairs. Damn. I had on an old T-shirt and cotton undies. Looking like this, even the tide wouldn't take me out.

"Abby, you still up?" he called from the foyer.

"You betcha, but what you see is what you get." I hurried down the stairs.

"You look great to me," he replied.

"Yeah, that's 'cause you see dead people all day."

He laughed and we kissed; then he put an arm around my shoulder. "I'm hungry. Anything besides cold pizza available?"

"Four-day-old Chinese. Very microwavable."

"Great."

Thirty minutes later, after the beef and broccoli was gone—and yes, I do eat green vegetables when they're smothered in soy sauce—we cuddled up on the sofa. Jeff took off his shoes, loosened his tie and rested his feet on the antique trunk that substitutes as a coffee table.

"You look tired," I said.

"A few hours in your company and I'll be recharged. How's your end of the case going?"

I told him about my day, then said, "Your turn."

"Did I ever tell you how much I hate bankers? They seem to take great pleasure in withholding things; mostly because they can, I guess."

"Are you talking about Verna Mae's money?"

"One of our investigative officers figured out someone made regular transfers into her account. Any chance of finding out who's been moving that cash for years is slim or fat, depending on your favorite saying."

"But can't you make them tell you? I mean, you're the cops."

"The money came through the Cayman Islands," he answered. "You'd have to be a head of state before those guys would even think about sharing information without a year of legal wrangling. Anyway, I'm guessing it's no coincidence the payments began a few months after Will was born. I suppose it could have been blackmail payments or—"

"Child support," I offered.

Jeff smiled. "You read my mind. How do you plan to investigate that angle? Because this is your territory."

"About the only clue I have concerning the abandonment is the baby blanket. Burl won't give it up."

"Why?"

"Says it was collected during the execution of a search warrant and—"

"He's reaching. Hanging onto an old unsolved case. But technically, he's right. I'll ask him to send it to me if you really need it."

"I have photos. If they don't help, I'll take you up on the offer."

Jeff pulled me close and kissed me. "Enough shop-talk. You're ready for bed. Why not help me get ready, too?"

"I can manage that." I removed his tie and started on his shirt buttons as we kissed again, but ten minutes later, when we were ready to move to a more comfortable place—like my bed—Jeff's beeper went off and he left to chase another murderer.

9

The trendy Rice Village shopping center has been around for as long as I've been alive, but in the last few years they've added enough pubs to make Ireland and England jealous. Nice for business so close to Rice University, where plenty of beer drinkers reside, but the parking problems have grown worse as a result. Cars cram not only the parallel slots in front of the stores but every narrow little street within a half mile. To avoid this, I walked the five blocks from my house to visit British Imports on Tuesday morning, the pictures I'd printed of the blanket tucked in my purse. Hoping for clues there was a long shot, but it was better than interviewing everyone at the Galleria or Highland Village, two other places that might have sold expensive imported baby blankets back then.

Someone in a magazine article once described Rice Village as "like shopping in New England, only with humidity," and today I had to agree. Though it was just past noon, the temperature had already climbed to ninety. I was damp with sweat when I entered British Imports, and the air-conditioning offered welcome relief.

Standing inside the door, I blinked several times to stave off sensory overload. Floor to ceiling shelves to my left held knickknacks, blankets, sweaters, everything Shakespearean, books, posters and flags. The right side was reserved for china—and lots of it. Made me afraid to step in that direction. I'm clumsy enough to get thrown by a stick horse and could see myself toppling over ten-grand worth of Wedgwood.

I made a beeline for a stack of blankets but found nothing babyish. They were mostly plaid lap blankets with fringe or heavy cable knits from Ireland. I was about to approach the man behind the counter, a fiftyish guy who, in keeping with the neighborhood, looked very much like a university professor. He had a trimmed red beard and graying hair, and even in the warmth of June wore a sweater vest.

But before I could introduce myself, a well-dressed couple beat me to the punch, mentioning they had just returned from England. The storekeeper greeted them in a British accent, treating them like old friends. They began a conversation about train rides through the countryside. Since I had plenty of time and wanted the man's undivided attention, I made my way around the center glass counter and found three aisles of marmalade and candy, as well as a cooler filled with frozen items, most of them hot dogs. The labels called them bangers or beef sausage, but they were still little hot dogs. You didn't need a PI license to know that. The shelves above the cooler held dozens of cans of pork and beans. Hot sellers, no doubt. To the right of this section, a small corner had been set aside for baby items, mostly rattles and stuffed animals, but I did find blankets. Problem was, they all had Winnie the Pooh stamped or sewn on them.

By the time I'd examined every jar of marmalade and lemon curd, noted that tea comes in a hundred varieties and realized that toffee and chocolate are staples of the British diet, the couple left and I had my turn.

I walked up to the counter. "Hi, there," I said. "My name is Abby Rose."

"Gerald Trent," the man replied. "How can I help you?"

"I'm a private investigator and—"

"I'm being investigated, am I?" he said with a lop-sided grin.

"Oh, no. Nothing like that," I said quickly. "I'm tracking a clue on a case I'm working. Can I ask how long you've been here?"

"I opened shop in 1993," he said with genuine pride. My face must have shown my disappointment, because he said, "Is that a problem?"

"This clue dates back to 1987, so yes."

"And what *is* this cryptic clue, if I might ask?"

"A baby blanket." I took the pictures out of my purse and placed them on the glass counter. "But if you weren't here before 1993, then—"

"I wasn't, but Marjorie McGrady was. The shop was called the British Emporium back then." He took a pair of reading glasses from his shirt pocket and studied the pictures one by one. "Marjorie had plenty of rubbish in her inventory, but she also had some very nice items, things like this. Probably cost her a pretty penny to import, but then she wasn't the wisest woman when it came to running a store."

"So you've never carried any blankets like this?"

"Can't say as I have. Never heard of this Posh Prams brand, either."

"I researched the name on the Internet and found nothing."

"Could have come from a store in Britain she did business with. You should ask Marjorie, not me."

I smiled. "I'd love to. Can you help me find her?"

"Find her? She's my best customer," he said.

"Would you mind contacting her? See if she'll talk to me?"

"Don't mind at all, though if you wait five minutes, she'll probably show up." He laughed and reached for the phone. "Let's just see if she's home." He dialed a number without having to look it up, and explained to the person on the other end who I was and what I wanted. Then he handed me the phone. "She'd like to speak to you."

"Hi. This is Abby Rose," I said.

"Marjorie here," she answered. She was British, too. "You have one of my blankets, do you? Quality item if it's indeed from Posh Prams."

"You did sell that brand?"

"Yes, but I'd have to have a look-see at what you've got there to be certain. I imported a number of items from them."

"I could bring the photo to you, or . . . we could meet here at the store."

"I have no plans to leave the house today," she said curtly. "I suppose you could bring the picture by. Join me for tea."

Her enthusiasm was underwhelming, but who was I to complain? "Great. Where do you live?"

She gave me directions and told me tea would be ready at three on the dot. After I hung up, I said, "She didn't sound all that excited about helping me. Maybe I could bring her something from your shop to go along with tea?"

"Marjorie does like her sweets," he said with a nod. "Let me give you a few choices."

After I walked back home, I did a little more computer sleuthing on the Posh Prams angle, focusing on British importers, but still found nothing. I printed out an extra set of blanket pictures and added them to Will's file. Then I wrapped up the paperwork on a few cases I'd finished in the last few months—easy adoption reunions with happy outcomes. Nothing complicated like this case. By the time I faxed the completed files to Angel's office, it was time to leave for tea with Marjorie McGrady.

She lived in the Heights, an old and well-known residential area west of downtown. I turned off Heights Boulevard onto her street about five minutes before three and quickly found her restored home. Many of the houses in this area had been renovated in the last decade, making the Heights prime real estate. Her place looked like pictures I'd seen of British cottages, the stone and brick home surrounded by a low wrought-iron fence and a vibrant garden of violet heather and fuchsia wildflowers.

"No trouble finding me, I see," said the cherry-cheeked Marjorie McGrady after she answered the bell—a bell that played "God Save the Queen," if I'd heard right. She had on an old-fashioned halter-type apron complete with ruffles over her gray skirt and white blouse. I noticed a little jeweled Union Jack pinned to her silk collar.

I offered her the tin of toffee Mr. Trent had told me she liked, and this prompted a small smile that lasted about a millisecond. She placed the tin in her apron pocket and gestured for me to follow her. By the time we reached the dining room where tea had been set up, I knew I was right about the doorbell music. The entire house I'd passed through—foyer, parlor, as well as what I'd glimpsed in the kitchen—looked like Gerald Trent's shop gone mad. I'd never seen so much British crap in my life. Not quaint, organized, make you go "aaahh" crap, either. I spied an ugly, uncomfortable-looking green velvet sofa and gaudy gold-brocade wing chairs in the parlor. Portraits of the royal family and their many castles lined the hall. Plenty of photographs of places and people looking definitely regal hung there, too, but I didn't recognize anything or anyone. She just had stuff everywhere, even little British flags in the flowerpots and fake crowns hanging from the ceiling.

Mrs. McGrady gestured to the mahogany table where a silver tray held a floral china teapot and matching sugar and creamer. I noted a basket of what looked like buttermilk biscuits as well as a bowl full of jam and another bowl of . . . what? Whipped cream?

"Have a seat, Ms. Rose. I don't often have guests for tea. Don't care much for company, to be honest." She made an attempt at another smile, her gunmetal gray curls framing a round, puffy face. Matched her puffy body. Yes. Puffy. That was the word that best described Marjorie McGrady.

I took the chair she pointed to and sat in front of a china cup and saucer with a different pattern than the teapot. "Please call me Abby."

"If you wish. And I'm Marjorie. I've chosen a Darjeeling, if that's acceptable. But if you'd rather—"

Just then a clock bonged three times—bonged so loud I nearly jumped out of my skin. My punishment for being early, I decided. I turned and saw the offender, a standing replica of Big Ben. How could I have missed *that*? Maybe because my attention had been drawn to the life-size stuffed Shakespeare in one corner and the massive sideboard next to him that held stacks of mismatched china and a glass display case showing off a copy of the velvet and jeweled crown used for British coronations. And I thought Verna Mae's house was overdecorated.

"I do so love the sound, don't you?" said Marjorie, her eyes moist with joy. "Very much like the original, you know."

"Never heard the original," I said, resisting the urge to massage my temples. That damn clock was loud enough to jar the pecans off the tree I could see through the dining room window.

"I'll pour, if that's acceptable," she said. "I must have my tea directly at three every day."

"Go for it," I replied. "Those are scones, I take it?" I nodded at the basket.

"Yes. Strawberry jam and clotted cream for accompaniment." She took a plate from the sideboard for me and used silver tongs to place one on the plate. She did the same for herself. I followed her lead, splitting the scone and spreading each half with jam and cream.

The sugar was cubed, making the tea far too sweet for my taste, but all negative thoughts were obliterated by the scone. My mouth rejoiced with each delicious bite. When I'd finished the first half and politely taken a few miniscule sips of tea, I said, "What part of Britain are you from?"

"Oh, I'm not from Britain," she said, smoothing more jam on another scone. "I'm from Waco."

I blinked. "Oh. But you lived in England, I take it. I mean, your accent . . . your home . . ."

Her gaze met mine. "I have visited London and the English countryside often, and find being British far more comfortable a demeanor for me than Texan. When I ran the shop, the accent helped quite a bit with sales. It's natural for me now." Her eyes glistened with what I decided was either humor or insanity. I wasn't sure which.

"Very . . . authentic," I said. "Tell me about the store. Why did you sell?"

"I wasn't very handy at shopkeeping," she said. "Had a difficult time parting with my items, as I'm sure you've noticed by a glance around here. My dear husband bought me the British Emporium so that I'd move some of my collection out of our home. Then the bloody bastard died on me. Still haven't quite forgiven him. After a period of mourning, I sold the Emporium and returned to what offers me the most comfort." She spread her arms. "This and Mr. Tibbetts."

"Mr. Tibbetts? You remarried?"

"Mr. Tibbetts is my cat," she said, her tone implying I was an idiot for not knowing this. "You'll meet him soon, now that the clock's sounded. He does like his clotted cream."

"Can't wait," I said, feeling as if I needed to put a "cheerio" in my voice. I turned and retrieved my purse—a leather backpack type that I'd hung on the back of the chair. I took out the pictures of the blanket and spread them in front of Marjorie. "Does this look familiar?"

Her hand went to her mouth to stifle her gasp. "Oh my word."

"You recognize it?"

"Hang on," she said, her fake accent momentarily lost. She bolted from the room, her puffy body bouncing with the speed.

I thought about following her, but when I turned, I saw Mr. Tibbetts lumbering into the room. I laughed out loud at the sight of him—all twenty pounds of black and white fluff. He was as puffy as his owner and knew where the cream was.

By the time Marjorie returned, he'd helped himself to the bowl.

"Mr. Tibbetts," she cried.

He raised his head for a second, revealing dripping whiskers, then resumed lapping.

Marjorie said, "If you'd like more cream, I can—"

"No, thanks," I answered, my eyes on what she held. "I'm far more interested in what you've got there."

She had a duplicate of the blanket from Verna Mae's house, same color, same two-inch satin binding. She offered it out to me and I took it, ran my hand over wool as soft as a cloud.

"I bought two of these," she said. "Sold one and kept the other. Mr. McGrady and I never gave up hope for a family, and if I had been blessed, my babe would have rested in this blanket. I was forty-five at the time. That's what a fool I was."

I found the label. POSH PRAMS.

"The woman who owned Posh Prams died not long after she sent me those blankets," Marjorie said. "She had the most wonderful baby things. These last two blankets, however, were far nicer than any she'd sent before."

"Do you remember who bought the other one?" I said.

"I don't recall the customers all that well. Mr. Trent is so good at remembering his customers, knows all the regulars by name. Myself? Besotted by my inventory. Yes, that sounds materialistic, but I love England, the queen, all the history and pageantry. I had my genealogy chart done and am related to the royal family. Remotely, yes, but all the items I've saved only strengthen that connection. I do remember my inventory, but not much else."

"Did you keep receipts, by chance?"

Her already bright cheeks fired up. "Paper takes up

room that could be best used for other items. I'm afraid I wasn't all that adept at bookkeeping."

"You saved nothing from the year you sold that blanket? Which was probably 1987, by the way."

"Ah, 1987. I parted with so many wonderful things in the shop that year." She sighed heavily.

Mr. Tibbetts, snout now covered with cream, paused and offered a liquid meow in sympathy.

"Since you had those identical blankets and kept one yourself, is there anything you could pull from your memory about the sale?"

"I should be able to, shouldn't I? They were pricey. One hundred and fifty pounds each. Worth every quid, too. See how well this one has held up?" She reclaimed the blanket and held it against one cheek.

"Someone well-to-do bought it, perhaps?"

"Most of my customers were well-to-do. Of course, when you buy items for your baby, price sometimes means nothing and—" She blinked hard. "Oh, my goodness. It was *then. Him.*"

"What do you mean?" I could tell from the far-off look in her faded blue eyes that she was remembering something.

"I'm almost certain a young black gentleman picked it up. Very young."

"You mean he bought it?"

Marjorie McGrady eased down into a chair. "No, he didn't. Someone else did. A telephone order. The details are all so fuzzy, but I recall thinking he was the limo driver. I probably wouldn't even have remembered that much if I hadn't seen his photo a week later."

"Really? Where?"

"In the newspaper. How could I have forgotten all this? He was arrested. A man in possession of one of my beautiful things had been *arrested*. Shameful turn of events."

They didn't put photographs in the paper of your everyday car thief or cat burglar—not then, not today.

This must have been far more serious. "Arrested for what?"

"Murder, I believe."

At that appropriate moment, Mr. Tibbetts knocked the bowl off the table, and clotted cream splattered everywhere.

10

"Mr. Tibbetts!" cried Marjorie McGrady. "Look what you've done!"

The cat, however, was too busy licking cream off the floor to pay any attention. Diva would have raced up the stairs in terror if she'd done anything like this, but not Fats Domino. He wasn't about to miss a drop.

While I picked up the shattered china bowl, Marjorie hurried to the kitchen for sponges and cleaners. She returned a minute later with a small pail, and we started in on the mess.

I worked on the Union Jack area rug beneath the table while Marjorie wiped up the wood floor and baseboards.

"This man who picked up the blanket," I said. "You're sure you recognized his picture in the newspaper?"

"Yes, it's all quite clear in my head now that I know this has to do with my blanket. He seemed like a polite, quiet young man when he'd come to the shop. Shocking for him to be accused of murder, I remember thinking."

"What time of year did this happen?" I saw newspaper archives in my future and wanted the timeframe narrowed down as much as possible.

"Right after Easter. I bought the blankets in March on a whim when we'd had a late cold snap. Isn't the blanket the softest, most lovely thing you've ever seen?"

"Yes indeed," I said, wringing out my sponge. I sat back on my heels. "Think I'm finished here. You mentioned you thought he was the limo driver. He arrived in a limo, then?"

Mrs. McGrady stopped her work and cocked her head. "I'm not quite sure. Perhaps the manner of that particular order made me think of a limo."

"Why's that?"

"Phone orders only came from regular customers, and I assumed the buyer had a big car and a driver. Many of my patrons were very wealthy." She paused, her forehead creased with thought. "Or maybe, and forgive me for saying this, but he *was* a young black man. In my mind back then—and yes, this is very wrong—he could have been . . . a servant sent out on an errand."

I nodded, knowing that was most likely why she'd come up with this limo idea. Not helpful at all.

Mrs. McGrady frowned. "I can see you're quite disappointed in me. The fact that I am not a—how do we say it these days?—a "people person" has been modified by the insight of age. I don't give a bloody damn what someone's skin color is anymore. People are asses no matter who their ancestors are."

I smiled. "At times, I think I agree."

I left Mrs. McGrady's house a little after four and stopped at the central branch of the library in downtown Houston. I was due to pick up Kate for our trip to Bottlebrush this evening—she had a client until six—but I wanted to see the newspaper photo of this murderer. Because online archives don't have photos attached, I couldn't go home and look up the article on my computer to view the photo Marjorie mentioned. I had to see it on microfilm.

I parked the Camry in the library lot, careful to put my parking ticket in the side pocket of my capris where I could find it. Last time I'd lost the stupid thing and ended up paying sixteen bucks for a full day after only an hour's worth of research. I also reached around the .38 in my glove compartment and raided my car-wash quarter stash. I'd need change for copies.

Once on the main floor of the library, I bypassed the escalators, went straight to the bibliographic research area in the far right corner, sat down and got to work. The *Houston Chronicle* was archived back to 1985, and though I feared I'd get dozens of hits for murders in April 1987, that wasn't the case. Seems less than four hundred people had been murdered the entire year, and only one in April had a picture of the accused alongside the article. The killing had taken place at night in a bank parking lot, and the victim was a University of Houston coed named Amanda Mason. Her murderer had been picked up at his parents' home only hours after the shooting, thanks to an anonymous tip. Amanda Mason's wallet, watch and jewelry were hidden in the guy's dresser drawer—he was an eighteen-year-old kid named Lawrence Washington. *What a brilliant criminal,* I thought.

I put several quarters in the printer, and while it was copying, I plugged Lawrence Washington's name into the archive search engine. A dozen hits popped up. The one that first caught my eye read ACCUSED KILLER HAD BRIGHT FUTURE. The other articles dealt with appeals, rehashing the murder and an interview with Lawrence Washington's father, who proclaimed his son's innocence. There was a related piece about how much crime took place near ATM machines since they'd begun to pop up everywhere. I wanted to dig deeper, read every article right this minute, but I'd be late picking up Kate if I scratched that itch right now.

After copying everything I could find, I took out my phone and called Jeff. I got his voice mail, so I left a message for him to hunt up anything he could on Lawrence Washington and the old murder conviction. Jeff had joined HPD in the nineties, but I was sure he'd be able to find out something about the case. As I was finishing the message, I realized this brief bit of cell phone indulgence had incurred the wrath of a man at an adjacent table.

He informed me that cell phones should be banned in libraries and looked about ready to knock me cross-eyed, so rather than respond like the smart-ass I am, I told him I was sorry and left to pay my parking fee, copies in hand.

11

I left downtown at rush hour—big mistake—and was late picking up Kate anyway. She was waiting in the parking garage next to her car as planned, wearing one of her "soothing" pastel suits—this one aqua. She's a firm believer that color affects her patient's mood and carefully chooses what she wears to work every day.

When she climbed in beside me, I handed the articles to her. "Could you read these out loud? Help make the drive to Bottlebrush more interesting?"

"No apology for making me stand around in a damp old garage for twenty minutes?" she asked.

I glanced at her as I stopped to pay more parking money—and this time I hadn't even parked. "Sorry. I was at the downtown library at five o'clock and hit gridlock."

She shook her head. "I'm sorry myself for being so cranky. Terry and I had a fight this morning, and I can't seem to shake my bad mood."

I laughed. "You and Terry fought? First time ever or what?"

"He's pressing me again to get married, and you know what a fence-sitter I am on *that* subject." She began shuffling through the pages I'd handed her.

"I'm staying on the outside of that particular dispute, seeing as how I'm O-for-one in the marriage department."

"Look who you've hooked up with now? Jeff is perfect for you."

"And Terry's right for you, Kate. He adores you."

"Why can't I commit?" she said.

"You're the shrink, not me."

"I know. This is my problem." She sighed and looked down at the stack of copies. "What *is* all this?"

As we headed for the freeway, I explained what I had learned today and that I hadn't had a chance to read through the articles. "Start with the one that mentions the killer's bright future," I said.

She found that particular article and began to read: "He was voted 'Most Likely to Succeed' and 'Most Athletic' at his high school and had just signed a letter of intent to play baseball for Texas A&M. Yes, Lawrence Washington was going somewhere. But now he's going to jail for the rest of his life. Washington, eighteen, was sentenced to life in prison yesterday, convicted in the execution-style slaying of University of Houston coed Amanda Mason."

"That sounds cold," I said, merging into a line of slow-moving traffic on the 610 loop.

Kate went on reading. "Friends and family can't explain why the bright young man who would have graduated tenth in his class in a few months would commit such a horrific crime. No one, not even the principal of Hurst High, can recall him ever raising his voice, much less getting into trouble. But according to one friend, Washington's mother has breast cancer and the family faces huge medical bills. Perhaps that's why Lawrence Washington put a gun to Amanda Mason's head and pulled the trigger, fearing she would identify him after the robbery if he let her live. Sadly, her cash withdrawal from the ATM near where her body was found that night had been a mere fifty dollars. Fifty dollars for two young lives wasted."

Kate sighed again. "How depressing. Makes me feel guilty for whining today."

"We've got it pretty good, huh?"

Kate took out her cell phone. "I'm calling Terry right now to apologize."

"Good idea, and when you're done, read me the rest of the articles. I need to know everything about this Lawrence Washington, even though I'm praying right now he's not connected to Will—especially when it comes to genetics. He's a black athlete, and that makes him a good candidate for biological father. Unfortunately, he is also a killer."

Kate had been ready to use her phone, but closed it and said excitedly, "The murdered girl could have been Will's birth mother. Yes, and he killed her to—"

"The timing's wrong, Kate. Amanda Mason died in April of 1987 and Will was born probably in October or late September of that year."

"Oh. Right. Reading these articles out of order is confusing." She reopened her phone and called Terry.

We were almost to Bottlebrush by the time she'd made up with him and finished reading the articles to me. One was a short piece on Washington's having exhausted his appeals, another a human interest story on the life and death of Amanda Mason that included interviews of her brokenhearted family. Several more articles had appeared when Washington was due for parole in 2004. Amanda Mason's family and their supporters made sure he stayed in Huntsville State Prison.

Since we'd had to navigate plenty of traffic on the freeways, the ride had taken more than two hours. Dusk was giving way to night when we parked in front of Verna Mae's house.

Before I unlocked the front door, I nodded at the bassinet planter. "There sits my first clue something wasn't right with Verna Mae."

"She was clinging to the most important event in her life," Kate said.

Once inside, I felt around on the wall for a light switch and then illuminated the foyer.

Kate took in the antique coat rack, an expensive-looking side table holding Lladro figurines of mothers and babies, and the plush carpet on the stairway to our right. "Nice place."

"Kind of suffocating, if you ask me. I say we start in her bedroom. That's where Burl and I found the blanket and the albums she'd made of Will's life story. I want those if Burl left them. I didn't get to examine them closely enough."

Kate said, "It *is* stuffy in here. Mind if I find the thermostat and turn on the air-conditioning?"

"Go for it," I said. "Meet you upstairs."

She took off down the hall, flicking lights on along the way, while I took the stairs. I turned on the light in Verna Mae's bedroom and found things were not as I remembered them. The oak dresser drawers were half open, the closet door stood ajar, even the linens on the bed were in disarray. I set down my purse and went to the four-poster, knelt and pulled out the box where we'd found the blanket and albums.

Empty. *Damn.*

No wonder Burl turned the keys over with a smile. He'd come back and taken what he wanted, left the place a mess. As Jeff said, the guy was still fixated on an old case he'd never solved.

I shoved the box back under the bed, more than a little pissed off, but when I did, I heard a tiny jingle. I removed the box, flattened on my belly and sank into carpet so thick you could sleep on it. Reminded me of my old digs in River Oaks, the mansion I'd grown up in and didn't miss one bit. With my cheek pressed against the carpet, I looked under the bed and spotted a lump that appeared to be a set of keys. They were more than an arm's reach away, and I had to squirm my shoulder under the frame to grab them.

Wiggling out from beneath the bed, I thought, *Got one back on you, Burl.* I sat cross-legged to check them out. One key was small, maybe for a padlock, and had a white, round tag marked B-109. The other looked like a house key. I pulled Verna Mae's set from my pocket for a comparison, but no match. Did

Verna Mae have more surprises to offer after her death? Like another house?

It dawned on me then that Kate hadn't joined me. Where the heck was she?

I retrieved my purse, stashed the keys and called her name as I made my way to the landing. She didn't answer.

"Kate," I yelled louder. "I found something."

Still nothing. In fact, the house was so quiet you could have heard a hummingbird's heart beat.

My own heart sped up. Something wasn't right.

I rushed down the stairs and followed the path made by the lights she'd turned on, aware that the smell of the spring night—a blend of honeysuckle and humidity—filled the house. Maybe she'd gone outside, leaving the door open so as not to get locked out.

Why? I wondered.

"Kate," I called, my voice cracking with fear. Where was she, damn it?

I ran down the hall, which suddenly seemed like the length of a football field, and stopped dead at the kitchen entry, my hand covering my mouth.

My sister was lying on the cold tile floor.

12

I rushed over, knelt by Kate and as soon as I touched her shoulder, she moaned.

"Talk to me," I said, stroking her cheek. "Tell me you're okay."

She turned toward me, blinking to clear the cobwebs. "I-I am okay. I think. Help me get up. This floor is hard."

"Are you sure you should move?"

"Don't get dramatic on me. Someone bopped me on the head, that's all."

Once I helped her sit up, she rubbed the back of her skull then held out her hand. "See? No blood. Just a little bump."

Brave talk, but she was pallid as paper. I touched her left cheek. "You're getting a bruise here."

She laid her face against her palm. "Probably from the fall. Believe me, I was never in hand-to-hand combat with anyone. That's more your style."

"Someone hit you hard enough to knock you out, Kate. We need to call an ambulance . . . and call Burl, too."

"No ambulance," she said sharply. "I don't want any traditional drugs or doctors unless I'm close to dying—and I'm not. Calling Burl's a good idea, though."

She stood with my help, and once on her feet, she tottered a little.

"You're as dizzy as a drunk trying to get out of the

tub," I said. "I reserve the right to overrule the 'no ambulance' call." I guided her to a kitchen chair before raiding the freezer. I opted for a package of frozen mixed vegetables for an ice pack. Being close to her favorite things ought to comfort Kate.

"Abby, I am *not* explaining this to Terry while I'm lying in some emergency room taking up space better used for real sick people. Are we clear?"

"Clear," I said. "For now."

After sitting at the table alternating the veggies between her head and her face, her cheeks regained some color. I found Burl's card, called him and told him what had happened. He said to sit tight, he was on his way.

Kate asked for water, and I found a spotless glass in a cupboard above the dishwasher. There were plenty to be had. The cabinet was crowded with expensive crystal glasses and china dishes. I filled a tumbler, brought it to Kate, then sat across from her. "What happened while I was upstairs?"

She took a generous swig, then held up the glass. "Heavy. Not your eight-for-a-dollar Wal-Mart special."

"What happened?" I repeated sternly.

"Wish I knew. I went looking for the thermostat, turned on the air and then thought I'd get a drink of water after all my yapping in the car. That's the last thing I remember."

"You didn't see anyone?"

"If I did, that memory's been erased."

I reached out and squeezed her arm. "Are you sure you're okay? That bastard could have—"

"Quit it, Abby. I'm fine. Did *you* see or hear anything?"

"I sure didn't hear what happened down here, but someone searched Verna Mae's bedroom, took the picture albums. We probably interrupted whoever it was. Maybe with me upstairs and you down here, they felt trapped. . . . You turned your back, they saw their chance, knocked you out and ran."

Kate sipped her water. "Whoever it was never made a sound. I had no clue someone was lurking around ready to pounce on me."

"I'd have heard you yelling like a Little Leaguer's mother if you'd seen whoever bopped you."

She smiled. "I *can* holler when necessary."

"Stupid me thought Burl had come back and raided the place just like we were doing, but obviously that's not the case."

"Why would someone want an obsessed woman's picture albums, Abby?"

"Damn good question. Verna Mae's death has to be connected to Will somehow. Maybe there was a clue in those articles and photos and the killer wanted them."

Just then Burl rushed in through the open back door, his gnarled fingers gripping a pistol in one hand and holding a crime scene kit in the other.

"Whoa," Kate said, her gaze fixed on his gun.

"Sorry. Didn't mean to scare you. You okay, little lady?"

"Yes, sir," she answered. "Abby used to beat me up worse than this when we were kids."

"We've only known each other a short time," Burl said, "but I don't doubt it. Let me make a quick check of this place, make sure no one's hanging around."

When he returned to the kitchen a few minutes later, he stashed his gun in his holster, came over and lifted Kate's chin, examining her cheek. "I'm thinking we should call the paramedics."

"Thanks but I've heard that suggestion and declined. I stay away from traditional medicine as much as possible. I'm Kate, by the way." She held out her hand.

They shook, and Burl said, "If you two would stay where you are, not touch anything, I'll get busy on the door. Looks like the lock was jimmied and someone ransacked the upstairs."

"Those albums are gone," I said. "You didn't take them by chance?"

"No, but I should have." Burl began his evidence collection, taking fingerprint powder and a brush from his kit. Kneeling in front of the door, he said, "Whoever it was, they parked out by the shed. I saw fresh tire tracks." Using the camera hanging around his neck, Burl snapped off a photo before dusting the door and knob for prints.

Meanwhile, I got up, ready to refill Kate's water glass.

When I moved, Burl whirled as fast as the snap of a whip. "Don't you even think about snooping around until—"

"Water?" I said, holding up the glass.

Burl sighed. "Sorry. Little edgy. I feel like I screwed up again by not taking Verna Mae's photo collection."

"It's not your fault," I said. "Who knew someone would want a bunch of old pictures? I'm wondering what else might be missing."

"I took a mental inventory when we were here last Friday night," he said, "but since it wasn't a crime scene, I didn't make a video. Any small stuff taken? We may never know."

"Yeah, well, I'm finding out who broke in," I said. "No one hurts my sister and gets away with it."

Kate smiled. "I think our thief might have poured gasoline on a fire, Chief Rollins."

He nodded. "I think you're right."

Not until I pulled into a parking spot near Jeff's apartment did I remember the keys I'd found under the bed. Burl had insisted Kate and I leave, saying she needed a good night's sleep. He made us promise before we left that we'd call him next time we decided to come to town.

I'd taken Kate home rather than drop her at the parking garage for her car. Terry could take her to work tomorrow. Then I'd had to deal with Terry, who'd been waiting up for us. After Kate explained what happened and went straight for arnica gel to heal her bruise and feverfew to ease her headache, he blasted me for putting Kate in harm's way. She reappeared in the middle of his explosion, however, and explained we had no way of knowing our trip would put either of us in danger. He took a deep breath and seemed to calm down. As I was leaving I heard Kate say, "Terry, I make my own decisions. Don't go off on my sister again, okay?" Maybe Kate's concerns about committing to Terry for a lifetime were founded on more ripples in their relationship than she'd talked about earlier.

I'd made a beeline for Wendy's after I pulled out of their driveway, so I was carrying a friendly white bag when I knocked on Jeff's door. He was expecting me. He'd finally returned my call on our way back from Bottlebrush, and when I told him what happened, he said to meet him at his place. He rarely spent much time at his apartment since we'd been together, but when he needed to grab a few hours of sleep and get right back to work, he spent late nights here.

He answered the door quickly, pulled me inside and before I could talk, wrapped me in his arms and kissed me.

"Kate okay?" he whispered against my lips.

"She says so," I answered. "That's the story she's sticking to, anyway. Stubborn doesn't stop with me."

"You two could have been—"

I put a finger to his lips and we started kissing again, the squashed bag of hamburgers falling to the floor. They stayed there, forgotten until we were lying in bed after a nice long hour of lovemaking.

"I brought food," I mumbled. I was lying on my side, head on his chest, one leg bent over his thighs.

"Didn't notice," he said. "Tell me about this break-in."

After I summarized the evening, Jeff said, "What was in those albums again?"

"A history of Will's life from the brief look I had,

but maybe there was more. I don't know." I got up and began gathering my clothes. I was hungry, and those burgers were salvageable, smooshed or not.

Jeff put his hands behind his neck. "Those clippings connected Verna Mae and Will, something the press knows nothing about yet. Something that the killer might not have wanted us to know."

"I like that. *Us.*" I hitched my bra and pulled up my panties. "Does that confirm the cases are connected? Could Will showing up in Verna Mae's life again have triggered her murder?"

He stared at me for a second. "God, you're gorgeous."

I grinned. "You're not so bad yourself. Now answer my question."

"You know my thoughts on coincidences and murder. There aren't any. That said, we've got nothing concrete to indicate that her death is connected to her strange attachment to Will." Jeff got up, retrieved his boxers and slipped them on. "So what's for dinner?"

"Squashed hamburgers and cold fries."

"Mmmm. Can't wait."

Jeff's kitchen is smaller than his bed, so we took our reheated food and the only other item in Jeff's fridge, a jar of dill pickles, into his agonizingly plain living room. The one item that hung on his wall held meaning, though—a wedding photo of his parents, both long dead. They were standing outdoors, Mount Rainier in the background. Jeff was not a native Texan, but I didn't hold it against him.

Then there was the upright piano that took up one wall. The always silent piano. The piano I'd asked about more than once. He never would talk about it. Something painful was connected to that thing, and maybe one day I'd hear about it—or better yet, hear him play. He did have long, wonderful pianist's fingers.

We sat on his dark green love seat, our legs intertwined. The love seat and a recliner were the only furniture in the room aside from a scratched-up coffee table and a few lamps.

Before crunching a pickle, I said, "Did you find out anything about Lawrence Washington?"

Jeff tore open a ketchup pack and squirted it on his paper plate. "Oh, yeah. That man's life is an open book. Inmates have no secrets—at least no secrets connected to how they ended up in prison."

"According to what I read at the library, the guy was headed to A&M on full scholarship—a smart kid, with a loving family. Any idea what made him commit such a terrible crime?"

"Washington never talked except to say he was innocent, according to the officer who snagged the case—guy's retired now. Washington's family needed money but weren't poor enough to qualify for county assistance. They had no insurance, either. Those are the kind of people who fall through that giant crack that exists between a rock and a hard place."

"Sounds like you feel sorry for them."

"The family. *Not* the killer. There's no excuse for what he did." Jeff's voice had gone hard.

I rubbed his knee. "Hey. I agree."

He looked at me. "Sorry, but if you haven't noticed, I've got no sympathy for killers."

"Think I could talk to Washington? See if he remembers picking up the blanket from the British store and what he did with it?"

"You're thinking the blanket makes him the birth father? I'm not so sure."

"It's possible, Jeff. He's black, he was an athlete and he picked up a blanket that Verna Mae kept hidden away for nineteen years."

"The blanket is not proof, Abby. Washington could have been doing a favor for a friend by picking it up."

"You're right. That's why I need to talk to him. Can you please arrange that?" I asked.

"I can get you in, but you'd need a background check first."

"If you recall, I already had a background check when I signed on with Angel."

"Forgot about that."

"You worried about me walking into a prison?" I asked.

"No . . . well, maybe a little. What makes you think Washington will talk to you, anyway?"

"My charm?"

Jeff's gaze traveled to my chest and then down my bare legs to my toes. I hadn't bothered to put on the rest of my clothes. "That might work," he said. "But I don't think they'd let you in dressed like you are right now. Might start a riot."

I grinned. "Can you go with me?"

"Nope. My plate is full. DeShay might be willing. He's ticked I'm not giving him much to do on this one."

"Great. When can we go?"

"I'll look into this tomorrow. Maybe you two can connect some of the coincidences, build something circumstantial between Verna Mae's death and Will's abandonment. Right now, all I know is that a woman was beaten, robbed and—oh, I forgot to tell you—shot."

I sat up straighter. *"Shot?"*

"Dr. Post faxed the preliminary autopsy report today. The Olsen woman was beaten then shot. Thing is, she was probably close to death from the assault. She hardly bled from the chest wound."

"Raped?"

"No evidence of rape. We do have a bullet, though. Real evidence you can hold in your hand. I plan to run the bullet through the system, see if I can trace the gun."

"This is crazy. What could Verna Mae have done to make someone so angry?"

"Maybe he wasn't angry—and you agree this had to be a male perp?"

"Or a woman strong enough to knock the white out of the moon," I said.

"Maybe the bad guy was trying to make her tell him something and beat her unconscious, then shot her to make sure she never gave up what she knew and never identified him."

"What about the gang angle you were following? Could this have been a test for a wannabe member?"

"I've been working the streets, but our informants say the Olsen murder wasn't a gang casualty. We do know she shed blood in her car, probably from a blow to the face, but they found no prints other than hers."

"You've got nothing except the bullet?" I asked.

He shook his head. "Nothing. Cases like this get damn frustrating when you pass the magic forty-eight-hour window. Leads dry up. I'm counting on you to see if our cases intersect."

"Nothing like a little pressure," I said.

"I trust you. Go interview Lawrence Washington, see what you come up with."

I rubbed my foot up and down his leg. "One more thing and then we can quit with the shoptalk."

I got up and retrieved my purse, pulled the keys from the side pocket and tossed them to Jeff. "What do you think of these? Is the tag from a storage facility?"

"Most likely. But where'd you find them and why are they important?"

"I'm not sure they are. I found them under Verna Mae's bed and wonder if they fell out of the album box."

"You took evidence from a crime scene?" From his tone, I expected Jeff to pull a pack of Big Red out of his shorts and cram every stick into his mouth.

"Not intentionally," I said quickly, sitting back down. "I had no idea it would become a crime scene. I found the keys before I found Kate out cold, and with all the excitement, I totally forgot about them until I arrived here."

"You're the one who told me Rollins is clinging to that blanket like it's the Holy Grail, so I don't think he'll be too happy you have these."

"I'll give them back." *After I copy them,* I thought.

"You mean after you copy them?" Jeff said.

"Did I say that?"

"Work with Rollins on this. It's not like you can call up every storage facility within a hundred miles and ask if Verna Mae Olsen rented space. They won't tell you a damn thing."

"You're right, but they'd tell a chief of police."

"You got it. If Burl wants in on this investigation, it's the perfect job for him. He may not have the time, but he sure has the desire."

"How long before you hook me up with DeShay and I can get into the prison?"

"I don't know. Depends on how many people get murdered tomorrow."

"Let's hope that for a multitude of reasons the number is less than one," I answered.

He sat up and brought me to him, his lips close to mine. "I'll help you get into the prison, but prepare yourself. It won't be fun."

We kissed and I tasted pickles and onions, but the way he held me, the shift from passion to protectiveness, told me he might just be a little worried.

And now I was, too.

13

Before Jeff's partner picked me up Wednesday morning for the trip to Huntsville State Prison, I made a quick run to Marjorie McGrady's place—calling first, of course. She agreed to see me, and I showed her the newspaper photo of Lawrence Washington. She remembered the layout of the article, where the story had been placed on the page more than his picture, and stared at the photo for a long time before deciding he was indeed the man who'd picked up the blanket. I stared right along with her, and though I decided Washington and Will bore a vague resemblance, it wasn't enough to add to the list of reasons he was the birth father.

After I returned home, DeShay Peters picked me up in his unmarked police car and we started north on I-45 toward the prison. The first hour of the drive was dedicated to a discussion of DeShay's latest girlfriend. We had come to the conclusion that she was too high-maintenance for him. DeShay, forced to wear a coat and tie for the job, would rather be wearing baggie jeans and Houston Texan T-shirts, whereas Tisha spent hours shopping at the Galleria for shoes when she wasn't getting her nails painted with little American flags.

"Good," he said, leaning the driver's seat back a little. "Tisha's history. Now, Abby, tell me more about your side of this case. You know Jeff. The man's good, but he'd rather chew gum than talk. I only got the Cliffs Notes version of what we're doing today."

I told him what I'd learned so far, and by the time I was done, the rifle towers and razor wire surrounding the old redbrick units that make up Huntsville State Prison appeared on the horizon.

"I try not to look on either side of the highway when I drive by here on my way to Dallas," I said.

"Why?" DeShay asked, sounding surprised.

"Because Huntsville State Prison is a nasty old dungeon filled with hatred and violence."

"As far as I'm concerned this is the best damn place in the world, even if half the population are brothers. Not to say I don't work every day at getting more white guys locked up. White guys do just as much evil shit as the next man, but they got so damn much money, they get mouthpieces who can actually talk for them. Black dudes? They got nothing but mamas who cry a lot. Damn injustice, Abby. You hear what I'm saying?"

"I hear, all right. Jeff tell you my ex is here? *He's* a white dude."

"Say what?" DeShay sounded genuinely shocked.

"Yup. Killed two people."

"If it'll make you less jumpy, he's not here, Abby. He'd be in Livingston."

"No," I said. "He's here. On death row."

"Death row's been moved. 'Course when they give him the needle, they'll bring him here. You gonna come and watch?"

"Are you kidding? I never want to see him again, alive or dead. He blackmailed my adoptive father, nearly killed me and then for some stupid reason, when he was about to drown in a flash flood, I saved his sorry ass."

"That's the difference between you and him. It's called a conscience."

"Yeah, I have plenty of that," I said, nodding. "My daddy used to say conscience is like a toothless old hound. It might not bite you, but you can't keep it from barking. Mine barks all the time."

"Jeff talked about the case that brought you two together after we were partnered up, but he never said your ex was the bad guy. How'd you hook up with someone like that?"

"He was smart, could charm the skin off a snake and I thought I loved him. Didn't take me long to figure out his charm came courtesy of Jose Cuervo. He was an alcoholic, and I divorced him. But did I keep my distance? No. Big mistake. He killed my yardman, partnered up with the lawyer who'd arranged my illegal adoption and then murdered him, too. All for money. It's very sordid and makes me sound like a fool."

"You are *no* fool, not if Jeff Kline, the smartest guy I ever met, is head over his ass about you."

I laughed. "Feeling's mutual."

"You like the PI stuff?" DeShay asked, pulling into the parking lot of the Goree Unit, where Washington had lived for the last eighteen years.

"More than I thought," I said, noting the turnoff was almost in the shadow of the humongous cement statue of Sam Houston that for some bizarre reason guards the interstate. The thing was ugly, white and about six stories high. What in hell were the folks in Austin thinking when they contracted for this? That statue was scary enough to give kids nightmares.

DeShay parked after we were checked through at the gate—a police badge is handy at locked entrances—and as we got out of the car, I said, "I hope you plan to help me out with this interview. If I go wrong, pinch me or something."

"Jeff would send me out of this life if I hurt you."

I slugged his arm. "You know what I mean."

"Hey, I'll be right next to you the whole time. Just give me a look and I'll step in, but this is your deal."

Once we were escorted inside, DeShay turned over his weapon, and since I was civilian, I gave up my driver's license. We passed through a metal detector, and a young man wearing a gray uniform with navy epaulets led us down a narrow, bleak corridor.

We were taken to the empty visitors' area. The long room was split by a counter with chairs facing mesh and Plexiglas that divided the prisoners from their visitors. Despite the air-conditioning, the old room smelled of mildew with an undercurrent of body odor and urine—those smells leaching from beyond the divider. And then there was the hint of eau de sour mop.

The guard gestured us to chairs and said the prisoner was on his way. Then he stood in one corner, hands behind his back, his young, smooth face impassive.

"This place makes me feel so small." I didn't add scared, but my heart was pounding so hard I felt every beat in my temples. Gates and bars and ancient, chilly rooms had a definite effect on me, I was learning. Not to mention the unsmiling faces of the gray shadows who worked here. How could they do this day in and day out? Where do you stash your fear before you step beyond those heavy doors?

Through the distortion of the scratched, smudged Plexiglas I saw a guard let Washington into the room. He wore no cuffs or shackles as I'd expected, and they left him alone. Tall and not as dark-skinned as DeShay, his prison-issue pants and shirt were as white as the Sam Houston statue.

He sat across from us, and I stifled an "Oh, my God." The grainy, copied picture from an old newspaper had not told the truth. This man's resemblance to Will shocked me. Sure his skin was darker, his eyes brown not amber, but he could have spit that boy out, that's how sure the resemblance was.

"Why am I here?" Washington's soft voice hardly carried through the mesh and glass.

I couldn't answer right away. All doubts had disappeared now that I was being confronted with a resemblance almost as honest as a mirror. Will's father was a murderer. That wasn't quite what he or his family had hoped to discover.

Washington stared straight into my eyes, awaiting my response, and when I didn't answer, he repeated the question.

"I'm sorry," I said, focusing on this familiar face. "It's just that you look like someone I know."

"Get to the point. I have work to do in the laundry." Even tone. Not insolent or sarcastic.

His gaze and demeanor spoke of intelligence and self-control. Not what I expected from a man sentenced to life in prison. Guess I thought he'd be as egotistical as my ex. I took him in more fully and thought I also saw sadness in his eyes. A profound sadness so tangible it made my heart heavy. This was an awful place, and every bit of pain he'd been subjected to rested in his eyes. I didn't want to feel sorry for him, but I did. I just did.

DeShay cleared his throat to encourage me to speak, and I managed to find my voice. "My name is Abby Rose and this is Sergeant Peters. I'm working in conjunction with HPD on the murder of a woman named Verna Mae Olsen. I'm hoping you can help me."

"Then you'll put in a good word with the parole board?" Washington asked, eyebrows raised.

I looked at DeShay for this answer.

"Depends on what you got to say, bro," he said.

"I am *not* your brother." Washington's eyes glinted with anger.

"I think we'll move on," I said quickly. "Maybe you'll find a reason to help after I've explained why I'm here. I'm working for a young man named Will Knight. Basketball player at UT. Ever heard of him?"

"Who hasn't?"

"He's my client and he's—" I stopped, remembering the guard on the far side of the room. Would he leak the connection between Will and Verna Mae to the press? Was this how information got out? But . . . Jeff wouldn't have helped me get here if he hadn't been willing to risk that possibility.

"You know a superstar," Washington said. "I'm impressed. What does that have to do with anything?"

Sarcasm had surfaced now, but I could tell he was interested.

"Will Knight was adopted as an infant," I said. "He hired me to find his biological family. That search led me to Verna Mae Olsen. Did you know her?"

He looked down at his hands folded on the divider's ledge. "Never heard of her."

"She was murdered after my client and I paid her a visit. See, she found Will on her doorstep in 1987. We discovered a baby blanket at her house after she died. A very special blanket. A blanket I've learned that *you* picked up from a British import store about nineteen years ago."

Washington's head snapped up. He glared at me, the muscles of his forearms bulging with tension. I began to wonder about the strength of Plexiglas about then.

The angry silence that followed seemed to slash through the mesh. I'd never felt so intimidated and yet so exhilarated at the same time. That blanket meant something to Lawrence Washington.

"I *never* bought any blanket." He enunciated slowly, every word cold and bitter.

Semantics, I thought. *You may not have bought it, but you sure as hell picked it up.* Arguing with him wouldn't get me anywhere, though, so I said, "I believe Verna Mae's connection to Will might have something to do with her murder. I need more proof. Please tell me about the blanket."

"I don't know anything about any blanket or any baby or any woman who got killed. That's *all* I have to say." He held my gaze.

I swallowed. Jeez, this was unnerving. But though Washington's presence was intense, I could tell by his eyes, the shifting back and forth, he was thinking hard. Had I surprised him? Had he been unaware until now that Will Knight was most certainly his son? Had he never noticed the resemblance when he watched Will play basketball on TV? That wouldn't really have surprised me, however. I'd looked at a photo of my birth mother before I knew who she was and never saw the obvious resemblance between us.

I leaned forward, holding his gaze. "What's going on, Lawrence? Why are you so upset?"

He laughed. "Upset? Not me. But you? I think you're as crazy as a shit-house rat."

DeShay half rose and pointed his finger at Washington. "Watch your mouth, *inmate*."

I put a hand on his forearm. "No problem, DeShay." Looking back at Washington, I had no choice but to press harder. "Tell me who bought that blanket. Was it you? Or did someone send you to pick it up?"

It was then that the thought of this man conceiving a child with Verna Mae flashed through my mind—sort of like a teeth-rattling smack to the face. I couldn't picture her as a seductress of teenage boys. No. That theory was all wrong. Had to be. Maybe Washington picked up the blanket for her that day and now that she'd been murdered, he wasn't about to talk. Why should he risk being even remotely connected to another crime?

Washington straightened, his lips tight, his eyes closed. "I have nothing more to say."

Everyone has their currency, I thought. Problem was, I had no clue what was important to Lawrence Washington. Big mistake. I didn't know enough to be sitting here. Yup, I'd screwed up again.

I had nothing and Washington knew it. He stood and yelled for the guard to take him back to the laundry.

Out of the side of his mouth, DeShay whispered, "Abby. He's splitting."

"That's okay. We'll be back—when I'm better prepared."

DeShay sighed. "You're the boss."

As we were led out, I spoke to the young guard. "Washington have many visitors?"

"Not since I've worked here. He sees the chaplain every day, though."

"Every day? Is the chaplain here?" I asked.

"Sure," the guard said.

"Could we see him, please?"

The chaplain, we soon learned, had an office behind several sets of locked doors deep inside the facility. We had to wait in a hallway outside while he finished a session with an inmate. I moaned to DeShay about my poor preparation for the Washington interview and he cheered me up by saying I'd done pretty damn good for a rookie.

Finally, the inmate left and the chaplain came out to greet us, his wispy red hair and freckled arms telling us a little something about him before he even spoke. The Irish skin never lies. Not that a man of God would lie, but you never know.

"Jim Kelly," he said, reaching for my hand first and then shaking hands with DeShay. He was casually dressed in Dockers and a plain white polo shirt.

After we introduced ourselves, he grabbed a hall chair and dragged it into his office. We followed him into a closet-size room.

A pewter cross hung on one wall and a giant box of tissues sat on an otherwise bare desk. The wastebasket alongside the desk was filled with crumpled Kleenex. Though the sadness that shrouded Lawrence Washington had touched me, that full wastebasket gave me an odd sense of satisfaction. It shouted loud and clear that prison is hell, as it should be. At least some of these men cry, and that had to be a good thing.

Kelly sat behind his small metal desk and gestured for us to be seated as well. "I'm told you want to talk to me about Mr. Washington, but you understand I'm required to keep inmate confidences."

"We know." DeShay sat in the hall chair while I took the padded one I assumed the inmates used. "Just want your take on the guy. We need his help on a case and he's not obliging."

Kelly steepled his hands. "I see. That surprises me."

"Why?" I asked.

"Because I have always found him to be a gentle, cooperative man."

"Really?" DeShay said with a laugh. "You mean gentle for a murderer?"

Kelly flushed, his earlobes turning crimson. "You've met him once, Officer. I've known him for years."

"He sees you every day?" I asked.

Kelly looked at me. "Yes. Are you wanting me to put in a word? Help him see the importance of his cooperation?"

"That would be great," I said.

"Then you'd better have a compelling reason I should do that, Ms. Rose. I have a strong bond with Lawrence and I will not break that trust by convincing him to do anything not in his best interest."

"Strong bond, huh?" said DeShay, his voice iced with sarcasm. "You know why he's here and you can forget he killed a girl? God says that's okay?"

Whoa. What was with DeShay? Why had the chaplain struck a nerve with him? Kelly seemed like a good guy.

"God forgives what others can't," Kelly said calmly. He'd no doubt heard plenty of what DeShay was dishing out.

"God's forgiven Lawrence?" I asked.

"If there was anything to forgive, yes," Kelly replied.

DeShay groaned in mock agony. "Oh, so he's innocent in God's eyes? You guys with collars think—"

"You think he's innocent?" I said quickly, interrupting DeShay's off-putting attitude before he did more damage.

Kelly intertwined his fingers. "I believe he is."

"Why?" I rested a hand on DeShay's forearm and squeezed, hoping he'd keep his mouth shut.

"In my opinion, Lawrence Washington does not think or act like a criminal—and I've seen plenty of hardcore criminals. What's even more convincing is that the other inmates have told me they think he's innocent, too. Believe me, *they* know."

"He could have lashed out in anger the night he committed the crime," I said.

"Do you know the details of that murder?" asked the chaplain.

"I researched it, so yes." *But not enough,* I added to myself.

"Did what you *researched* sound like someone *lashed out* at that poor young woman?" Kelly said.

"I read it was an execution-style murder," I said.

"Good. I've made my point." Kelly leaned back in his chair.

"Has he told you he's innocent?" I asked.

"That's confidential, but do I really have to answer that question?" Kelly replied.

"I guess not," I said.

"Do you plan to tell me why you need Lawrence's help?" Kelly asked.

"Sure, if it will get us some answers." I related all I'd learned so far while a sullen DeShay kept quiet. Something had definitely turned him off to Jim Kelly. I finished my summary, saying, "I have to tell you this. Will Knight and Lawrence Washington look very much alike. If Washington can provide us with a DNA sample, we might be able to prove those two are father and son."

DeShay piped in. "We already have a DNA sample, Abby. He committed a crime in Texas."

Kelly's relaxed attitude disappeared as he sat straighter. "You cannot check for paternity with a CODIS sample, Sergeant. Federal law is very strict about how you use the database."

DeShay sighed. "Guess you know the law almost as well as you know your best buddy inmates. You and God gonna help us on this one?"

Kelly smiled. "I might do that, Sergeant, because you see, I think God is the one who sent you both here."

On the ride back to Houston, I called DeShay immediately on his attitude change after we'd sat down with the chaplain.

"Sorry," he said, "but some things get to me. See, the reason I wear a badge is because my sister was murdered when she was sixteen. Drive-by shooting. Some damn bleeding-heart minister convinced my mother to forgive the crackhead who killed her. Mamma actually testified during the penalty phase on the bad guy's behalf. Then she dropped dead the next day. Had a massive stroke. Now that's God talking, you ask me. The Big Man called her on her mistake."

"So you're mad at her, too?"

"No. I only wish things would have turned out differently."

"You go to church anymore, DeShay?" I said quietly. If his mother's faith had been that strong, he'd probably been raised in a religious home.

"Don't feel comfortable there, you know?"

"Yeah. Forgiveness may be a choice, but it's not an easy choice. And before you get all pissed off again, I'm in that boat myself. I'm having a hard time forgiving my adoptive Daddy. I thought he hung the moon, but after he died, I found out he was a liar. A liar with good intentions, but still a liar. Then I married an even bigger liar who blackmailed and killed and generally messed up my life and plenty of other folks', too. I haven't forgiven either of them."

DeShay changed lanes to avoid a convoy of trucks traveling the interstate toward Houston. "You're a lady who leads with her heart. Sounds like that got you into trouble. Not all bad, putting your emotions out there. Me? I deal with them by working the streets, loving my job."

"Me, too. Even when it gets . . . emotional and scary."

"You got the smarts to do this investigating thing, Abby. Be careful with that Washington dude, though. Bad guys are pretty much all psychopaths, and psychopaths are convincing SOBs."

"What if he *is* innocent?" I asked.

"Washington's guilty of something or he'd be talking. They all want that get-out-of-jail-free card and we hinted we might offer a good parole report. Somehow, that wasn't enough. That tells me something."

I glanced out the passenger window. DeShay was right. If Washington was innocent, why had he walked out on the interview? Was he protecting someone? The mother of his child—who probably was *not* Verna Mae? I could be wrong about that, though. DNA doesn't lie. If it wasn't Verna Mae, who was the birth mother? I didn't know, but maybe looking deeper into Washington's past would help me answer that question.

After DeShay dropped me off at home, I went straight to the garage and climbed in my car. I couldn't fix the mistake I'd made by rushing to the prison prematurely, but I could take the keys back to Burl, explain why I had them and enlist his help as Jeff had suggested.

About five p.m., I walked into the Bottlebrush police station, and Burl came out to the front desk to greet me.

"What's up, Abby?"

"I'd like to take you out to dinner and, well, apologize. Then maybe you'll help me with something."

"If you're apologizing for not telling me you and your sister were coming to town last night, there's no need, Abby."

"It's not that. I have to talk to you. Anywhere we can grab dinner?"

"You think the Missus would like it one bit if I went out to dinner alone with a woman who looks like you? Believe me, she'd hear about it before I paid the check."

"I'm paying the check," I said.

"No. We'll go to my place. That will make everyone happy."

We left a few minutes later, with me following Burl home. He lived on the outskirts of Bottlebrush in a sprawling brick one-story home. When we arrived, he introduced his wife, Lucinda, who had come out on the front porch to greet us. She responded by giving me a punishing hug while reminding me we'd already met on the phone.

"Pretty thing, isn't she, Burl? You married?" she asked as she and Burl led me into their house.

"Divorced," I answered. I was proud of that particular piece of paper.

"You're free. Great. Our oldest, Burl Junior, is—"

"Lucinda. Quit." Burl looked over his shoulder at me. "He's twenty-one. She thinks he needs to get married as soon as he graduates next May."

"He's a little young for a thirtysomething like me, wouldn't you say?" I smiled, glancing around. If there was an opposite of the place I'd visited this morning, this was it. Warmth and comfort filtered out from walls crammed with photos of a smiling family, not to mention the smell of the home-cooked meal that saturated the air and had my mouth watering.

"Hope you like fried chicken," Lucinda said when we entered the country-style kitchen. "We'll have plenty for ourselves. The boys are gone doing their thing. One has swim practice; the other's into martial arts, so he's out breaking apart planks of wood. Boys do like to destroy stuff. Burl Junior's up at A&M taking a summer Spanish class."

An oval table covered by a green woven cloth was set with bright plates, all different colors, cloth napkins and tall glasses of tea. Steaming bowls of mashed potatoes and green beans surrounded a platter of golden chicken pieces.

"You knew I was coming?" I asked.

"Burl called me to set a place for you on his way home. We talk a lot. Or I do, if he's telling it. Anyway, this is a better dinner than you'll get in town. Not a decent restaurant to be found unless you're looking for eggs and grits. Casey's Café does serve up an acceptable breakfast after church."

"Sit, Abby," Burl said, "or Lucinda will talk you to death before you get to taste the best fried chicken in the world."

So we ate, and I found no time for talk during that meal. I was too busy savoring every mouthful. Lucinda managed to get in plenty of conversation, though. By the time she was finished, I knew everything that had happened in Bottlebrush that day, down to the woman who'd broken a liter of Dr Pepper in a supermarket aisle and thought she could just walk away without telling a clerk. The way Lucinda told it, the woman had more nerve than a sumo wrestler turned cat burglar.

Burl leaned back in his chair, a contented smile on his face. "I'm curious. What do you need to apologize for, Abby?"

"A set of keys I spotted under Verna Mae's bed. I grabbed them, but when I found Kate hurt, I forgot all about them." I rose and went to my purse, which Lucinda had set on the kitchen counter. I removed the originals and handed them to Burl. "Here you go."

He stared at the keys in his palm. "You gonna give me the copies you made, too?"

"And why would I make copies?" I said evenly.

"Hand them over." He sounded just like Daddy used to when I got caught in a lie.

"Is there a reason I can't keep a set? I mean, the estate belongs to Will and he's given me free rein."

"Think for one second and answer that question yourself," he replied.

"Okay. So you don't want me messing with evidence," I answered.

"Aren't you glad we never had girls, Lucinda?" Burl said.

"I don't know, sugar," said Lucinda. "This one might make me proud if I were her mother. You gotta admit, she's working her case."

"Yes, ma'am," he said. "But she still needs to give me the copies."

I did. One set, anyway. "Looks like the key with the label might be for a storage unit, right?" I asked after I handed them over.

"Yup, and just 'cause I have these, doesn't mean you can't know where these keys lead me."

"Thanks. See, that's what we need help with. Finding what they belong to."

"We?"

"Sergeant Kline and me. I am working with HPD on this."

"How could I forget? You want to fill me in, then? 'Cause I got a feeling you're holding back."

"I am not holding back. That's why I invited you to dinner, to tell you everything I've learned—though coming here was a far better idea." I smiled at Lucinda. "If I ate like this every day, I'd have to make two trips just to haul butt."

She laughed. "I think you two should go in the other room and talk while I clean up."

"Let me help you with the dishes," I said.

"Go," she said sternly. "Both of you. Now."

We went to the front room and settled into worn armchairs. I told Burl about Lawrence Washington and my visit to Hunstville today.

"Have you had time to tell your cop friend you're convinced Washington is Will's daddy?" he asked when I'd finished.

"No," I said with a grin. "I was too busy copying keys."

"Even if he is the daddy, it still doesn't explain much. We got a bleeding-heart chaplain who thinks the guy's innocent, a blanket connecting Washington to Verna Mae, and a resemblance that says Will and the prisoner are related. Thing is, Washington's been locked up tighter than oil in a barrel for a long time. How does he figure into Verna Mae's murder?"

"Good question. If there had been an argument over the baby or some other problem between him and Verna Mae because she was supposed to care for the child, maybe he got someone on the outside to murder her. Maybe—"

My phone rang and I dug it out of my purse. It was Jeff.

"Hey, there," he said. "I dropped by your place and you weren't home."

"I'm with Burl. Filling him in on the case."

"Good. Then you better share this piece of news, too. Just got the DNA report. Verna Mae Olsen is *not* Will's birth mother. She's no relation. Period."

14

"No DNA match?" I said.

"Nope. Why don't you sound surprised?" Jeff said.

"DeShay and I met with Lawrence Washington, and call it intuition, but I left the prison pretty certain he would never have slept with Verna Mae." I went on to tell Jeff about the resemblance.

"Abby, a resemblance isn't evidence any more than your incorrect conclusion—logical though it might have been—that Verna Mae was Will's birth mother."

"Go ahead. Rub it in. I deserve it." This was damn depressing. Did I really know what I was doing on this case or was I in over my head?

"Don't get all down on yourself," Jeff said. "You mess up, you start over."

"Thanks for the pep talk," I answered, still feeling dumb for not preparing better for the prison interview. "See you tonight?"

"Probably not. Tied up on a new case. No one forgot to do murder in Houston on this fine June evening, I'm sorry to say."

"Okay. We'll talk later." I hung up.

Burl nodded. "No match, just as you suspected."

"Verna Mae is definitely not Will's mother," I said.

His whole body seemed to relax. "I never thought so, but it makes me feel better to have proof. Her being so big and all and me being an inexperienced buck, I never asked the one question I should have.

I'm relieved she didn't give birth but still mad at myself."

"What's her connection to Will, then? I mean, she loved that kid, Burl."

"You *think* she did. That's not a fact."

"Yeah. People keep reminding me about those pesky facts." I closed my eyes, let out my breath and thought for a second. "Maybe someone left Will on the porch and she and Jasper kept the child for a week or two. When Will's skin darkened and his features began to look more African-American, Jasper told her to get rid of the baby."

Burl nodded. "Knowing Jasper, that explanation makes sense to me. She musta got attached to Will. Real attached."

"That would explain her scrapbooks," I said.

"Yeah, but there's more to this," he said, shaking his head. "Whoever broke in and stole those books knows something we don't, something worth breaking the law for."

I thought for a second. "Okay, what if Will's abandonment wasn't random? If someone intentionally left the baby with Verna Mae, she would have known whom to contact once Jasper screwed things up, maybe asked them to pay her to keep quiet about the baby."

"Not random, huh?" Burl said, sitting back.

I nodded, liking this idea. I knew better than to fall in love with it, though. "If we knew of anything else taken from the house last night besides those albums, that would sure help."

"No way to know," Burl said. "I didn't find anything but those tire tracks. I'm working on a match, but the cast wasn't good. Don't hold your breath."

"The books . . . Verna Mae's connection to Will, you think that's all the thief wanted?"

"Could be," Burl said. "They missed the keys, though."

"Oh, yeah." I smiled. "Guess we have something after all. Changing the subject, have you heard anything about the cold case at the CPS office yet? If that's how Verna Mae found out where Will had been placed, it could lead us somewhere."

"Bet she paid someone to steal Will's file and trash the place as a coverup," he said.

"If you can get a hold of the case file, maybe they collected fingerprints or had a lead. Could be names in the file we could check out."

Burl sighed. "Abby, they won't even *have* a case file."

"But you said—"

"Ever hear of the statute of limitations? I called over there hoping they'd help me track down whoever worked that case, see if the guy is still around. If you expect fingerprints, you're dreaming."

I stood, feeling a little stupid. I should have realized there'd be no file—unless they were very, very behind at the county sheriff's office and hadn't thrown out anything in two decades. "I'm tired and discouraged," I said. "Maybe on the drive home I can sort things out."

Burl got up, put an arm around my shoulder and squeezed me close. "Turn on the radio and give it a rest."

"Yeah. I might do that." Funny, but I welcomed his fatherly embrace and marveled at how murder and secrets had joined two strangers in friendship so quickly.

I took Burl's advice and sang along with Dave Matthews and Norah Jones in the car. Definitely relaxing. Once I was home and climbed into bed, I was fast asleep in twenty minutes, Diva purring next to me as happy as a lizard on a rock.

Thursday morning I spent a long time in the shower, organizing my thoughts on the case. I dressed in shorts and a T-shirt—it was supposed to get into the mideighties today—and went to my office to call Jeff for the names and numbers of the officers who'd arrested Lawrence Washington. He told me one officer was dead, the other a retired detective named Randall

Dugan. Jeff had never met either of them. He said he'd phone Dugan and tell him to expect a call from me.

Every newspaper article I'd read about Washington's case said they had a mound of evidence, but details might provide me with something useful. Who better to give me the inside scoop than the officer who'd worked the case? Thirty minutes after speaking to Jeff, I called the retired policeman, and he answered with "Dugan here," in a raspy, abrupt greeting.

I gave him my name, reaffirmed my police connection to the ongoing murder investigation and said, "Do you remember the Lawrence Washington case?"

Silence followed and went on so long I finally said, "Mr. Dugan? Are you still there?"

"Yeah, I'm here. Kline said you needed my help with a *fresh* case."

"Did Sergeant Kline mention the fresh case may be connected to your old case?"

"Oh. That's right."

Memory problems? I wondered. "Lawrence Washington," I prompted.

"I remember him. Shouldn't be sitting in Goree, where they practically wipe those inmates' asses for them, I'll tell you. What do you want to know?"

"I recently interviewed Lawrence Washington. Apparently you have no doubts about his guilt?"

"Are you nuts? He did that girl for a lousy fifty bucks. Shot her brains out. We found her ID and the money in Washington's bedroom two hours later."

"I read that much in the old newspapers. What about the weapon?"

"No weapon."

"Did you find out Washington was the shooter through a tip?" I asked.

"Officer's best friend." I could picture Dugan smiling.

"You had Crime Stoppers back then?" I said.

"They've been around for thirty years, lady. How old are you, anyway?"

Apparently not old enough to know better than to ask dumb questions. I was glad he couldn't see me blush. Before I could cover my embarrassment with some smart-aleck remark, Dugan said, "The tip on Washington wasn't for Crime Stopper money. Came in straight to the precinct, and we followed the lead. Once we collared the kid, he never denied he did it."

"What did he say?" I asked.

"A whole lot of nothing. Wouldn't even talk to his own lawyer from what I heard."

"Did you ever find out who gave you that tip?"

"No. But not for lack of trying. That was Frank's deal. Finding out who called."

"You mean your partner, Frank Simpson?"

"Yeah." A quiet "yeah" followed by, "God rest his soul."

"I assume Frank was as convinced as you were about Washington's guilt?"

"Man, I miss that guy. Visit his grave with Joelle on our retirement anniversary. We retired on the same day, you know. But he only lived three months and then, *wham*!"

I heard a slapping sound so loud I pulled the phone away from my ear for a second. Dugan's words had begun to run together, and I guessed his emotion had been boosted by a few Miller Lites.

"Joelle is your wife?"

"No. Frank's wife. Frank was too good to live, you know what I'm saying? Some guys are just too good to live."

"Frank thought Washington was guilty? He agreed with you?" I repeated.

"He *never* agreed with me," Dugan said with a laugh. "That's what I liked about the guy. He could keep me in line. I couldn't agree with him on Washington, though. We had the evidence, an uncooperative kid who had dumped his wheels that night. I figured he thought the car had been spotted near the scene and got rid of it in some junkyard. Anyway, we had everything, toots."

Toots? My turn to wonder how old someone was. "Did Frank ever come around to your way of thinking?"

"Nope. I testified in court, which let him off the hook. He still had his doubts about Washington. He and I had a few cases like that, but not many. Frank always held onto his doubts to the bitter end. I swear that's what killed him. The fucking doubts." I heard the clink of a bottle or glass, and then Dugan swallowed.

"What exactly were those doubts about Washington?" I asked.

"He said the case was too pat. Too easy. He worried about the easy ones. Joelle said Frank was still talking about that one 'til the day he died."

"Joelle? Does she live around here?" I asked.

" 'Course she lives around here. Why?"

Why? I thought. *Because I need to talk to her.* But aloud I said, "Just wondered. I think it's great you two keep up with each other."

"We always keep up with each other's families. That's who we are. You still haven't told me how the fresh murder connects with this. I want to know."

I explained about Verna Mae's death, the scrapbooks, the blanket and the will leaving everything to my client.

"Okay, Washington knocked up some girl before he did our vic. So what?" "So what" had become one word.

"There's a lot of money involved, money my client knew nothing about. But others may have. I don't have to tell a retired police officer what the prospect of a few hundred grand does to some people."

"This still isn't fitting together for me," he said.

"Washington picked up the blanket at an upscale store and it ended up at Verna Mae's house."

"How in hell does that prove he didn't kill my vic?" he asked, sounding angry. "You're wasting my—hey. Wait a minute. How much did you say that blanket cost?"

"A lot, but—"

"Maybe Washington didn't want money for his sick mother. Maybe he killed Mason to buy his girlfriend some fancy-ass blanket for their kid." I could tell Dugan was liking this idea.

"The woman who sold the blanket doesn't think he bought it. He was picking it up for someone else."

"She doesn't *think* he bought it? She's not sure?"

Obviously cops never really retire. "You're right. I don't have any proof Washington didn't murder Amanda Mason." I waited for Dugan's *I told you so.* The words remained unspoken, but I could hear even more attitude in his tone as I segued into a good-bye. I wasn't about to convince him that he might have arrested the wrong guy. Not in a million years. Frank's wife was the one I needed to talk to.

Joelle Simpson was my next stop. Maybe what her late husband had told her would provide enough information for me to return to the prison and question Lawrence Washington again, this time telling him I had doubts about his guilt, just like Frank Simpson and the chaplain. Maybe then he'd talk.

After I hung up from Dugan, I'd called Frank Simpson's widow and told her I needed her help on one of her husband's old cases. She'd acted like I was a long-lost high school friend. "Could you come today?" she'd asked. "Frank would want you to come right away if he were alive."

A little stunned by this instant and eager cooperation, I got in the Camry a few minutes later, directions in hand. She lived in the northwest suburbs not far from a busy mall, and the traffic was horrendous at mid-morning. Maybe because I'm paranoid about being rear-ended—something that's happened twice in the last year near shopping malls—I looked in the mirror more than usual during the halting trip to Joelle Simpson's neighborhood—and realized I was being followed.

If you're going to follow someone, why drive a flashy apple-red Lexus? I'd noticed that car as I'd left my house. Noticed because none of my neighbors own a car with gold hubcaps and windows tinted too dark to be legal. That same car or its twin was several vehicles behind me. Vanity and gridlock will get you every time.

I was in the left-turn lane and my tail wasn't. Guess that would have been too obvious. Easy enough to go past me at this intersection and make a U-turn. Whoever it was could easily pick me up in a few seconds. But I'd be waiting.

I made my turn, went two blocks and pulled into a driveway, hoping the tail would think this was my destination and drive on by. Then I could read the plates. Less than a minute later, the Lexus came cruising around the corner and slowed, obviously spotting my car.

At that wonderful moment, someone pounded on my driver's side window. I was so startled I nearly jumped through the sunroof.

A man in his sixties holding a golf umbrella pressed his face to the glass. I glanced back at my tail and saw that the car had also pulled into a driveway, but in the first block. Damn. I couldn't see the plates. I rolled down my window.

"You selling something?" the man asked, his irritation obvious. " 'Cause if you are, we don't need your Avon or your Tupperware." He pointed at me with the handle of the umbrella as if scolding a child.

"Um, no," I answered sweetly. "I'm kind of lost. Can you help me?" I glanced back at the Lexus idling a block away.

"Oh." This seemed to deflate the man. Here he'd been ready to scare off one of those perfume predators who he probably didn't realize rarely sold door-to-door these days.

"Where you headed?" he asked.

I gave him Joelle Simpson's address.

"You're almost there." He pointed down the street with the umbrella, telling me to drive three more blocks and turn right.

Since the guy was gesturing while giving directions, I might still be good. The tail would think I'd simply gotten lost, and once the Lexus was behind me again, I could make the plates and call them in to Jeff.

After I pulled out of the driveway and headed toward Mrs. Simpson's house, I watched in the rearview as my tail backed out and headed in the opposite direction. My heart sank like a rock with a hole in it. I couldn't read anything. The Lexus was too far away. The adrenaline rush that had surged through me at the prospect of obtaining a solid lead vanished like hailstones in July.

I drove on to the Simpson house thinking how my sister had been knocked silly at Verna Mae's place and now I'd been followed. Someone was paying close attention. Who? The only people aware of me working this case were Burl, HPD, Angel . . . and my sister . . . my aunt, oh, and the chaplain and then there were all the people I'd interviewed and—holy hissy fit. The whole frickin' world knew.

I'll be on the lookout for my friend in the Lexus, I thought, as I parked in the Simpson driveway. I only hoped Jeff or Angel hadn't put some babysitter on me. That would be worse than a bad guy hanging around.

A smiling Joelle Simpson, her ginger hair gray at the roots, greeted me at the door of her modest brick home before I could even ring the bell. She wore a loose-fitting cotton dress and no makeup, and had an almost ageless oval face. She must have avoided the Texas sun her entire life.

She grasped my hand in both of hers and smiled broadly. "No one's ever asked me anything about Frank's cases before. I really hope I can help." Her attitude was a welcome departure from the prison visit yesterday and my conversation with Frank's partner earlier today.

As she led me inside, my initial take on the house was that it seemed like a cozy bungalow filled with comfy furniture. Then I took in the photographs filling the walls—photos in stark contrast to the smiling, sweet Joelle Simpson and her warmth. Not family photographs, but the work of someone with a serious hobby. No Texas landscapes or old barns or fields of bluebonnets. They were all people . . . haunting character studies. Some were in color, some in black and white—people young and old, crying, or with heads bent, or clinging to children or other loved ones. A few were so searing in their portrayal, I had to look away.

"Frank," Mrs. Simpson said quietly. "He took them."

"They're . . . amazing. Who are these people?"

"Families of the victims. He got their permission, if you're wondering. Most of the time, he'd invite them here later on, after he'd developed and framed their pictures. The families wanted to see, and the pictures offered an opening for them to talk about the day their lives changed forever. They welcomed the chance to sit and talk with Frank, sometimes for hours."

"Sounds like Frank had a big heart," I said.

She blinked back tears. "Funny, that's what killed him. A heart attack. I told our grandchildren his heart was so big it just burst. He was the kindest man I ever met."

I reached out and squeezed her arm. "I didn't mean to upset you."

"That's okay, Abby. Can I call you Abby?"

"Of course."

"I'm Joelle. Anyway, the occasional sadness, the bouts of tears, it's all part of missing him and I expect it will go on forever. Now tell me more. You mentioned Lawrence Washington on the phone."

"Yes. Did Frank talk much about him?" I'd learned from Dugan that he had, but I needed Joelle's take on this.

"Frank knew something wasn't right about that case, said he thought the boy was innocent. Let's go get Frank's book."

His book? I wondered, as she led me up a narrow

staircase and into a converted bedroom with wall-to-wall shelves. They were filled with hardback and paperback books as well as a slew of albums, each labeled with a month and year on the spine. On the left wall I noted more framed photographs, and one jumped out at me. It was an eight-by-ten black-and-white of Lawrence Washington sitting with his cuffed hands resting on a small table. He was leaner than now and wore a Texas A&M T-shirt, his tired eyes staring into the lens, dark and as sad as I remember from yesterday. If I had seen this picture first, rather than the one from the newspaper, I would have known Will and Lawrence were most certainly father and son.

"I'm not sure of the month," Joelle said, stepping toward the 1987 shelf.

"April," I answered, wondering why Washington agreed to the photograph. Maybe he'd wanted someone to remember the worst day of *his* life.

She pulled the album and brought it to a card table set up in the center of the room. "Frank used to have half of this space set up as a darkroom, but I finally had some friends remodel it about a year after he died. Took me that long to accept he wouldn't walk through the door with a new roll of film in hand." She pulled her lips in and out a few times, the album held tightly against her chest.

"I lost my daddy not long ago," I said. "I understand."

"I'm so sorry." Joelle reached out and squeezed my hand.

"What's with all these albums? More pictures?"

"Not exactly. I added more shelf space so I could organize these. He had them everywhere. I've always wished one of his old police buddies would write a book and use them—they all say they're going to write a book, you know."

I smiled. "I have a detective friend. He tells me that half the force say they have a book in them."

"Frank kept information about every case, though

I'm not sure he was supposed to do that. I'm hoping one day, because of him, a wrong can be righted." She set the album on the table.

We took folding chairs side by side and Joelle began turning the pages. Not only were there pictures and newspaper clippings, but Frank Simpson had kept notes about each case. Amanda Mason had been murdered in April, and Joelle pointed out a photo of Frank standing between a middle-aged couple. The picture was nowhere near the quality I'd seen hanging on the walls.

"Who took this?" I asked.

"Randall."

"Randall?" I said.

"Frank's partner, Randall Dugan. He took some of the pictures for the books."

This seemed so strange, the families posing like that, but kindness and compassion can open almost any door, and from what I'd seen of Frank's photos, he had been filled with both.

"These people are related to Amanda Mason?" I asked, pointing at the picture.

"Her parents." She turned the page. "And here's Lawrence Washington's parents. Frank considered them victims, too. They were as devastated by their loss as the Masons."

Frank was standing next to a porch swing where Washington's parents sat. Mrs. Washington wore a bandanna around her head, a scarf that had slipped, revealing her baldness. Mr. Washington seemed like a giant next to her, his belly spilling over his belt and his long legs stretching so far his feet weren't even in the photo. Their anguished expressions showed how devastated they were. I'd never thought about those left behind, those who suffered when a child they loved was sent to prison.

"He didn't often take pictures of the suspect's family, but these people touched Frank. He talked often with Mr. Washington, kept in contact until Frank dropped dead. Now I'm the one who visits. Mr. Washington's not well. Diabetes. I need to get over to his place this week, as a matter of fact. Check up on him."

"And Mrs. Washington?" I asked.

"Cancer took her after Lawrence's trial. Double tragedy for Thaddeus."

"Thaddeus?"

"I'm sorry. Lawrence's father."

"Mind if I take more time with the book?" I asked.

"Sure. Don't remove the cellophane coverings, though. When Frank put later books together, he learned not to use cellophane. You might tear something if you peeled it back now."

"No problem," I said, my eyes on the notes I was eager to read.

She stood, and I looked up. Her slumped shoulders and concerned expression made me think of a new mother leaving her baby in the hands of a stranger— a rather ironic comparison.

"You don't have to leave. Help me with this," I said.

"I-I thought you might want privacy. Sure you don't mind?"

"Of course not."

She reclaimed her chair, smiling.

The notes were neatly typed on what appeared to be thin paper and the black ink had already faded— might totally fade with time. I began to read.

Amanda Mason. 20-year-old WF. Found in Worthington Bank parking lot at 21:00, 4/24/87, after tip phoned in to precinct. Bullet wound to back of head. Pronounced at scene by ME. Morello and Kent processed. Dugan and I went to interview Thaddeus and Clara Washington, parents of suspect Lawrence Washington. Anonymous tipster said evidence linking LW to the murder was at the home. LW was with parents watching TV. Suspect stated he spent evening at a church youth meeting. Victim's wallet with fifty dollars and jewelry found in LW's room. Window unlocked. Fur-

ther investigation indicated LW would have had time to commit the murder after church function, since he did not arrive home until 90 minutes after the event ended. Came home on foot. Claimed he had been out selling his car. Refused to give name of buyer. Dugan theorized LW dumped vehicle, maybe because it contained evidence or suspect feared it had been spotted at the scene. He may have come in through window, hid evidence from parents before going back out window and entering house through the front door so as not to arouse parents' suspicion. Ground outside bedroom window disturbed but no usable footprint impressions. LW's shoes dirt-free. Dugan dismissed this. Said LW had time to clean them. Only fingerprints on the dresser drawer where victim's personal items found belonged to suspect and suspect's mother. Leads on tipster all dead ends. Call came from pay phone near suspect's church. No relationship between LW and victim uncovered. LW's family with medical bills. Mrs. Washington has breast cancer that spread to bone. Dugan considered financial need the motive. Deputy DA Foster handled case. LW refused to help with his defense. Convicted in four days. Sentenced twenty to life.

I sat back. All this circumstantial evidence pointed to Lawrence Washington, even as laid out by Frank Simpson. I turned to Joelle. "Aside from intuition, why did Frank believe Lawrence was innocent?"

"Frank told me Lawrence's polygraph indicated no deception, but since Frank knew psychopaths can beat a polygraph every time, that was only part of it." Joelle rested a hand on the page, her gaze on Frank's typed words. "It was more the boy himself. From the interviews, Frank believed he was protecting someone. Protecting the person he might have been with during those missing ninety minutes."

"Protecting the killer? Or someone else?" I was

thinking about the mother of his unborn child, wondering how taking the fall for this murder would protect her. I didn't know.

"I don't know," said Joelle, echoing my thoughts.

"Frank never learned who could be so important that Washington would give up his own freedom and future to protect?"

"No. He was so frustrated that Lawrence wouldn't talk."

"Was Lawrence protecting his father, maybe?" I asked. After all, he might have been the one desperate to find money to help his sick wife.

"Thaddeus? A killer? Absolutely not. You'd be just as certain if you ever met him."

"A brother or sister, then?"

"Lawrence was an only child. I think that's why Clara went downhill so fast after Lawrence was sentenced. She just didn't have the will to fight the cancer."

"Is there more?" I asked, turning the page. But what followed were pictures and notes from another case in May of that year. My stomach sank with disappointment. This wasn't as much as I'd hoped to learn. Frank's gut feelings weren't enough to help me. I mean, the chaplain had those, too, but faith in a convicted man's innocence was about as useful as a handful of dust.

"There is more," Joelle said quietly. "Just not here. These were books Frank showed to the families, to his police friends, but . . . he did things on his own, looking for answers, you know? The department might not have been happy if they'd known, and he never wanted to let the brass down, have them think he was some kind of . . . 'rogue' is the word he used."

Joelle pushed away from the table. A filing cabinet stood in one corner, and she walked to the shelf beside it, took a key from behind a book and opened the cabinet. After removing a folder stuffed to overflowing, she came back and handed it to me. "Take this. After meeting you, I know he'd want you to have it."

15

I saw no sign of the red Lexus on my way back from
Joelle's, maybe because I kept glancing at the file sitting on the passenger seat rather than in the rearview
mirror. I couldn't wait to read Frank Simpson's notes.
Maybe a dead cop's dedication to his job would yield
some solid clues.

On the drive home I encountered the same stop-
and-go traffic, giving me time to think about other
avenues I hadn't explored on this case. Verna Mae
hadn't lived in a vacuum. Who were her friends or,
better yet, her enemies? Who did she talk to and what
did they discuss? And who had she left out of that
will? Surely one relative had to have been lurking in
the background thinking they'd inherit.

That side of the case was Jeff's territory, but I needed
to know, too. He'd been so busy lately, he hadn't shared
much of anything, so before I took home the file and
concentrated on its contents, I wanted to talk to him.
Okay, I wanted to see him, too. Smell cinnamon on his
breath and, if I got lucky, make him smile.

I reached him on his cell, and he said he wanted to
see me, too, if only for a little while. We agreed to
meet at the Beck's Prime hamburger place on Kirby
for lunch, one of our favorite places to eat.

Thirty minutes later we were sitting across from
each other at a small table reminiscent of McDonald's.
But the hamburgers? A whole other world. This was
fast food with a reason to exist. I'd indulged myself

with a chocolate shake along with my burger, and then kept stealing from Jeff's mound of ketchup-drenched fries. It's not like you can order your own fries when you've given in to a milkshake.

We ate in silence for awhile, me with my grilled onions and cheddar dripping out the sides of the burger and Jeff making amazingly neat work of his pickle and jalapeño pure Angus concoction.

I picked up a napkin and wiped mustard from the corner of my mouth before saying, "You ever find any of Verna Mae's friends?"

"The woman had acquaintances, not friends. She belonged to a garden club and that's about it. By the way, I've discovered I love interviewing garden clubbers a whole lot more than guys with bad attitudes."

"What did they tell you?"

"Nothing we don't know already. EZ TAG records offered far more. I learned she made lots of trips to Houston, used the toll roads. Made at least one trip a week over the I-10 bridge before heading south on the Sam Houston Tollway. Made the same trip back. I have dates and times. She usually made a day of it."

"She went south from I-10?"

"Right."

"If you were heading for downtown, you'd stay on the freeway, right?"

"I would, but then some folks will drive ten miles to avoid traffic on I-10."

"True. Any pattern to her visits? Maybe she had regular meetings in town."

"Lots of Wednesdays, but she came plenty of times on other days of the week."

"Like the Friday she died," I said. "Did you ask the garden clubbers if she ever mentioned where she was going on her trips out of Bottlebrush?"

"I asked. Like I said, the ladies were nice, but no help," Jeff answered. "They talked flowers and shrubs with the Olsen woman. The only other place they saw her was at church."

"Last Friday?" I asked. "You have a time line on her activities that day?"

"She used her EZ TAG coming toward Houston at two-fifty p.m., but never used that prepaid cell phone we found near the body. So we checked *your* cell records, to see how she contacted you before she was murdered. She phoned you from a gas station pay phone in the vicinity of the coffee shop."

"Why buy a phone and not use it, Jeff?"

"Good question. I don't have the answer. She purchased it that morning at a Target store east of Houston. Wish I could ask her about phone records. We checked her landline in Bottlebrush and got nothing. No toll calls to Houston. No long-distance calls period. My guess is she always used prepaid phones or calling cards, and probably did so for a reason. We find that reason, we're a step ahead."

"What about relatives? Any luck finding someone who might have been interested in her money?"

"DeShay's on that. So far, he's got nothing. She was estranged from her in-laws—hadn't spoke to them since the husband's funeral. Rock-solid alibis. They didn't ask about money when the notification was made. The deputy who visited them said they acted like they hardly knew the woman. Her parents are gone, have been for years. No kids. No siblings. Nada. The lady was a loner."

"An obsessed loner," I said. "But maybe that's redundant."

"Unless she went to the Galleria every week, we don't know what she came to Houston for. You check out her closets? Was she a shopaholic or something—and I cannot believe I just said 'shopaholic.' " He rolled his eyes. "That's what I get for hanging around garden clubbers."

I laughed. "I wouldn't say she was a big shopper. She appreciated nice things, had well-made plus-size clothes, but not an overflowing closet or a designer wardrobe. With luck, that storage unit key will tell us

why she drove into town week after week. Burl is
checking into that."

"Glad you turned over those keys to him. He
sounds like a guy with some smarts. Did you learn
anything from Dugan?"

"Not much. Simpson's widow helped me far more.
I have his file on the Washington case."

"Simpson copied HPD files?" Jeff's pupils con-
stricted, enhancing that glacial blue stare I'd seen a
number of times when he was bothered by a case. He
reached in his shirt pocket for gum.

"No," I said. "He did his own investigating. Is
that wrong?"

"If he worked a closed case on the clock, yeah."

"He's dead, Jeff. And his wife . . . I think she'll
need his pension."

"Chill, Abby. Who do you think I work for? Inter-
nal Affairs?" He smiled.

"Thanks," I said.

"For what?" He folded two sticks of gum and laid
them on his tongue.

"For the smile. I don't get enough of those."

He reached across our tiny table and took my hand.
His fingers trailed down mine when he pulled his hand
away. Suddenly I wanted to be home alone with him,
murders and prisons and evidence forgotten.

"Tell me more about this file," he said.

"I haven't gone through it yet. Just took a quick
glance. I did learn a few things talking to Simpson's
wife, and there are these photographs he took—the
guy had an amazing talent, by the way." I told him
more about my visit with Joelle and ended by mentioning that I thought I'd been followed there.

His gum-chewing speed switched to double time and
he stared at me, eyes narrow in thought. Finally he
said, "You should have called me when you spotted
the tail. I could have given a description to any patrol
units in the area. Hell, you could have taken a video
with your fancy phone and we'd have it right now."

"What? Stick my phone out the window so I could take a picture? Oh, wait. I could have jumped out of my car, waved my arms like I was as crazy as a road lizard and shouted, 'Hey, are you following me?'"

"You should have called me, Abby." No smile. He was as serious as the tax man.

"I have my .38 in my glove compartment," I said.

"When's the last time you took target practice? You know you have to keep up your skills, make sure—"

"Don't get parental on me, Jeff. I hate that."

He sighed, closed his eyes. "You're right. I worry, that's all."

My turn to smile. "That's what a girl likes to hear."

After I left Jeff, I made the short drive home, came in through the back door and immediately spread out the contents of Frank Simpson's folder on my kitchen table. His organizational skills? Not so good. Soon Diva arrived—she has a nose for anything made of paper laid out on a table—and thought she might help me rearrange things. I quickly carried her off and bribed her this time with a catnip toy. I didn't need her taking a nap on Frank's notes.

While Diva knocked herself out with her fake mouse, I sat and began the process of making order out of chaos. Some notes had been jotted on scraps of paper or on the back of his business cards, others on full notebook-size sheets. At least he'd been good about dates and times. Guess cops do have to pay attention there. When I was done putting everything in chronological order, the compilation spanned years and wasn't as much information as I had initially thought. The papers and cards were messy and crumpled after being jammed in the folder, making it seem like there was a lot more.

I decided to put all this in an accordion folder, arranging the notes by years, and was about to get one from my office when I heard Kate's familiar rap on the back door. I let her in.

She wore a pale green silk blouse and matching

straight skirt, and her dark hair was gathered with a jeweled clip. Despite the flattering clothes and hair, she looked exhausted.

We hugged and then I held her at arm's length. "You okay?"

"Just went to the chiropractor. Whoever hit me the other night knocked a few things out of place. I'm better now."

I touched her bruised face, surprised at how well she'd healed in two days. "Damn. I am so sorry for dragging you into this. No more. I promise."

She pulled away, her gaze on the table. "Don't you dare say that. We take care of each other and that's not about to change. What's all this?"

"Information concerning the Amanda Mason murder . . . from the cop who worked the case."

Kate went to the table and sat, picking up one of the scribbled-on business cards. "Wow. How'd you manage to get a hold of this?"

"I'll explain in a minute. Now, while I fetch a folder to organize this mess, make sure Diva doesn't jump up and send everything flying."

Kate saluted. "Yes, ma'am. I am now officially on cat duty, ma'am."

I grinned. If she could joke around, she wasn't hurt too badly—but I still felt guilty.

Once we had all the years sorted into their separate compartments and I had brought Kate up to date on the case, I scooted my chair close to hers and started with the 1987 information. Much of what was there were small notebook pages of people Simpson had interviewed about Amanda Mason.

"Looks like Officer Simpson was searching for any connection between Mason and Lawrence Washington and found none," said Kate.

I picked up notes from Simpson's interview with Mason's parents. "These are sketchy. She didn't live at home. They gave him her apartment address. I remember seeing something titled VICTIM NOTES. Where is that?" I shuffled papers and cards.

"Simpson took a photo of her parents, right?" Kate said.

"He did, and—wait. Here it is." I sat back and read aloud from a notebook page:

"Parents say Miss Mason lived on own for last two years. Juvie record for shoplifting. Finished high school in detention. Turned it around, according to father. Theology major at U. of H. Mother called me 5/1/87 at 09:00. Worried daughter's past would be made public. Victim had contact with drug dealers and gang members in high school. Assured mother press would not hear about this from us. Not relevant."

I looked up.

"That's it?" Kate asked.

"Not exactly. Apparently Simpson wasn't so sure about the relevancy. He follows with a list of her old friends. William Collins, Byron Thompson, Neil Cohen, Jamie Smith, Ross Dayton, Celia French, Lori Edwards . . . You want more? 'Cause there's plenty."

"He thought one of her friends might have killed her?" Kate asked.

"I think police do a lot of eliminating, from what Jeff says. But gosh, Frank Simpson did plenty of interviewing if he followed up on all these people."

"He was thorough," said Kate.

"We have years of notes, Kate. When does 'thorough' turn to obsession?"

"Maybe we should jump to a later year. Unless you want to follow everything just as he did."

"I do," I said, spotting something else. I removed a photocopy of the picture caught by the ATM machine with the date of the murder printed in ink at the bottom. Amanda Mason was withdrawing the fifty dollars that would later be found in Lawrence Washington's room. The girl had short hair and looked more like sixteen than her actual nineteen years.

Kate leaned forward to see, then her fingers flew to her lips and she gasped.

"Kind of creepy looking at a ghost, huh?" I said.

"It's not that, Abby. My God, she looks like you."

"She does not," I shot back.

"Look at her. Her eyes, the shape of her face. She could be our sister."

"Yeah. Our *dead* sister," I said, pushing the photo away.

"Sorry," she said. "I didn't mean to upset you."

"It doesn't bother me, okay?" But we both knew it did. This case had been one disturbing episode after another, and her saying I looked like a murder victim made me realize it wasn't getting any better.

16

The next morning, on the one-week anniversary of Verna Mae's death, I got in my car and set out to visit Lawrence Washington's father. Though I had an address from Simpson's notes, I found no phone number despite searching the white pages, directory assistance and my online resources. All I could do was drive to his home and hope he was there.

By the time we'd finished with Simpson's notes last night, Kate and I had ended up cross-eyed and cranky. They did indicate that Washington continued to stonewall about the unaccounted for ninety minutes, the time gap that had helped a jury convict him in a circumstantial case, but other than that, Simpson seemed to have made a mountain of paper out of molehills. Names and dates and what might well be useless pieces of information were swimming in my head even now.

I turned onto Lyons Avenue after traveling the freeways north and east to Houston's Fifth Ward, a section of the city struggling to overcome the street crime that had at one time made it the most dangerous part of town. Renovations were ongoing and included condos and newly painted houses spotting the neighborhoods. The work wasn't finished, however. Poverty decimates culture and recovery is slow no matter what the politicians promise.

After several wrong turns, I finally found Thaddeus Washington's house and discovered he had been one of those who had benefited from neighborhood improvement projects. His one-story was small, probably no more than 1,000 square feet inside, but the siding was a fresh yellow and the porch slats gleamed with bright white paint. The swing I'd seen in the photograph swayed in the warm morning breeze.

The steps to the house had been replaced by a plywood ramp, and when Mr. Washington cracked the door open, I saw why. Even through the six-inch gap I could see he was in a wheelchair.

"Can I help you?" he asked, his voice wary.

"My name is Abby Rose and I want to talk to you about your son, Lawrence. I saw him the other day." I offered my card but he didn't take it. I already had my ticket inside.

He widened the door and said, "You saw him?"

"Yes, sir," I replied. He had nappy gray hair, but the face that I'd seen in Simpson's photo had changed little over the years.

He backed up the wheelchair and told me to come in.

That's when I saw the .357 Magnum lying across his blanketed stumps. I guess a gun helps if you can't run. I wondered when he'd lost his legs—probably from the diabetes—since in the picture both had still been attached. But that's the type of personal question preschoolers ask strangers.

He noted I was staring and said, "Don't pay this gun no mind. Probably don't need it, but word gets around for folks to leave you be when you stay protected. People don't mess with Thaddeus Washington. And I know what you're thinking—that I'm a foolish old man." He laughed then, a hearty laugh.

"I don't think you're foolish and I hope I'm not intruding," I said.

"Intruding? What the hell are you talking about? Not every day a pretty girl visits. A girl who knows Lawrence." He grinned, revealing dentures a little too big for his gums. "Come on in and have a seat on the divan. I'll get you some coffee and then you better tell me all about my son." He turned and started toward the adjoining kitchen visible beyond the pass-through bar.

"I stopped at Starbucks on the drive here," I lied. "I'm already wired on caffeine." I was still avoiding coffee like I might one of Kate's veggie "meat" loaves, but didn't want to sound impolite.

Mr. Washington wheeled to face me. "Starbucks. I own some of their stock. They keep sending me these little cards for three-dollar coffees around dividend time. Guess I can give them to you."

My turn to laugh. "You own stock in Starbucks?"

He grinned. "You probably think it takes me an hour and a half to watch *60 Minutes*, too."

"I certainly do not," I replied, still smiling.

He gestured for me to sit on a red chenille sofa with fringe on the bottom. Had to be fifty years old, but it was in pristine condition thanks to the plastic cover. He steered his wheelchair around so we were facing each other. "You a lawyer?"

"No. Why would you think . . . oh. Because I visited your son?"

"You're not police. I can tell them. So who are you? And don't hand me that card again, 'cause I couldn't read it anyway. My glasses are in the other room."

I explained who I was, how I'd talked with Mrs. Simpson and read Frank Simpson's file on his son's case.

"Frank thought Lawrence was innocent. Do you?" he asked.

"Something tells me he is," I answered quietly. Even if I wasn't totally sure, this was what Thaddeus Washington needed to hear, what I needed to hear myself say.

"I'm afraid he'll never get out of that place. All the lawyers been used up long ago. He won't let me come see him anymore. How did he look?"

"Healthy," I answered, leaving out the sadness that seemed to overpower everything about Lawrence. "You say he won't let you visit?"

Mr. Washington gestured at his lap. " 'Cause of this."

"You should know better than to try to take a gun into a prison," I said with a grin.

Washington smiled. "Good one. I think I like you. Wish Lawrence had your attitude. He says the prison is so old it's too hard to get the chair in there, but I think he don't want to see me like this—or for me to see him with a screen between us. So we talk. And write. It's okay, I guess."

I could tell it *wasn't* okay. "I think there's far more to what happened the night of the murder than a robbery gone bad. If I can find the truth for my client, maybe that will help Lawrence." I paused, and took a deep breath before I said, "You see, I think my client is your grandson, Mr. Washington."

His hand found the .357, tightened around the grip, but not in any threatening way. I sensed that the gun was his friend and he needed to feel its presence. "My *grandson*? What the hell are you talking about?"

I spilled out the whole story, my words coming fast, my mouth growing drier with each passing minute. I had to keep looking away, down at my hands, out the side window, anywhere to stay away from his intent stare. His sadness seemed just as deep and strong as what I had seen at the prison, the same expression that Frank Simpson captured in Lawrence's eyes with his 35mm camera.

Mr. Washington said, "You're saying Lawrence has a child, this Will Knight, and we never knew about him?"

"Oh, I think Lawrence knew he was about to be a father. He picked up that blanket, after all. Did he have a steady girlfriend?"

"Not that me or Clara knew about. You had to understand Lawrence. He was a shy boy. It was only when he was on the baseball field that we saw the other side of him. The aggression. The need to win. He wouldn't have told us nothing about a girlfriend."

Aggressive enough to murder? I wondered.

"You know something?" Mr. Washington went on, squinting as if looking back in time. "I do recall Clara and I thought Lawrence might have had a crush on a girl. He spent a lot of time at that church, and we thought God wasn't the only one he was visiting. She must have been a fair-weather friend, though, 'cause she never showed up to visit him in jail and never went to the trial."

"She was in his youth group, perhaps?"

Mr. Washington said, "If he had a girlfriend in that group, she was white. We found out after Lawrence's arrest that they was all white kids over there. Lawrence being a big-cheese athlete, seems they invited him. Place is north of the space place—NASA. Long drive from here, and I don't mean in miles. What bothers me to this day is that if Lawrence hadn't been in that neighborhood, maybe whoever really killed Miss Mason would have been caught. That cop Dugan got himself a scapegoat in Lawrence. Black kid in a white neighborhood? Could it get any better for the police?"

I hated to admit it, but he was right. "Officer Simpson did indicate in his notes that the church was close to where Amanda Mason was killed."

"Yup. I go that way for my diabetes checkups. Got a doctor in the Medical Center and then have to visit a lab way in the other direction. Medicare makes some sense, huh?"

"Not to me or you. Who takes you?" I asked.

"Joelle borrows her friend's van. Don't know what I'd do without that lady. Got to say, I hate driving by that prissy church. Place gets bigger and fancier every day. I see their ads in the religion section of the paper all the time. Not Baptist like Lawrence was raised, neither. Nondenominational, he said. Clara and I were troubled he wanted to abandon his church home, but he was old enough to decide. God doesn't care where you visit Him, I guess."

"You think a girlfriend might have had more to do with this desire to change his religious affiliation than any conversion?"

"Remembering how I was at that age, I would've bungee jumped off the Transco Tower for Clara—if I'd heard of such a thing as bungee jumping and if she'd asked me to." He smiled, but it was a small, sad smile, the kind memories create.

"No idea who this girlfriend was or if she even really existed?"

"Nope," he said with a shake of his head.

"Did you mention a possible romantic interest to Officer Simpson? Because if he wrote about it in his notes, I missed it. In fact, he indicated Lawrence had nothing going on with anyone as far as he could tell."

Mr. Washington hung his head, fiddled with the binding of his plaid blanket. "I mighta told the police officers there was no girlfriend. Wasn't exactly a lie. See, I was afraid if Miss Mason attended that church, if Lawrence knew her, dated her, well, that would be like pounding a nail in my own son's coffin. I told myself they could figure it out themselves." He looked up. "You get what I'm saying?"

I nodded. "I understand, but suppose he did have a relationship with someone in that youth group—not Amanda Mason, which we know for sure—but maybe another girl. Would Lawrence have confided in anyone about her?"

"Maybe today he might have, but not back then. Not if she was white. Besides, Lawrence didn't talk much, and never about that sort of thing. He went about his business . . . school, playing ball, planning his future. We raised a fine young man, Ms. Rose." Mr. Washington's voice cracked and his eyes grew moist. "He may have sinned and conceived this child you're talking about—and that whole idea still ain't sunk in—but he would never take a life. Not ever."

I believed him. This man may not have known anyone in that church group, but he knew his son, and about now, the scapegoat idea was sounding pretty damn good to me. "I have the church's address from Frank's notes—the Church of the Reverent Life, if I remember right. You say they're still in the same location?"

"Bought up property around them and built an even bigger complex not long ago. They're right off the freeway feeder in south Houston."

"I suppose the ministry there has turned over since Lawrence attended," I said.

"The assistant minister, the one who visited Lawrence after he went to prison, is still there. Read in the paper he took the big job—Pastor-Teacher or something like that. His name is Rankin."

"Pastor Rankin visited Lawrence in Huntsville?"

"Yup. I got to the prison early one Saturday and couldn't get in 'cause he was there. Sort of ticked me off him taking away my time with Lawrence, but those are the rules. He was the youth minister back then, and his wife ran the Bible study for the kids. 'Course I had to hear all this from Frank, not my son. God, I wish Lawrence and I woulda talked more." Mr. Washington shook his head.

The would-haves and could-haves. I knew about those, too. "I thank you so much for your help, Mr. Washington. Guess I need to find out about these friends from Lawrence's group."

I walked to the door with Thaddeus Washington wheeling behind me.

When I opened the door, his chair suddenly rammed into me and Mr. Washington shouted, "Get down!"

I fell forward onto the threshold, instant pain blasting through both knees. I squeezed my eyes shut. That's why I didn't see who was shooting at us, though I did hear glass breaking. That's *all* I heard, because Mr. Washington's return fire deafened me.

"Some idiot in a hotdog red car," he yelled once I was on my feet and my assaulted eardrums began to function again.

Damn. I missed getting that plate number again.

17

I've been shot at before, and it's not something you get used to. My hands were shaking when I called Jeff and explained what had happened. He said to sit tight, he was on his way.

Meanwhile, Mr. Washington called 9-1-1, but someone else must have done the same, because a few seconds after I disconnected from Jeff, two HPD squad cars came to a screeching halt in front of the house.

Fortunately we avoided a SWAT team appearance or helicopters descending on us when a neighbor woman came out and explained what she'd seen to the patrol officers and assured them that Mr. Washington and I were not the threat. The threat had sped away in a red car.

Then it was all happy reunion time with the four officers who'd responded. Seems Mr. Washington and his gun were well known to these guys. Meanwhile I had two blue-red indentations across both knees and an attitude that matched the pain. I'd missed that Lexus-driving jerk again.

By the time Jeff arrived, I'd shown my PI license to every smirking, uniformed face, tried to explain why I was here and listened to their skepticism about this assailant being the person who'd followed me yesterday. There were a million red cars in Houston, I was told, and since Mr. Washington had a history of firing at drive-by shooters, perhaps one of his old enemies had returned for payback.

When Jeff and DeShay showed up, the atmosphere changed. Jeff made sure Mr. Washington and I were unhurt before turning his attention to senior Officer Smirk—okay, it said SCHMIDT on his uniform. Jeff said, "You call out a crime scene unit?"

"It's a broken window, Sarge. We—"

"Call one. Now. And get the other officers out of here. You can stay." The icicles in Jeff's tone must have pierced Schmidt's Kevlar vest, because Schmidt sent the three officers back to their patrol units with a "Yes, sir." Then he called on his walkie-talkie for a crime scene unit.

Meanwhile a gloved DeShay was pointing with a pencil at a bullet lodged in the wall right above the sofa—oh so close to the place I'd been sitting not thirty minutes ago. "We need this bullet," he said.

"You think this incident is related to the case the woman was telling us about?" Schmidt asked.

"*Tried* to tell you about," I piped in.

"The woman's name is Ms. Rose and she's working with us," Jeff said, looking at the bullet hole, his head tilting right then left.

"Guess that's a yes," Schmidt said quietly.

"I think you'd be right, Schmitty," Mr. Washington said from his spot at the kitchen entry. He'd already apologized several times for knocking me down and now held a bright blue plastic ice pack. "This might help, Ms. Rose."

I hobbled over and took it from him. "Thanks. I think what just went down puts us on a first-name basis. I'm Abby."

"Thaddeus. Just so you know, he wasn't aiming for neither of us."

This observation got Jeff's attention. "What's that, Mr. Washington?"

"From what I could tell—'course these things happen in a split second, so I could be wrong—he hit what he wanted to. The window. I mean, he was a damn twenty feet away and missed us by ten."

"A warning shot," Jeff said, nodding in agreement. "Get a look at the shooter?"

Thaddeus shook his head no. "Black glove and shiny gun through the driver's side window, that's all. I did hit a taillight, though. You might want your crime scene folks to take a look in the street."

Jeff smiled. "You got off a shot?"

"You betcha."

Jeff glanced down at me. I was sitting on the floor next to Thaddeus, holding the frozen gel pack across both knees.

He said, "Seems Miss Abby Rose is one of the lucky ones. She makes friends willing to defend her wherever she goes."

After I gave Schmitty a formal statement, I left at Jeff's insistence, even though I wanted to see what the crime scene people came up with. He told me the house was so small I'd be in the way, so I tried not to pout when I said good-bye. There is nothing more unattractive than a pouting girlfriend unless she happens to be a *Playboy* centerfold candidate. Those types could chew tobacco and men wouldn't care.

But if I thought the excitement was over, I was milking the wrong cow. My cell phone rang about halfway home.

"This is Blinks Security. Vega here," said the caller.

Yes, *Blinks*. I still wonder when Brinks will file suit.

"What is it, Mr. Vega?" I had a sick feeling in my stomach. Your security company does not call to say, "Everything's fine at your place, if you're wondering."

"You've had a break-in, Ms. Rose. West U. police are already on the scene. We arrived first, by the way."

I sighed. "Of course you did, and I'm so proud. I'll be there in twenty minutes."

I'd hired the security company and had a system

installed after a suspect in another case walked right
into my screened-in porch with her trusty gun in hand.
A lot of good it did me today. I felt like I'd had my
clothes stolen while I was skinny-dipping. Embarrassed, angry and foolish about summed it up. See, I
was now certain that *someone* had gotten *someone's*
license plate number even if I hadn't. Mr. Red Lexus
got mine, probably when he ran out of Verna Mae's
house the other night. The bastard had been on my
tail ever since, and apparently following me had been
as easy as catching fish with dynamite.

I returned home to meet with Vega and the West
U. police, a visit that didn't last long. Vega said he'd
have my broken lock replaced before nightfall. Then
when the police and I did an inventory and discovered
the only thing missing was the Washington file, they
left as happy as blowflies on manure. Who cares about
a pile of paper?

I sat at my kitchen table, fists supporting my chin.
I didn't want to call Jeff and tell him what had happened. I was too upset. The Washington files were
gone, the files I had promised Joelle Simpson I'd take
care of, stolen while I'd been giving a statement, stolen no doubt by Mr. Red Lexus. Had he shot at and
missed us for just this purpose? To delay me across
town? Probably. After seeing me with Thaddeus
Washington, he put two and two together, created a
diversion and headed straight here to find out what I
had that led me to Lawrence's father. At least he
hadn't hacked into my computer. That would have
required time considering how well-protected it was.
No, my computer wasn't important to the thief, anyway. I'd left what he wanted in plain sight.

I squeezed my eyes shut, feeling a headache coming
on. Damn. First Verna Mae's scrapbooks and now the
files. Someone did not want the old case and Verna
Mae's death connected—and that meant bigger secrets
were out there somewhere.

I had to tell Jeff. Despite the disinterest by the local
police, the thief could have left evidence in my

kitchen. Yeah. Big fat fingerprints all over the place. Probably even spit on the table to make sure we had DNA. *Right.* Like he'd never seen *CSI* or *Forensic Files* or any other crime show that offers crooks recipes for success.

I sighed and took my phone out of my purse, but before I could even speed-dial Jeff's number, Aunt Caroline rapped on the back door and then came prancing in like she always does. Could this day get any worse?

"Abby, I heard you were robbed. What did they take?" She was wearing a pink polo shirt and golf shorts, her electric beach tan just a little too dark this week.

The break-in probably happened an hour ago and she already knew. The woman never ceases to amaze me, and I don't mean that in a good way. "Nothing antique or encrusted with jewels was stolen, but thanks for asking if I was home or I was hurt or any of those less important details."

If she hadn't applied so much plum blush I might have detected embarrassment over her being more concerned about material things than her niece. Her reaction, however, was par for the course, and I didn't give a flying flip anyway. How would I explain to Joelle?

"Who told you?" I asked.

"The news is all over the neighborhood, so Marion Callaway called me immediately, which is more than you did."

"I only just found out and who the hell is Marion Callaway?"

"Your neighbor down the block. You really need to be more sociable, get out and meet people. I met Marion at the country club, we got to talking and I found out she lives right near you. We've been friends for several weeks now."

Great. Aunt Caroline had her own CIA agent in my neighborhood. "Listen, I'd love to give you all the tantalizing details, but there aren't any, and I don't feel much like visiting, so—"

"Marion said she's seen that car several times hanging around your place and didn't think it belonged to anyone she knew. Then this happens and she sees the police and—"

"She *saw* the car?"

"Oh, yes. Didn't see the driver, but Marion is quite good with numbers. I swear she could keep her golf score in her head. God knows, she always keeps track of mine. I only hope when I'm as old as her I—"

"*Numbers?* What about numbers?"

"She remembered the license number. I think she said she was calling it in to the West University Police right after she hung up from me. Unlike you, she knew I needed this information immediately, even before the police." Aunt Caroline smiled—the last face-lift was already wearing off, so she could actually smile without splitting her lips at the corners—and for once her smug face didn't make me clench my teeth.

I called Mrs. Callaway after Aunt Caroline left, and the woman was more than happy to give me the license number she'd already phoned in to the West U. police. She was a talker like Aunt Caroline, and I listened with half an ear while she rambled on about crime and being a good citizen and how my aunt was proud of me for me getting my hands dirty in the real world. This implied that she and Aunt Caroline wore gloves—expensive ones—to keep their hands clean. After I disconnected, I called Jeff with the plate number but got his voice mail, so I left a message.

But I wasn't done with phones. I'd no sooner hung up when Will called.

"How's the case going, Abby?" he asked. "Did . . . did the DNA result come back yet?"

Abby, you idiot. How could I have forgotten to at least call Will's parents, let alone him? Probably because I had tunnel vision right now. One thing kept leading to another in this case, and Will had been the beginning of the trail—a meeting that seemed so long ago now.

"I am so sorry, Will. I should have phoned you right away."

"I probably couldn't have talked to you anyway. They're pretty strict about us focusing on the game at camp."

"Nice of you to let me off the hook, but I'm still sorry. I found out Wednesday evening that Verna Mae was not your birth mother."

A short silence followed, then Will said, "It kinda makes me feel better. Does that sound bad?"

"No, not at all. I think we both knew deep down she wasn't your birth mother. I am making progress in other ways." *Should I tell him his father might be in prison for murder?* That answer came easy. I had to be honest. It was my job. I filled Will in.

"Man, this blows my mind. He's in *prison*. Do you think that officer was right? That he didn't kill that girl?"

"I have no hard evidence, but Frank Simpson never gave up on Lawrence, and that says a lot. Now that I've lost his files, though, I—"

"You didn't *lose* them. Someone took them," Will said.

"I feel responsible, and the fact that someone wanted them that badly tells me they're worried about what Simpson kept."

"You mean they wanted the evidence that might prove the man who is probably my birth father is innocent, in prison for a crime he didn't commit?" Will, my usually subdued young client, was angry. And so was I.

"Officer Simpson didn't have hard evidence, so I'm not one hundred percent sure about anything Will, not even about Lawrence Washington being your birth father. But I promise you, I *will* learn the truth."

"But you believe this man in jail is him. My birth father."

"Yes, Will. I do," I said quietly.

"Okay, I want to see him. See the man who's probably my grandfather, too. When can that happen?"

"Listen, I understand this is upsetting, but give me more time, let me find out what's true and what's not. Lawrence wouldn't have even let me in to see him without police help. I doubt if it would be wise to take you to Huntsville."

"I'm sorry, Abby. This just pisses me off. It's so wrong."

"I'm sure your parents have told you more than once that what's fair and right doesn't always happen. In this case, I'm hoping we can fix that."

But while I was reassuring him of my commitment, I was thinking about something Will had just said. He wanted to see his *grandfather*. Lawrence might not be willing to give up any DNA to prove paternity, but I was certain Thaddeus wouldn't hesitate. Grandparent genes had to be good, though I hadn't had a case yet where I'd needed them. If they could identify Billy the Kid's relatives after a hundred years, not to mention Thomas Jefferson's mixed-race offspring, then surely I could get the proof we needed.

"Abby? You still there?" said Will.

"Sorry. Are you back from camp?" I asked.

"No. I have a few more days to go. We aren't supposed to use our cell phones except for emergencies, but I couldn't stop thinking about that poor dead lady and what you were doing. I'm hoping no one rats me out about phoning you."

"You do what you're supposed to in Austin, and I promise I'll have more answers when you return." Okay, so I'd offered up more than a little hope that Lawrence Washington was innocent, though I wasn't totally sure, had left out a few details—like how Lawrence was stonewalling and how I'd been followed and warned and had basically put myself and my sister at risk. But that's what I'd signed up for when I chose this life, and Will didn't need to know all that.

18

My mentor Angel always says the element of surprise is a PI's best friend, so Saturday morning I made no phone call before taking off to visit the Church of the Reverent Life. Besides, everyone's welcome at church, right?

My exhilaration about learning the license number had evaporated after Jeff called to say the car had stolen plates. We agreed that whoever was following me had probably opted for a new car by now and I'd seen my last red Lexus for awhile.

Before I left, I checked up and down the street, looking for any occupied vehicles. Nothing. Maybe the file had satisfied whoever was following me, at least for now. Minutes later I drove off to find the church, being watchful for anyone making all my same turns.

Finding the church was easy. *You could play a Rockets game in this place,* I decided as I parked in a lot with enough room for about 10,000 cars. I walked toward the monstrous main building, remembering what Thaddeus had said. Hell, the building even had a gold roof, as did the adjacent day care center, youth center, fitness center and retirement center. Yup, this probably served as the center of the universe for lots of folks.

I opened one massive brass-plated sanctuary door rather than try to find the church offices. Who wouldn't want to see the inside of a place like this? I entered a large marble vestibule—even the walls were a mottled beige marble—and walked through into the sanctuary. *Holy opulence, Batman.* There was red velvet stadium seating, a pulpit so far from where I stood I'd need binoculars if I sat in the back, and a pipe organ so big a photo of it would weigh five pounds. My jaw must have dropped, because when someone lightly touched my shoulder, my teeth came together loud enough to rattle the rafters. And those rafters were way up there.

"Can I help you?" said the man beside me. He had a full head of white-blond hair, styled in the popular bed-head look. I guessed he was around forty. And his eyes. Wow. Almost as clear and blue and gorgeous as Jeff's. (I did say *almost*.)

I offered what I was sure was an awe-filled smile, both for him and for this place. "Unbelievable," I said, again scanning the sanctuary.

"It is, isn't it? I'm certain God is proud of what we've built."

I offered my hand, and the guy shook it eagerly while his other hand gripped my upper arm. He was staring at me with what seemed as much admiration as I held for the church building. Maybe a little too much admiration, although I was flattered by his obvious interest.

"I'm Abby Rose. I came to see Pastor Rankin."

"I'm B.J., the pastor's administrative assistant. Seeing him right now might be a problem," he said with an apologetic smile. "He's awfully busy. We have brochures about our church if you're interested, and I'll have an assistant pastor call if you leave us your information. Please feel free to join us Sunday."

"I really have to talk to him today. Could you ask him to spare a few minutes?" I pulled a card from the pocket of my linen skirt and handed it to him. I *had* put on a skirt and a lime cotton shirt fresh from the dry cleaner. Once I'd tried to wear pants to church and my daddy about had a fit and fell in it. Even now

I could hear him saying, "No funny business in church, Abby. You act like a young lady who's been taught right."

"A private investigator," the man said. "Interesting." He'd only taken his pale eyes off me for the instant it took him to read the card. They were fixed on my face again and I held his gaze even though I felt a strong urge to look away. I was beginning to understand what they meant when they said "magnetic stare" in romance novels. It had been a long time since I'd met someone worth looking at besides Jeff. I felt a little guilty, but a girl does need a distraction or two.

"Where can I find the pastor?" I asked. You want something, sometimes you gotta push.

"I'm sorry, Miss Rose, but—"

Just then a resonant, powerful voice rang out through the church, saying, "Friends and welcome visitors." The man standing at the pulpit stopped speaking to look down at a paper he held in his hand.

"Pastor," B.J. called. "Hang on a second." He strode down the nearest aisle.

The pastor said, "I wish you wouldn't—"

"You have a visitor," B.J. said.

Pastor Rankin squinted in my direction. "Oh. A parishioner? Someone in need?"

B.J. had made it to the pulpit, and the two spoke quietly for a second before they both started back up the aisle toward me.

When Pastor Rankin was within ten feet, I had to stifle a smile. From the pulpit, you would never know the man was diminutive, not much taller than my five-four. He also had a tragic comb-over and eyes that reminded me of two rabbit pellets in an Amarillo snowdrift. How could a magnificent voice like that—unmiked, mind you—come from *him*?

He offered a hand, and at least his firm grip matched his voice. "Miss Rose, right? How can I help you?"

"I have a few questions. I promise I won't keep you long."

Rankin opened his mouth, but it was B.J. who spoke. "The pastor has a routine and—"

"Please?" I said, focusing on Rankin.

He glanced back and forth between B.J. and me and settled on me. "Of course. Let's talk in my office." He looked up at B.J. "I promise I'll watch my time."

The assistant gave a resigned shrug. "It's your call."

While B.J. went back down the aisle to parts unknown, Pastor Rankin led me back through the vestibule and down a long corridor decorated with oil paintings and watercolors with religious themes. Nice merchandise. I'm not up on my artists, but I was willing to bet some of these painters were famous, their work was that good.

Rankin opened a heavy oak door with his name engraved on a brass plate, and we entered the spacious office. He gestured to an upholstered chair facing his desk, and I went over and sat down, taking in the room.

The first thing I noticed was the *People* magazine on the center of the desk. Is that where inspiration for sermons comes from these days? The bookshelf to the left of the desk did hold a collection of Bibles, and some of them looked quite old. To my right, a seating area with green leather chairs surrounded a coffee table with an inlaid beveled glass top. Looked pricey. Everything here spoke of money—vases on the windowsills and custom-made drapes with billowy swag toppers.

The Pastor sat behind his desk, and the chair must have been ratcheted way up, because he seemed taller again, like he had at the pulpit.

"Miss Rose, I sense you have a mission. A calling."

"Really? What makes you say that?"

"I see a light surrounding you—a soft, golden light."

From what I knew of this church, it edged toward the fundamentalist side, and California New Age auras wouldn't be the order of the day. Yet here was the pastor telling me I was lit up like a firefly. "I guess you could call this investigation a mission." I pushed my card across to him and said, "I'm working on a case concerning a baby who was abandoned a long time ago. That child is now a college student and hired me to find his birth family."

"B.J. said you were a private investigator. I find that a fascinating profession for a woman. Especially one as young as you." Rankin stared at me, his head tilted, his thin lips curved in a smile.

I shifted in the chair. This wasn't a come-on. The way he looked at me made me think he was trying to solve a mystery, read something in my eyes. Or maybe he was hallucinating and that's what this light thing was about. *Kate, where are you when I need you for a diagnosis?*

He said, "A baby brings you to our church? Perhaps that's why I sense such a strong bond between you and God. Sorry to say, I don't recall any of our parishioners ever mentioning an abandoned child. Did one of our congregation accept one into their life?"

"Let me explain by starting earlier in time, before that baby was left on a doorstep. There's a man who might be connected to that child. He's in prison now, but once attended here, probably in 1986 and 1987. You might remember him."

He was fingering the *People* magazine and held it up. "Do you know what fascinating material you can gather from a publication like this? The world is a different place than when I was first called to the ministry. These days you have to—"

"His name was Lawrence Washington," I interrupted, my voice sounding harder than I intended. I had a feeling this man could get distracted easily— by faces, by reading material and by golden auras. "According to what I've learned from the police, he was a member of a youth group—and you were the youth minister then."

"Lawrence. I remember him." He opened a drawer

and shoved the magazine inside. "It's been so long since I've heard anything about him. Is he still . . . there? In prison, I mean?"

"Yes. Can you tell me what you remember about him?"

Pastor Rankin folded his hands and leaned forward. "I recall he was a good young man who made a horrible mistake." He was giving me that intense and puzzled stare again, but I didn't shift my eyes from his, though I wanted to.

"Can you tell me about that youth group?" I asked. "Like any names you might recall? See, some of my evidence has . . . disappeared."

"And this has caused you anguish. I can read that much in your face." He was smiling, head cocked. "Would you like to join hands? Pray, perhaps?"

My daddy used to say, "Don't wait to hear the alarm go off before you build the fire escape." Alarms were sounding, and I hadn't come prepared to deal with someone like this. The best I could do was keep him on track. I said, "Um, not right now. The names of the youth group members would help."

He leaned back in the chair, stared up at the ceiling for a second. "That was so long ago, Abby Rose. All I remember is how Lawrence was brought to our youth ministry by friends from his high school, and we were so glad to have a black boy join us. Christ does not discriminate, and all are free to worship here."

Christ does not discriminate? A black boy? The way he said this had me thinking about this man of God in a different light. Damn. I didn't want to think about lights. *Just push forward, Abby. Get over the need to squirm while you do your job.* "Do you recall even one of his friends, Pastor Rankin?"

"You'd think I would, but I have been cursed with the worst affliction a pastor can have—I'm horrible with names. I do remember hearing about the young woman he . . . he *did away with*. She was found in a bank parking lot less than a mile from our original building, and it *was* our youth group meeting that night. The police came with questions, but sadly, we couldn't help the black boy. Our meeting ended long before the girl was killed, as I recall."

"You visited him in prison, Pastor Rankin," I said. "I've visited myself, and it's not something you forget. Can you tell me about that?"

"Tell you what we spoke of? That would be wrong, even if I could recall our conversation. Confidentiality is sacred. But I can offer you this by way of explanation. The gospel of St. Matthew teaches us that both the righteous and the sinners will be judged according to six requirements: giving food to the hungry, providing drink to the thirsty, showing hospitality to the stranger, clothing the naked, visiting the sick and visiting prisoners. By rendering these acts of compassion to the least of our brothers, we perform them for Christ Himself. It was my sacred duty to visit him."

"To sum up—and correct me if I'm wrong—the visit was just part of the job?" I'm not good at hiding my opinions, and if it made this guy like me just a little less, be less fixated on my face, I was all for cynicism.

His gaze shifted to a heavy oak lectern where a massive Bible sat open, the red satin bookmark dangling. He started flicking at the corner of my business card with a fingernail, his other hand balled into a tight fist. " 'Remember those who are in prison, as though you were in prison with them.' Hebrews 13:3. I sense your distrust, a certain distaste, and I am sorry for that. Your spirit is admirable, however. Like you, I perform my duties and am glad to do so. If it helps your cause, the black boy and I prayed together, but he told me nothing about his crime . . . nor did I ask."

"He may have spent years in jail for a murder he didn't commit. Will your duty to God help me find the truth? Perhaps free an innocent man?"

He smiled, folded his hands in front of him. "God has guided you here, brought your precious light, and I would never refuse you anything if only I could remember more. I simply can't."

But despite his calm tone, I noticed his face had

reddened. Maybe he had a blood pressure problem—
or my light had given him a sunburn.

"What would help you remember?" I asked. "Pictures of Lawrence after his arrest? I could bring one."

"You simply do not understand, Abby Rose." His
sanctuary voice had reappeared, his loud voice. Great
for a Sunday service, a little much for an office. Obviously the guy was coming unglued—which, now that
I thought about it, might not be a bad thing. Maybe
he'd let loose with something unexpected.

"Think hard, Pastor. Tell me what Lawrence said
to you in Huntsville. Tell me about the night of the
murder. Help me learn the names of the kids he hung
out with. Tell me—"

"*Stop.*" Rankin covered his face with his hands.
"You *don't* understand."

All of a sudden he was crying big old crocodile
tears. If I wanted to drive this man crazy, it would be
a short trip. "What is it that I don't understand,
Pastor?"

He took a deep breath to compose himself. "1987
was the *worst* year of my life, Abby Rose. We had to
deal with tragic events that had nothing to do with
the black boy's troubles."

I wasn't sure I felt comfortable asking what those
events were, and turns out I didn't have to.

He said, "We lost our daughter that year. The pain
is fresh even today and supersedes any memories of
prison visits or youth counseling or anything else from
back then."

"I'm really sorry, but even though it was a horrible
time—"

The door opened and I smelled an overpowering
perfume before I saw the woman. "Andrew, I heard
you—oh, my heavens. I *knew* something was wrong."

She rushed to Rankin's side, bent and held his face.
"What's happened?" She looked my way. "What's
going on?"

"I'm a private investigator and I came to ask a few
questions about a case I'm working—one that dates

back to 1987. I seem to have dredged up some bad memories, and for that I apologize."

"We lost Sara that year," the woman said softly, rubbing tears off her husband's cheeks.

"I really had no intention of upsetting the pastor."

She straightened, tugging at the short purple jacket that matched her skirt. She was shapely, and though I could tell she was in her fifties, she had aged well.

"I'm sure you had no idea about our child," she said. "How could you possibly know?"

Rankin said, "She came about Lawrence—you remember the black boy? But all of a sudden my thoughts leaped to Sara and—"

"Shh, Andrew. It's okay," said his wife. She looked at me. "Perhaps you should leave for now. Call me later. I'll try to help you, but right now, my husband needs me for reasons I don't need to explain."

"Certainly." I stood. "Sorry to have caused a problem." I was happy to go, because if I heard him say "the black boy" one more time, I might have had to slug a man of God, tears or no tears.

Mrs. Rankin smiled sadly. "Forgive me . . . forgive us. When you lose a child, the pain never goes away." She rested a hand on her husband's cheek again. "Andrew is a very sensitive man; so strong for others, but when it comes to Sara, well . . ."

"I'll ask for you when I call, Mrs. Rankin," I said.

She came around the desk, extended her hand and then rested her other over mine when we shook. "It's Noreen. And you're?"

"Abby."

"Abby Rose," said the pastor, pulling a handkerchief from his pocket. He blew his nose. "Isn't that a beautiful name? Perfect for a spirited, glowing young woman. I have never before seen light surround someone like it does you, Abby Rose."

Mrs. Rankin glanced at her husband, and though she tried to mask her confusion, she failed. "Andrew, what are you talking about?"

"You can't see it? Maybe Sara has returned, resides

in Abby Rose and—no, no. That's not right. I'm a little dizzy, Noreen. Where are my pills?"

Oh, yes. Find the pills right away, I thought.

"Please excuse us, Abby." She smiled, showing off bleached, perfect teeth to match her smooth, lovely skin—the kind you can only get from plenty of pampering. She was concerned, however, and I didn't blame her.

I picked up my purse and left, closing the door as softly as I could. That whole interview had been bizarre, and what had I learned? Zip. I was about to head back in the direction I'd come in when I saw a sign pointing the opposite way that read CHURCH LIBRARY. I decided this little visit wasn't over yet. The library in the church I'd attended as a child kept a history of everything, so maybe this one did, too.

When I entered, I was immediately reminded of the Hearst Castle library. There were shiny, walnut floor-to-ceiling shelves, a ladder on a slide to reach items on the top, thick pale peach carpet and soft overstuffed chairs where you could sit and read. Above me was a stained glass dome that, if I'd been paying attention, I could have probably seen from the parking lot. Guess I'd been too dazzled by gold roofs.

The library was magnificent and peaceful. But I hadn't come here for peace. I closed the door behind me and began scouring the shelves. I soon found what I was looking for in books that had been bound in identical leather volumes with gold engraved numbers—all the saved copies of newsletters, prayer lists, articles about special members of their congregation, church trip journals. I even got to climb that cool ladder. A few minutes later I found the years I wanted—'86 and '87. The volume with an '86 newsletter had a picture of a very young Pastor Rankin and his wife flanking their youth group.

I climbed down and laid open the book on a study table and took out my phone. I'd only clicked off one picture before the door opened.

It was Mrs. Rankin. She flashed her brilliant smile

again and definitely looked more relaxed than when I'd left her. "I thought you'd gone, but I'm so glad you found the library. Isn't it wonderful?"

"The whole building is amazing, but I think this room is my favorite."

"Did you find anything helpful?" she asked.

I closed the book. "A photo of Lawrence. Funny how he hasn't changed all that much since he was sent to Huntsville."

"You've seen him recently?"

"Yes."

"He's the one who hired you, then?"

"No, not Lawrence." I wasn't sure she needed to know about Will. Not right now, anyway.

"You're keeping a confidence," she said. "That's something we understand very well here. I have prayed for Lawrence often over the years and am so glad he has an advocate. This is a sign God doesn't want us to forget what happened." She stepped toward me, still smiling, her diamond stud earrings blinking in the sunlight coming through the tall velvet-draped window behind me. "Did he seem in good health when you visited?"

"As far as I could tell."

"He always said he didn't kill that girl, and frankly, I believed him. Told the police as much. Even though he was a very competitive young man, an athlete, you know, he had a soft spirituality about him. We were so lucky to have known him."

I came around the study table to stand between two armchairs. "But *you* haven't gone to see him?"

"Andrew went to the prison, then I tried, but Lawrence struck everyone from his visitor list quite early on."

"I didn't know that. By the way, is the pastor feeling better?" I was feeling a tad guilty about playing up to folks I didn't exactly like.

"He is better. You had no way of knowing what an emotional man he is, always has been. He's off to practice his sermon, so no harm done."

"Would *you* have time for a few questions now rather than later?"

She lowered onto the edge of a chair. "If Lawrence needs our help, of course. Though I'm not sure what I can offer."

I sat opposite her. "You met with the young people in his group every week, right?"

She nodded.

"Did Lawrence have a special attachment to anyone?"

Noreen Rankin smiled knowingly. "You mean was there a teenage romance going on? I can't speak to that, but you know adolescents. They wouldn't share that information with me. During our meetings we focused on our purpose, which was for those young people to become generous, God-loving adults who'd become assets to their church home. We read the Bible, we discussed the Bible. Anything that went on between them that didn't involve God stayed outside of our meetings."

"I was hoping that since Lawrence was the only African-American in your group at the time, maybe you could recall a little more about him than the others."

"I wish that were so, but Andrew and I both had such a difficult time that year. We thought surely Sara would be safe on that mission trip and—" She bit her lip, took a deep breath. "Anyway, perhaps if you can get in touch with someone in Lawrence's group, they could better help you."

"If I knew who they were. I need more information. Can I spend a little more time in here?"

She licked her glossed lips, thought for a second. "Our library *is* open to everyone, but we do have our church historical society meeting here in about . . ." She checked the thin silver watch on her wrist. "Oh, my goodness. They'll be here any second and B.J. hasn't set up the chairs. Would you mind returning? Say, tomorrow?"

I stood. "Sure. Thanks so much for your help. Let me put this book away before I go."

"B.J. will take care of it." She gave me another one of her clutching handshakes and gleaming smiles. She really was attractive and warm and all the things you'd expect of a pastor's wife, but she reminded me too much of Aunt Caroline and her rich friends. I was *not* feeling the love, but then maybe that was because I was so focused on getting what I needed.

At least I have one *picture,* I thought, as I walked out to the parking lot. With my luck, the library would probably be ransacked tonight and every single thing related to Lawrence Washington would be gone when I came back.

When I started to pull out onto the freeway feeder road, a church van was just driving in. The woman made a wide turn and nearly hit my front fender. She offered an apologetic wave as she steered right and drove into the lot. I noticed in the rearview mirror that the van was wheelchair-equipped, and I thought of Thaddeus. He could use wheelchair-equipped anything, and I might have to do something about it.

19

On my way home, I decided I had to face Joelle with the news about the break-in and the stolen files. This wasn't something I could do over the phone, and now was as bad a time as any. I called first to make sure she was home, and she sounded so excited to hear from me, I felt even more guilty about losing the files. I also made a call to Will's mother and updated her, told her I had spoken to Will and what I had learned so far. Mrs. Knight's concern was for Will and how he was handling this news, but she told me she was still behind him one hundred percent. If he wanted me to continue my work, then that's what I should do. Her commitment shored me up for the unpleasant task ahead.

I drove on to Joelle Simpson's, and she welcomed me wearing baggy jeans and an oversize cotton shirt. If she paid a little attention to her appearance—kept her hair dyed, wore clothes that fit—Joelle would be a pretty woman. Perhaps in her mind she was still married to Frank and being frumpy was a way to protect her relationship with her dead husband by keeping any interested male at bay.

If dressing down didn't work, a house filled with grief-filled photographs sure could scare suitors away. This time a shiver climbed my spine as I walked that hallway to her living room and passed those haunting photographs. She offered iced tea and I refused. I needed to get this over with.

Once we were seated, her on the couch and me in a worn recliner that I realized too late had probably belonged to Frank, I said, "I hate to tell you this, but someone stole the file you loaned me."

She tilted her head, her face expressionless. "Really?"

"Yes. I feel so stupid for not taking better care of it. I should have locked it up or something before—"

"But that's wonderful." She smiled.

I was so stunned by her response I couldn't speak for a second. "You don't have a sarcastic bone in your body, so I assume you're serious."

"Don't you see, Abby? That means Frank was right. Lawrence Washington was innocent. Why else would someone want that file? This would have meant so much to Frank."

She might be making a leap in logic—or more like faith—but it did make sense, in a way. "I'm relieved you're not mad about me losing the files."

"They were stolen, not lost. That's a huge difference."

Will had said the same thing, and as the weight of guilt lifted from my shoulders, I smiled. "You don't have to make me feel better."

"I'm not, Abby. What would I do with the file if you brought it back? Believe me, I have plenty more things in this house that need to go. I feel like I can't move on until I've finished what Frank so desperately wanted after he retired. Even in death, if he helps to right one wrong, then his obsession with those old cases was worth it. I believe you are an angel sent to help him rest in peace."

First golden lights and now I was an angel? What was I missing when I looked in the mirror? "You are one of the kindest people I've ever met, Joelle. Thank you. Was there anything else Frank kept besides the files? Because even though I only had one real run-through on the information, I've learned he might have missed something—and that doesn't seem like him." I was thinking of the girlfriend angle that Frank apparently had failed to uncover.

She sat back against the cushions. "As I'm sure you've figured out, Frank wasn't the most organized soul in the universe. Maybe we should check the attic? Before he went back to San Francisco after the funeral, our son hauled plenty of boxes up there. I'm not sure what was in them and I don't go up to the attic. Pull-down stairs are hard to climb when you get past fifty."

So I was the one who climbed the pull-down stairs, my second climb in search of evidence today. It was hot and dirty up there, and I was dressed in a skirt and blouse. Not exactly attic attire. At least I hadn't been stupid enough to wear hose.

I removed my clogs to better navigate plywood and beams, and started my search. I found lots of old soccer and baseball equipment, a three-speed bike, a disassembled crib and plenty of clothes in plastic bags. I bypassed bolts of material, an old sewing machine, photography magazines, stacked police journals and Christmas ornaments while balancing my way to the cardboard file boxes I'd spotted in a far corner. The boxes weren't marked, but that was to be expected from Frank. The first few I opened held slides and photos damaged by years in the heat of a Houston attic. Nothing police-related. Looked like the beginning attempts at Frank's photography hobby.

I moved these aside and opened the last box. When I did, I discovered my trip to this corner had been worth it. Inside were evidence envelopes from HPD. The first one made me wince when I looked inside. It was marked "Rape-Murder, Jane Doe #2" and held a box cutter. I decided not to check any of the others unless they were marked AMANDA MASON. Close to the bottom of the box I did find that Mason envelope, and inside was a bullet.

Yes. Pay dirt.

I'd been resting on my already sore knees and

nearly slipped in my haste to get up, but I finally navigated my way back to the ladder, grabbed my clogs and was soon in the nice, cool hallway.

"Got something," I said, holding up the envelope.

Joelle smiled and pulled me by the hand toward the kitchen. "You need a drink. You're so flushed."

After I gulped down a huge glass of water, I thanked Joelle, left, and called Jeff from the car.

"I am drowning in reports. Glad to hear your voice," he said.

"Can I come see you? It's important."

"You've got something?"

"I do. You may think I'm crazy but—"

"I *know* you're crazy, but that's what you do the best and I happen to like it."

I smiled, thinking about the pastor. I could show Jeff "crazy" he might not like so much. "I'll be there as fast as I can," I said.

"Without a tail, I hope? Because someone has been stuck to you like a bad smell lately."

"Don't remind me." I hung up, but his reminder made me pay more attention to my driving than I usually do, alert for that tail. I didn't notice anyone, though.

Once I met up with Jeff in his cubicle on the homicide floor, I sat down and held out the envelope. "I found this at Frank Simpson's place."

Jeff took it but kept staring at me. "What happened to your hair? You been hanging around spiders? And your shirt looks like—"

"Shut up," I said, wiping at a gray smudge. "I got down and dirty in an attic."

"Down and dirty," he said, grinning. "You and I could use a little of that."

"Great. You're horny and I'm trying to—"

"Sorry," he said. "What have you got?"

"I think this is the bullet that killed Amanda Mason."

Jeff's expression went from playful to unhappy in a

hurry. "Simpson took more than notes and files? He could have gotten himself in big trouble, Abby."

"It was a closed case. Don't you get rid of evidence after awhile?"

"They do clean out the evidence lockers after appeals are exhausted. Sorry for being critical, but from all you've told me, I like this Frank Simpson. Stupid of me to worry about a dead cop getting in trouble."

"Reputation is important to you guys," I said. "I understand your reaction."

He smiled. "You understand a whole lot about me. Guess this bullet would have been destroyed if he hadn't taken it. You know the Mason case better than I do. How can this help with the Olsen woman's death?"

"Here's the deal. The gun that killed Amanda Mason was never recovered, was not part of the evidence they found in Washington's bedroom that night. They figured he ditched it. What if that gun is still out there? What if it was used in some other crime later on and you have ballistic evidence waiting to be found in your police database?"

"I would have said you were nuts an hour ago, that you were reaching, but guess what we discovered when we ran the bullet we pulled from Thaddeus Washington's wall?"

"What?"

"It matches the one the ME dug out of the Olsen woman's chest."

My mouth went dry. "Uh-oh. You mean Verna Mae's killer shot at Thaddeus and me yesterday?"

"That's the logical conclusion, a possibility I like about as much as I enjoy Kate's cooking," he said. "Maybe next time it won't be a warning shot."

I took a deep breath. "Yeah. Scary. What about looking for a ballistics match to the Mason murder?"

"It's a long shot—no pun intended," Jeff said. "But maybe someone's been hanging onto a .38 for a very long time."

"Would the Mason ballistic evidence still be in the system?"

"Probably never was. DRUGFIRE didn't exist in 1987."

"DRUGFIRE?"

"The ballistics database. We do have two bullets already and now this one. If the Mason bullet matches the others, we'll have hard evidence that everything that's happened in the last week is connected to Will's abandonment. Probably not usable in court since you found this in a dead cop's attic, but still a clue. Let me get this to the right people and we'll know."

I returned home and showered the cobwebs out of my hair along with the grime and sweat off my skin. Once I was dressed in sensible clothes—denim shorts and a crop top—I transferred the picture of the youth group from the camera phone to my desktop computer.

After enlarging it, I used my software to sharpen the images so I could read the caption beneath the picture. Even though I no longer had Frank's notes, I recognized a few of the names from his files. Good. I had them in writing again. Then I found something that made me sit back in my chair and say "Damn."

Diva, who had curled up on my lap, did not appreciate my tone or my shift in position and took off with a hiss.

Why had Frank failed to note this? He never mentioned this person in his files—unless I'd missed it. A bigger question loomed. Why didn't the Rankins tell me their daughter, Sara, had been in the youth group? According to the caption, Sara Rankin was right there in this photo for God and everyone to see, standing next to guess who? Lawrence. She had long blond hair, a perky smile and dark brown eyes much bigger than her father's. She and Lawrence were the tallest kids in the group.

Maybe Frank's investigation focused on the group members present the night of the murder and that's why his notes didn't include Sara Rankin. The pastor's wife mentioned that her daughter had been on a mission trip, so the girl could have left home long before Mason was killed. Still, the fact that their daughter knew Lawrence seemed like an awfully significant piece of information to omit from our conversation—especially since I'd asked who was in the group more than once. Had the same information been omitted before? Could Frank Simpson have known nothing about Sara Rankin and that's why she wasn't mentioned in his files?

Okay, I thought. *I should give those people the benefit of the doubt.* Perhaps the pastor and his wife were so traumatized by their daughter's death that year, they failed to remember she knew Lawrence, or maybe decided it wasn't relevant. No matter what the reason, this required a very close look. I took down the names of the other members in the picture and began Googling them, starting with Sara Rankin.

The first thing I expected to find was an obituary, and I did. Sort of. A notice appeared in the religion section of the *Chronicle* in December 1987, an invitation to celebrate the life of Sara Rankin at the Church of the Reverent Life. I found one earlier reference to Sara: January of 1987, in a list of Confederate Legion debutante candidates—a crew of young women selected every year as the most gorgeous and precious relatives of men who had served in the civil war—on the Confederate side, of course. This social ritual still went on today and always made me shake my head in amazement when I saw newspaper pictures of all those pretty young girls with ties to slavery. I figured they didn't even realize what they were doing—or maybe I was the one who knew diddly-squat. Better not judge without the whole story, I guess.

Having not learned much about Sara, I picked the next name on my list. Nothing. Not until I ran a search for Oscar Drummond did I get dozens of hits. He was a financial planner and his name and face were all over cyberspace—almost unrecognizable as the face from the photo, since he'd gained more than a few pounds. His big smile gave him away, though. To meet with him on a Saturday might be tough. All I could do was try. I got an answering machine when I phoned, but mentioned in my message that I was the late Charlie Rose's daughter. A mention of a late, rich father would get a quicker response from a financial planner and sure enough Mr. Drummond called back in thirty minutes, eager to meet.

Forced to change clothes again, I chose something more appropriate for dinner downtown. Not a skirt, but khaki pants and a pink striped shirt that did not show my belly button even though I was pretty proud of my abs. I'd been running and working out with Jeff for almost a year.

The downtown streets were still crowded with late afternoon shoppers, but I managed to find a parking place in a theater district garage. I enjoyed a pleasant breeze as I walked two blocks to Birraporetti's, a fun Italian restaurant with "a heck of an Irish bar," as they liked to advertise.

Drummond was waiting for me at the hostess station, as eager as a groom in the last hour of the reception. I hate mentioning my money. It makes people act like they wouldn't be surprised if I spit a few gold nuggets at their feet before I spoke.

Drummond's infectious smile was the same as in the photo. He wore a charcoal suit, probably Armani, but I didn't think he could button that jacket if push came to shove. Not over the banjo belly. I never mentioned when I called that this wasn't about forging a relationship with him to manage my millions, so he was about to be let down big time.

"How good is your memory?" I asked, after we were seated in a booth far from the noisy bar and had given our drink order.

"As good as it should be, Ms. Rose. I manage a hundred clients, and if it weren't confidential information, I could tell you what the earnings are to date on their portfolios without so much as a glance at my computer. I customize to meet their individual goals, as any good money manager should."

I took a card from my purse and handed it to him. "Wonderful. Then I'm sure your memory can help me."

He kept the smile going. "Your father was quite the entrepreneur. I wish we could have met, but you—" He looked down at my card and fought to hide his confusion. "You, um, have a business of your own aside from your late father's?"

"Yes. Not as lucrative, but far more satisfying."

He rebounded quickly. "Great. I assume you're looking for help building and maintaining your assets while you pursue your new project?"

"It's not about money, Mr. Drummond. Sorry."

Though he was beginning to understand I hadn't met him here to hire him, he was still optimistic. I suppose that's what financial planners specialize in—optimism.

"I'd be excited to help you with anything, Ms. Rose."

I'd printed out the youth group picture and I placed it in front of him. "Do you remember any of these people?"

He picked the page up, stared at it for a second. "Where did you get this?"

"At the Church of the Reverent Life."

"Whoa. That was aeons ago. What I remember most is that life did not turn out too well for a few of my friends. A good life takes planning and hard work, Ms. Rose. When we're done with your inquiries, I hope you'll let me give you a quick little summary of the services I—"

"I'm sure you remember Lawrence as one of those unfortunate people you were referring to?" I cut in.

"Yes. He was a good guy. Ballplayer. Never understood why he messed up his life like that. For a stupid fifty dollars. Never made sense."

"What if he didn't mess up his life? What if someone else messed it up for him, set him up?"

"Are you serious?"

"Serious as Greenspan. I know Lawrence's story, probably better than anyone does right now, but I want to learn more about Sara Rankin. This picture was taken in '86. Did she continue attending meetings in '87? More specifically, was she present the night Lawrence was arrested?"

Before he could answer, my chardonnay and his scotch on the rocks arrived. We both sipped our drinks, and then Drummond said, "I believe she'd left the country sometime within the month before the murder on a mission trip to Mexico."

"She didn't come back?"

Drummond pursed his lips, shook his head sadly. "They never found her body as far as I know. She fell off some mountain carrying water to a campsite. Sweetest girl you'd ever meet. I had a crush on her for a year."

"Did anyone else have a crush on her?"

"I think all the guys did, which I'm sure worried her parents."

"How old was she?" I asked.

"Sixteen. Having a minister for a father is probably difficult for a girl—especially ultraconservatives like Pastor and Mrs. Rankin. Sara was strong-willed, though. Used to argue religious points better than anyone. If she'd wanted to date, I think she would have."

"But she didn't?"

"I don't think so. She was too busy with social causes. Smart and pretty and caring. Can you blame me for liking her?" He drained his glass, then swished the ice around. "After spending more time with Lawrence during our meetings, she pulled her name from the Confederate Legion Debutante list, said she couldn't justify taking part after getting to know him. That annoyed the pastor, I can tell you."

"How did you know?"

"Overheard a little argument. He couldn't keep up his end, though. She was the better debater, and he adored her too much to see her upset about anything.

He told her he would respect her choice. Must have been difficult for the Rankins. They wanted to show her off, have her picture in the paper all dressed in white with their family history printed underneath like all those other debutantes."

"The debutante scene is still strong in Texas." I took another sip of wine realizing that's all I really knew. Despite our money and the mansion we'd lived in, Daddy kept his Rolex in a coffee can when it wasn't on his wrist. Society stuff has always been Aunt Caroline's territory, and I made sure she knew I'd rather show off new jeans at the rodeo than trip over some ball gown.

"They worshipped that girl," Drummond went on. "When she disappeared, they spent weeks looking for her, hired locals in Mexico to help, had search dogs flown in. Later that year, close to Christmas, we had this big memorial service . . . so, so sad. Sara was all they had. Besides God, of course. Their faith carried them through. I couldn't return to the church after that, watch those nice people hiding their grief."

"Could she have had a relationship with Lawrence?" I asked.

"You mean boyfriend and girlfriend? No way. I would have caught on, since I'm very perceptive." He straightened in his chair, pasted on his happy salesman face again. "If you'd like proof of just how well I use my better traits, I have some revealing charts that compare traditional index funds with a high-performing real estate trust."

I said, "If I decide to change the people managing my money, I promise I'll think of you first."

"I'm certain your people have told you that diversification is the key to long-term growth. If they haven't, then—"

"Sorry, Mr. Drummond."

Maybe I should have strung him along awhile, because he didn't have much more to offer when I asked him about the other people in the photos. None of them had kept in touch, and Oscar Drummond hadn't set foot in the Church of the Reverent Life since Sara Rankin's memorial service.

But, I thought, as I made my escape after we made uncomfortable small talk over veal marsala, *at least I know a little more about Sara.* Problem was, if she disappeared in March or April and died soon after, she couldn't have been Will's mother. He'd arrived on Verna Mae's doorstep in October.

I had a feeling there was a whole lot more to that story, though. The only avenue I had left to explore was the other girl in the picture—Jessica Roman. Maybe she had some answers, could even have been Lawrence's girlfriend. But to explore this avenue, first I had to find her.

20

I was dog tired when I made it home, too tired to revisit my Internet searches looking for Jessica Roman right now. I'd just finished microwaving a pizza when Jeff showed up. Nothing better than more chardonnay and a little sex for my dessert. I'm never too tired for that.

An hour later, we were lying in bed, my head close to Jeff's ear, when he said, "The bullet is a match. The same gun that murdered Amanda Mason killed the Olsen woman."

I sat straight up and shoved Jeff's shoulder. "Why didn't you tell me the minute you walked in the door?"

"Because I had other plans. What would you do with that information tonight anyway?"

"I don't know. Drink more wine, maybe. I mean, this is great."

"Great because it connects the crimes, but it still doesn't do much for Lawrence Washington or your client," Jeff said.

"It's evidence. Unless you're trying to convince me that Lawrence gave the gun to someone after the murder, or sold it, or pawned it, and then years later the same gun is used to shoot Verna Mae? Come on, Jeff."

"I'm trying to make you think this through. For one thing, you can't be certain Will is Lawrence's son."

"If you'd been in that prison and seen him, you

wouldn't have a doubt—they look that much alike. I
plan on asking Thaddeus Washington for a DNA sample tomorrow, since Lawrence won't cooperate. Then
we'll have even more hard evidence."

"Good idea. I'll handle that. Send someone out to
collect a sample tomorrow. You won't get your private
lab tech to work on a weekend."

"Yeah, okay. Thanks," I said.

Jeff tucked several strands of hair behind my ear.
"You're distracted. What's going on?"

"I keep thinking about Lawrence Washington, Jeff.
He claims he's innocent yet he won't cooperate about
this baby thing. That tells me he's either protecting
someone or he's got nothing to tell." I reached down,
grabbed Jeff's shirt from the floor and put it on. "Protecting the mother of his child? Protecting his father?
Protecting the son he never knew?"

"Maybe all three," Jeff said. "Or maybe he didn't
want to get his hopes up about getting out, feared the
parole board would bypass him again. Now that
you've got a little leverage with him, he might talk."

"Leverage?" I said.

"His father. I saw you two together. You got old
Thaddeus charmed. Rent a wheelchair van and take
him up to Huntsville. I'll call ahead, arrange the visit.
With his father urging him to cooperate, you might
get something out of Lawrence."

"Do you guys have a wheelchair van?"

"A wheelchair paddy wagon is a better description.
Not exactly a comfortable ride for the old guy."

"Wait. I have an idea on where to find a van, not
to mention some willing spirits at the Church of the
Reverent Life that might just lend me the
transportation."

The next morning, I called the church hoping to
talk to B.J. and learned you do not call a church on
a Sunday morning and expect to get any help. I didn't
even bother to leave a message. Turned out Jeff

couldn't get me into the prison anyway. Someone had stabbed one of their best buddies with a paper clip, and discipline was the order of the day. My need for an interview wasn't deemed important enough to override the warden's order for all inmates to remain in their cells.

Needing another means of transportation to get Thaddeus up to the prison, I found a United Way volunteer who'd rolled over the office phone to his cell. He told me they'd help whenever I needed them. I didn't even have to donate money, though I made a call and left a message for my very excellent financial adviser—who did not go by the name of Oscar Drummond—to get a donation to them in the mail tomorrow.

I turned my attention to Jessica Roman. I had been unable to find her through usual computer searches, but finally did locate her using one of my expensive pay-as-you-hunt Internet companies. Strange how a picture does not always tell a thousand words. She looked prim, serious and even a little nerdy in the old church photo, but it turns out I could have gotten tons of information about her from Jeff for free. Jessica Roman was a "massage therapist" with a rap sheet as long as a well rope. Apparently her God-fearing days had ended long ago.

I called Jeff, and he hooked me up with a vice officer who knew Jessica well. But Officer Marty Lamar didn't want me visiting Jessica at her "business" by myself and offered to take me. Seems he and Jeff were pretty good friends and he'd been told to look out for me.

Marty picked me up in the late afternoon. He wore jeans and a T-shirt, and I'd opted for the same. A minor cool front had blown through and knocked the temperature down to the high seventies today. He was short and muscular, maybe late forties, but had spent way too much time in the Texas heat. His skin was leathery and sun-damaged, but what was more striking was his cynicism. Every word he uttered told me he should consider changing jobs. Vice did not agree with him.

We headed to a very nasty section of the city where massage parlors lined the streets, and he took me straight to where Jessica did business—Vivi's. The sign on the door read ALWAYS OPEN.

"Guess you know Jessica pretty well?" I asked.

"I know 'em all," Marty said. "But my view is kind of one-dimensional. She might be nice and helpful and all those things normal people are. I've never bothered to find out and don't give a shit, to be honest."

His attitude reminded me how much I had to learn about crime, despite long talks with Jeff—but then Jeff was as different from Marty as sugar was from salt. Not that Jeff was sweet and soft. He just had something Marty might have lost along the way. Compassion.

When we walked into the very small, very rundown portable metal building, a woman at a front table jumped up.

"Cool your jets, Bitsy," Marty said. "I'm not here on a bust. Where's Jessie?"

Bitsy was a bleach blonde with lips painted as red as Twizzlers. She was about as "bitsy" as a longhorn steer. "She's, um, busy. Guy with a really bad back needed help."

"Yeah, right," said Marty. "You go fix his back and get her out here. Now."

"Sure. Whatever you say."

While she hurried down a small narrow hall, I said, "I'll bet for every one of these you shut down, another springs up."

"Every fuckin' day. This used to be the Ocean Club. Looks like a club, doesn't it?" He offered a wry smile.

I just shook my head.

Less than a minute later Jessie appeared, wiping her hands on her spandex pants. I sincerely hoped that white stuff she was shedding was massage lotion.

She stopped short of us. "I'm losing money by the

second. What do you want, Marty?" Despite her life-style, Jessica Roman had aged well. She still had the kinky red hair and high cheekbones in the photo—not to mention a very nice body. The boobs, however, were bra-busters, probably not original issue.

"Let's go out to the car. Have a little chat," Marty said.

She looked at me with skepticism. "Who's she? An assistant D.A.? 'Cause I'm clean. Off the crack, doing real massage—"

"Save it for some rookie, Jessie. Let's go."

We went out to Marty's unmarked Ford, and Jessica and I slid into the backseat. He started the engine and turned on the air-conditioning over Jessica's protest that it was cold in the car already. He pulled a turkey sandwich from a brown bag and started eating while I explained I was a PI and needed her help.

"And why should I help you?" Jessica asked.

"Because I said so," Marty answered with a full mouth, his icy stare catching her in the rearview mirror.

"Okay, okay," she said. "Shoot."

"A long time ago," I said, "you belonged to the Church of the Reverent Life."

"When I was fifteen. So what?" She lifted her chin, her hostility evident.

"Hey, this has nothing to do with religion or the lack of it, if that's your problem. Don't get all bent." I had to thank Will for the vernacular one of these days. Helps with the job.

"In return for me talking to you, I don't get busted? Is that the deal?" she asked.

"That's right," Marty answered over his shoulder.

Jessica rolled her eyes and sighed. "What do you want to know?"

"There was a kid in your group, Lawrence Washington. He ended up in jail."

"Yeah. Lawrence. Killed some girl. Not what I expected from him. He probably had an IQ bigger than Pastor Rankin's. He was one smart dude."

"You thought Lawrence did the murder?" I asked.

"To tell you the truth, no. But everyone's got a dark side."

"Yeah, including you," Marty said.

"Shut up," Jessie shot back.

"Back to the youth group," I said. "What do you remember about the pastor's daughter?"

"Sara?"

"Yes."

"Oh. This is about her and Lawrence?" Jessica settled into the corner of the backseat, her smile a surprise.

When in doubt, act like you know more than you do, I always say. "How long had they been a couple?"

"They clicked the minute they set eyes on each other. But how'd you find out? I thought I was the only one who knew," she said.

"Believe me, it hasn't been easy to get at the truth. Tell me about them."

"Her parents would have freaked if they found out, I can tell you that. After she was gone and Lawrence got sent up, I decided it wasn't something anyone needed to know, especially the parents. A dead issue. Fuckin' Romeo and Juliet deal."

"Jessie's been reading Shakespeare?" Marty said. "Stop the presses."

"Hey," she said. "There's a whole lot you don't know about me, so screw it shut, Marty."

I cleared my throat. "Getting back to Sara. Exactly when did she disappear?"

Jessie squinted in thought for a few seconds. "Right before the whole Lawrence thing. All of a sudden two people were gone in a couple weeks' time. Her mother said she went on some mission trip to Mexico, but Sara never said anything about going anywhere to me. Other kids went on those trips all the time, though, and Sara got a lot more out of that Bible crap than I ever did. It would have been her kind of gig. Not up my alley, I can tell you."

Marty said, "You're serving mankind in your own

special way, Jessie." He balled up the paper sack that
had held his sandwich and tossed it in her lap. "Take
care of that for me on your way back to work."

"Sure, asshole." She looked at me. "Anything
else?"

"You're certain Lawrence and Sara were . . .
close?" I said.

"You mean doing the nasty? Oh, yeah. I'm sure. I
could tell by the way they snuck their little church
school glances across the room. I would have liked a
little of that Lawrence action myself. The guy was
hot."

"They're all hot to you," Marty said. "Even the
scuzzy ones with hair growing out of their ears."

"Okay. I'm done here," she snapped. She opened
the door, launched the twisted bag at Marty's head
and left.

After Marty drove me back to my car, I thanked
him for his help, and he apologized for the interaction
between him and Jessie, saying he got carried away.
He said she was a smart woman wasting her brain and
it pissed him off, that he ran into way too many people
like her.

I was a little pissed off myself at the information
the Rankins had omitted. I decided another visit to
them was in order. Maybe they didn't know about
Lawrence and Sara, but I was beginning to think that
trip she took had been a mission all right, a mission
trip the Rankins organized to get their daughter away
from her black boyfriend. I needed to know when
Sara left, and if I got lucky, the pastor and his wife
might even come clean about what they knew or suspected about Lawrence and Sara.

The parking lot was packed when I arrived at the
church and discovered a late Sunday service was in
progress. I tiptoed into the sanctuary and chose one of
those movie theater–type seats in the last row. Pastor
Rankin was miked, and I had to admit the little man
could make you believe he was alone with you despite

the full house. No wonder they needed this huge place.

I'd come in on the tail end of the sermon and only knew Pastor Rankin had focused on God's grace, grace that allowed friend and foe alike to gather as one community. I didn't really listen to the words, but focused more on the rhythm of his delivery. *Does someone teach you to speak like that?* I wondered. *Or was he born with the ability?*

He finished, saying, "All of you are present on earth to glorify God, to expand His kingdom by proclaiming His word in the world."

I was surprised when the audience stood and applauded. No one applauded in my church, not for anything. This whole production reminded me of a Broadway play.

I hung around in the vestibule for what seemed like an hour as people visited with each other and the Rankins. The crowd finally began to disperse and then the pastor and his wife were alone, preparing to leave.

They both seemed surprised to see me. "I have a few more questions," I said after we exchanged greetings.

Mrs. Rankin said, "Did you just arrive?"

"No, I came in on the end of the sermon. Impressive, Pastor."

"I'm so thrilled you joined us tonight," said the pastor's wife when he didn't respond.

Rankin was wearing that odd smile that had made me so uncomfortable the other day, his eyes never straying from me. Finally he spoke. "You've brought the light again. More light to fill our church home and our hearts, Abby Rose."

I thought this aura business might have been a diversion last time, but now I wasn't so sure. He seemed so sincere, so mesmerized by me when it should have been the other way around.

As for Mrs. Rankin? She was definitely bothered and was staring at him with that same confused look I'd noticed yesterday. "Andrew, the only light you seem to be speaking of comes from God or from Jesus, our savior. Please remember that."

I decided it was time to fish or cut bait, get to why I was here. "Why didn't either of you tell me Lawrence knew Sara?"

Mrs. Rankin didn't miss a beat. "You never asked."

Now *that* answer pissed me off. Not wanting to burn my bridges, however, I bit my tongue and sweetly said, "Okay. I'll try to be direct. Did you suspect they were having a little romance?"

"Of course not," said the pastor. "I told you before, he was . . . *black*." He whispered the word "black," a tactic used often in these parts to let a listener know where a speaker stood on race relations. I already knew where the pastor stood, though. Blacks might be welcome to worship here, but they would never really belong in the fold.

"Sara had no boyfriend," Mrs. Rankin said. "She was very involved in charity work, school, many other things, too. Besides, she'd left for Mexico before the murder, so I'm unsure why it even matters that they knew each other."

"The police never asked about her either, did they?" I said.

"No. She wasn't here the night Lawrence was arrested. They had no reason to ask," she said.

"Some people happen to think Sara and Lawrence were close, maybe even intimate."

"Intimate only with God." Pastor Rankin had flushed so red I thought we might need to call the fire department. His eyes had filled, and I was worried he might plunge over the deep end again.

"I didn't come to upset you, Pastor," I said. "I'm trying to get at the truth."

"Oh, I know," he said. "The light of truth follows you everywhere. God is helping you in your quest. Allow Him to lead you down the righteous path. Give in to His wishes, and the truth will follow."

Problem was, Rankin's so-called righteous path led me to this church, but his unwavering stare made me wish I was somewhere else. "Are you certain you knew nothing about your daughter's relationship to Lawrence?" I asked.

"There was no relationship," Mrs. Rankin said, placing a manicured hand on her husband's sleeve. "You know how spent you are after a sermon, Andrew." She looked at me. "The sermons sometimes take him someplace else, a place where his senses are heightened. I think he needs to rest."

I said, "Well, I'm not resting until I learn the truth. See, there's a man sitting in prison for a crime he didn't commit. If Sara was the person you say she was, she'd want you to help him—not take a nap right now, Pastor."

"Yes . . . she would want to help," Rankin said. "Sara cared so much for the less fortunate, the—"

"Please let him gather himself before you continue," Mrs. Rankin said. "We *are* willing spirits, but a church this size has its stresses."

"I hate to be persistent, but I *need* to know about Sara's trip," I said. "When did she leave? When did you find out she was missing?"

"Maybe we should go into the office," Mrs. Rankin replied. "All I ask is that you be gentle with Andrew. He has not healed from our loss despite accepting God's will. Any questions concerning that time are distressing."

Andrew took my elbow as we walked down the hall to the office. "I feel so humble in your presence, Abby Rose. Your dedication to your cause, the determination in your eyes—how I wish I had half of your passion."

I fought the urge to pull away from his touch. How could someone go from being vibrant and in charge of a huge audience to downright disturbed in less than an hour?

Since they were vacuuming the pastor's office, we opted for the library and sat in those cushy chairs. I took a deep breath before I spoke. Having had a minute to think made me realize that being a little less pushy might be a better approach with them.

But before I could open my mouth and offer a kinder, gentler Abby, a lady in turquoise scrubs with little panda bears all over the fabric came rushing into the room. I recognized her as the one who had been driving the van yesterday.

"Pastor? I—" She looked at me. "I am so sorry to interrupt." She stood there, her fingers working, obviously distressed.

Pastor Rankin stood, his concern evident. "Is it Chester? Is he going downhill?"

The woman nodded.

Reading my questioning look, Noreen Rankin said, "This is Olive, our nurse's aide. She visits the shut-ins, makes sure they get medical care, takes them out to pick up their medicines. We don't know what we'd do without her."

Olive sure had a huge job if she was serving the gigantic congregation by herself. Maybe there was more than one aide, though.

"Noreen, Abby Rose," said the pastor, "I'm needed elsewhere. Will you forgive me if I leave?"

"Is someone sick?" I asked.

"Yes. Please return, Abby Rose. We have much to discuss and the light . . . I think I understand now. You've been sent to help me past the sorrow."

From the corner of my eye, I saw Mrs. Rankin close her eyes and shake her head. Maybe she needed to consider upping his meds.

The pastor left with Olive and I turned to Mrs. Rankin. "Tell me about your daughter. You must have loved her very much."

If Noreen Rankin was unnerved by her husband's less-than-normal behavior, she'd stuffed it down. She rested against the cushions, raised her eyes to the stained-glass ceiling. "She was our angel. Gifted in so many ways. God must have needed her, called her to His side."

"She left for the mission trip several weeks before Lawrence was arrested, correct?"

"Yes. Our ministry was working in central Mexico with a town in need of help. Sara felt the calling."

"But what about school? It wasn't summer, so she was supposed to be in school, right?"

"School is more than a classroom and textbooks, Ms. Rose. Her education never stopped."

"She went alone? Didn't that worry you?"

"Her father took her, left her in the hands of the pastor there. Andrew was much more in touch with reality back then." She looked me straight in the eye. "He does have some lingering emotional problems, as I'm sure you've noticed."

"But he is a wonderful speaker," I said with a smile, at a loss for anything better to say.

She just smiled back.

I had to fill the awkward silence, so I moved on. "When did you realize Sara . . . wasn't coming back?"

Mrs. Rankin fiddled with the hem of her pale yellow sweater and spoke softly, saying, "May. We got a call, that horrible phone call every parent dreads. She'd fallen and they couldn't find her body. What a nightmare. We spared no expense searching, but she was gone. I have spent years learning to accept God needed her and took her. I am at peace with that today."

"The pastor's not at peace," I said.

"He's not always in touch with the world outside that sanctuary. He thinks she'll walk through the door one day, still sixteen, still as full of life as ever."

I considered the timing. Sara could have left, but maybe she didn't die in May as her parents assumed. If she gave birth to Lawrence's child in the fall of '87, the mission trip was a cover to hide the pregnancy from her family. "Several months passed from the time she left until you knew she was . . . gone for good?"

"We kept hoping for a miracle throughout the year.

Andrew wouldn't give up the search. He was a strong man back then, poured his heart and soul into his ministry—I think sometimes to avoid spending every minute thinking about Sara."

"Why did you finally have that memorial service at Christmastime?" I asked, remembering what Oscar Drummond had told me and the small newspaper article mentioning the celebration of Sara's life.

"How did you know? From the books?" She glanced over her shoulder at the shelves.

"I located someone from the youth group. Oscar Drummond told me."

"Ah, Oscar. Nice young man. Anyway, I convinced Andrew we had to let go of Sara. In the years that followed, I thought I'd made the right decision, because Andrew seemed to be coping well. He moved up the ranks, brought so many more people to our church." The smile that had disappeared when Mrs. Rankin had been talking about her daughter's death returned.

"But things have changed?"

"He has his good days. Lucid ones. And I hope you'll be kind enough to not say anything about his unusual behavior tonight. We don't want to trouble those who need him and might falter if Andrew were forced out of his position here."

"Sure. I'm just looking for the truth, and I do appreciate your help. I knew Sara's death took a toll on your husband the first time we met, but I didn't realize the magnitude."

"Maybe Andrew is onto something about you, Ms. Rose, because I'm inspired by your dedication to your job. You've learned so much in a day's time, and I've done nothing to reach out to the others who must have felt our terrible loss back then. They were her friends, after all."

"Oscar would love to hear from you." And love to manage the church money, given half a chance. Plenty of money here, that's for sure. Enough money to help keep a big secret? But before I could think harder on this, I heard the muffled ring of the phone in my purse. "Excuse me," I said.

I answered and was surprised to hear Burl's voice. "I found the place."

"The place?" I said, confused.

"Verna Mae's storage unit. In Houston. I'm on my way there."

"Can I meet you?" I asked.

"Sure." After he gave me the address, I hung up and looked at Mrs. Rankin. "Thanks for talking to me. I know it wasn't easy."

"Can you find your way out?" she asked.

"No problem," I answered.

As I hurried to my car, I was willing to bet Sara had left home to hide a pregnancy and gave birth, maybe in that Mexican village. Was Mrs. Rankin telling the truth? Or did Sara's parents guess the real reason she left? They might have made up the mission trip story and the mysterious fall to keep the church from learning the truth about their daughter's *sin*— and they surely would have considered her behavior a sin. Maybe they hoped Sara would return after time passed—their "lost child" miraculously found. But then a real tragedy occurred—teenage pregnancies can be dangerous, and Sara could have died in childbirth. The Rankins found out somehow and left the baby with Verna Mae.

Then I thought of another scenario. Jessica Roman could have been Will's mother and was lying through her teeth today, thinking she could get busted for abandoning a child.

You don't know enough to be sure of anything, I thought, as I climbed into my Camry. I pulled out of the parking lot hoping that storage unit would yield something to tie everything together. I needed more than wild guesses.

21

The address Burl gave me was off the toll road that Jeff mentioned Verna Mae traveled every week. Had the storage facility been her regular destination? Would Burl and I find some important truth hidden there?

My heart was thudding against my chest as I made a conscious effort to stay within the speed limit. The last thing I wanted was to be delayed by a ticket. With it being past nine p.m. on a Sunday night, the highways were deserted. Burl thought he'd be arriving about nine-thirty, but I knew I'd get there before him.

Indeed, I arrived at the U-Store-It at nine-twenty, just as my cell phone rang. It was Burl. He was tied up in traffic thanks to a major accident on the Baytown Bridge. He told me I could wait in my car until he arrived, or go on home and he'd let me know what he'd found tomorrow. Yeah, right. Like I would do that.

He had no idea I had copies of those keys to unit B-109—the number I remembered from the tag—and since I was as fidgety as a zoo animal at feeding time, I *had* to use them.

I got out of my car and bypassed the card swipe–equipped barrier, a wooden arm blocking a direct drive-in route to the rows of storage units. Instead, I used the key similar to a house key and opened a tall iron gate.

I soon learned the B row was at the end of the A

row to my far right. As I walked toward the B units, doubts began to creep in. Burl would play this by the book, which meant he'd want a warrant or the manager out here. In fact, he might have a warrant in hand and a manager on the way to meet us.

Damn. I'd been chasing cookie crumbs for days and I knew in my gut this place was important. I wouldn't let a traffic jam make me wait while I chewed my fingernails down to the quick, not when I could be in and out before Burl knew the difference.

The front entrance had been well lit, and though each unit was supplied with a halogen light over its wide door, the farther back I walked, the darker it seemed. Hurricane fencing ran behind all the units at the edge of the property, but it wasn't tall enough to keep anyone out. Heck, I could have crawled over if I wanted to risk scratches and bug bites from the overgrown weeds. Could be an electric fence, though, or one that triggered an alarm.

I finally reached B-109 and used the hem of my shirt to hold onto the padlock securing the door, not wanting to destroy any prints that might belong to someone other than Verna Mae.

I keyed the lock, and the padlock snapped open. I slid open the door, and a blast of air-conditioning hit me as I peered into the darkness, the halogen light worthless since it was mounted to illuminate the driveway. I used the small flashlight on my key chain to hunt for a light switch. If there was air-conditioning, there was electricity. I focused my light on the left wall and saw what I was looking for. I flicked the switch. Nothing happened.

Great. No lights.

I swept my meager tool from left to right, and even with such little light, what I saw raised chill bumps on my arms.

"Damn," I whispered. The whole place had been set up as a shrine to Will.

On a small low table near the back wall sat Will's high school graduation picture. I went there first and squatted in front of the table, saw that the photo was flanked by candles . . . and so much more. To the left were snapshots of Will as an infant, held by a smiling Verna Mae. Definitely the same baby I'd seen in Verna Mae's albums before they disappeared. The blanket he was wrapped in grabbed my attention, too. I didn't need to see the POSH PRAMS label to know I had taken a picture of this blanket and had held its twin at Marjorie McGrady's house. To the right were photos of Will holding a baseball bat, playing basketball as a teenager, and the most recent of him in his UT basketball uniform.

When I started to get up, I noticed the velvet kneeling rail along the front of the table, the kind you see in church. A whole platoon of goose bumps climbed my neck this time. Verna Mae Olsen had more than a few spokes missing from her wheels. Did she come here and pray in front of this altar she'd made? Make the trip week after week for the last nineteen years?

I tried to ignore the sick feeling in my stomach and swept my light to the right and saw another set of framed pictures on a small covered table. I stepped over there. The large one in the center was Sara Rankin dressed in a white ball gown—the kind Mardi Gras princesses and debutantes wear. Her unsmiling expression made me think she might also have had on barbed wire underwear. I could think of only one reason Verna Mae Olsen had that picture here in the Church of Will Knight.

The photo next to it interested me, too. I picked up the framed picture and held my light directly over it, squinting in thought. Two women, one of them a much younger, trimmer Verna Mae than the one I'd met. She had her arm around a teenage girl about her same age. A sister or a friend, or—

I heard a muffled voice behind me say, "Thanks."

"Burl," I said, whirling, my face already heating up with embarrassment.

Uh-oh. Not Burl.

The man was dressed in black, his face hidden by

a ski mask. I stepped back, wishing I could melt
through the wall like a ghost.

"Turn back around the way you were," whispered
the man. A harsh stage whisper. Nasty voice. However, the gun he held offered far better incentive for
me to do as I was told.

I moved slowly, my legs rubbery and reluctant to
comply. I hung on to my puny flashlight and keys
while thinking about the gun I'd left in my glove compartment. Man, I could use that .38 about now.

If he got close enough, I could use a key to gouge
this guy's eyes—but he was breathing down my neck
before I even finished the thought. He wrapped a forearm around my chest, his gun hand and weapon crush-
ing into my left shoulder. He quickly snatched my
keychain and light and tossed them away, then yanked
my hands behind me. I felt plastic cuffs being
snapped on.

The adrenaline had kicked in, that all-over shaky
feeling like after I've avoided a major collision. Except
I'd avoided nothing. I was in a wild bull's pasture
without a tree.

"Down on your knees," he said.

My stomach tightened, and the image of Verna
Mae's battered face flashed through my mind. This
was her killer. My turn now. Would he put a bullet
in the back of my head or—

"I *said* get down," he rasped.

"Can we talk first? We—"

"Do it."

Damn hard to use your brain when you're so scared
even your underwear is quivering.

I bent one knee, ready to do what he commanded,
but apparently not fast enough. He pushed me, and I
fell forward onto the floor. I tasted dirt first, then the
blood from my busted lip. He sat on my back and tied
my ankles together.

Then a soothing mantra started in my head, a mantra born of common sense. "He could have shot you
already. He could have shot you already."

He got off me, and I heard him walking around. I turned my head in his direction but could only see dark feet traveling the perimeter of the unit. What the hell was he doing? Then came the sound of breaking glass. Now I got it. He was smashing open the picture frames. Yes, but—

I smelled the gasoline before I heard it splashing around me, the odor so strong instant nausea rolled in my gut.

Holy shit. A bullet would be welcome compared to burning to death. One by one, small crackling fires were springing up within a few feet of my head, their flames jumping in the darkness.

Then he lit the cloths draped over Verna Mae's makeshift altars and the whole unit brightened with a horrible *whoosh*. I took in a deep breath and held it, not wanting to inhale the smoke.

If being scared out of my mind wasn't bad enough, the worst moment came a second later.

He caressed the back of my head, his gloved fingers trailing down my back.

"Sorry," he whispered.

22

I heard him run away, and it only took about a nano-second for me to realize he'd left the door open. Between the wind and air-conditioning, the fire was spreading, engulfing the contents of B-109.

The door is open, Abby. Open. As in you can get the hell out.

I didn't have to stop, drop and roll: I only needed the roll part. Trouble was, I was facing the back of the unit. Rolling would only take me left or right and not away from the fire, and its heat was already making me sweat.

I quickly turned over onto my back and sat up. Pretty damn easily, too. *Bless you, Jeff, for getting me in shape,* I thought, as I scooted on my butt out of that place.

I'd made it all the way to the A units when Burl found me. Thank God he didn't ask questions. He just uttered, "Damnation," before cutting me loose. Ever the careful cop, he took a Baggie from his pocket and stashed the plastic cuffs inside before pulling me to my feet. Then we ran.

Flames were flicking into the sky by the time we reached the entry gate. Burl helped me into the passenger seat of his Land Rover and called 9-1-1. The station must have been close, because we heard sirens almost immediately and the first fire truck pulled in only minutes later.

They had a swipe card—probably fire code regulations or something—and drove their truck in. Burl spoke to the cops who'd come barreling in on the heels of firemen and then returned to me.

He pulled a bottled water from the back floorboard. "Here. Drink this."

I twisted open the top and drank greedily.

"We need a paramedic for you, Abby?" he asked.

"No. I have a busted lip and a bruised ego, but other than that, I'm fine."

"Were you in B-109 when the fire started?" he asked.

"Yes. And I am so sorry, Burl. I—"

"How's your breathing? You inhale any smoke?"

"I got out of there pretty fast, so I'm really okay," I said.

"Good. Now what the *hell* do you think you were doing, girl?" The anger had finally surfaced, and I couldn't blame him. I was pretty mad at myself.

"I know I should have waited for you, but—"

"You got more buts than an acre of monkeys. You could have been killed."

"But I wasn't," I said. "And you know something? That's weird. He had a gun. He could have put a bullet in me."

"Maybe he thought you'd die in the fire."

"He left the door open, Burl. He *knew* I could get out. He didn't want *me*. He wanted to destroy that place."

Burl nodded in agreement. "Makes sense, and from the looks of that fire, we may never know what was so important."

"I saw some of it. Had a little flashlight and—oh, no."

"What?"

"My car keys. They're in there."

"Don't count on finding them anytime soon," said Burl, looking up at the black cloud hanging over us.

* * *

After I filled in the cops and the firemen on everything that happened, Burl drove me to Kate's place so I could get a house key. I'd lost that, too.

On the way, I explained everything I could remember about the inside of the unit, and Burl said he'd get with the firemen tomorrow about examining whatever could be salvaged from the fire. As expected, Burl had a warrant to search the contents, and I guess that still counted even if there was nothing but ashes left. I called Jeff, but got his voice mail, so I didn't leave any message aside from asking him to call. Some things you do not leave as a recording.

I rapped on Kate's back door. She must have been in the kitchen, because she answered right away.

"What happened to you?" she said, focusing on my fat lip. She pulled me inside by the wrist, and I winced. Plastic cuffs are brutal, I'd learned.

She looked down and saw the red abrasions. "Oh, my God. Where have you been? Who hurt you?"

"I'll explain everything, but I will need my house key before I leave. Lost my car keys, too, but I have a spare at home."

She put an arm around me and gently led me to the kitchen barstool. "You need help getting up?"

"I'm fine, Kate."

"I have something to help heal your lip, so—"

"Do I have to drink it? Because I'd rather have coffee than drink any of your—coffee! Yes. I want a huge mug of dark, strong coffee."

"You're not making sense. You've been saying for the last week that you might never drink another cup of coffee in your life. Were you hit on the head or—"

"Go get your magic potions and fix me up, doc. Then I'll explain."

After my lip had been slathered with goo and some different homeopathic ointment had been applied to my wrists and ankles, I told her everything over freshly brewed Starbucks Kenyan. It tasted *so* good, and I was thankful my coffee aversion had ended.

Near-death experiences tend to make you appreciate what's important in life, I guess.

"Verna Mae had created a shrine to Will?" Kate asked after I told her what I'd seen tonight.

"I can't think of a better word. She must have gone there and prayed for him, what with the kneeling rail and candles. But with the picture of Sara Rankin there, too, she obviously knew way more than she let on when Will and I visited her—the visit right before she was found beaten and shot. I'm wondering now if that's why she called to meet with me that Friday— to tell me about Sara."

"How did Verna Mae learn what's been so hard for you to discover?" Kate asked.

"She knew from the beginning, is my guess. Knew exactly whose baby had been left in her care."

"Left by Sara? I'm confused. I thought she died in May and Will was born in the fall."

"I'm guessing Sara died during childbirth or right after, not in a fall. The Rankins had that service in December because they knew she was dead."

"And they gave the baby to Verna Mae?" she asked.

"I don't know."

Kate said, "Maybe Sara did fall. She could have been in a coma from a head injury. I've heard of co-matose women being kept alive so they can deliver at term. What if her parents pulled the plug on life support after Will was born? Are they the type who would do that?"

"I can't answer that. I only know that something, maybe something more than grief, drove the pastor to the edge. Could his grief be mixed with guilt for pull-ing that plug?"

"Certainly. Especially if his religious teachings told him to keep her on a machine and he didn't," Kate said.

"Okay. That makes sense. Now, is there a connec-tion between the Rankins and Verna Mae?"

"Maybe she attended their church," Kate said.

"I never explored that possibility," I said. "It's on my to-do list now, though."

Kate stared at me, her coffee cup held between her hands. "I'm still confused. Why would the Rankins manufacture such an elaborate cover-up before Will was born?"

I explained my theory about their daughter being a sinner. "I think they would have been humiliated and embarrassed by Sara's behavior, don't you?"

"From all you've told me about them, yes."

"There's more, Kate. Verna Mae is dead because she knew something I don't. At least something I don't know *yet*.

"I'm worried, Abby. Please turn this over to Jeff? You got lucky tonight, but—"

"This is my life, now. This is what I do. A woman died an awful death. Lawrence Washington has been sitting in prison for a crime he didn't commit. Someone set him up, and that has to be made right. For Will, for Thaddeus and for Joelle Simpson."

Kate leaned over and took my face in her warm hands. "Okay. I understand. . . . But please be careful, Abby."

The call from Jeff woke me at three a.m, so I knew he'd heard about the fire or he would have waited until morning.

"Still have your eyelashes?" he asked. He was joking, but I could hear concern beneath the humor.

"I'm fine. Are you working twenty-four shifts now?"

"I crashed here at the precinct. Then I get a wake-up call from someone saying Burl Rollins wanted to talk to me. I think you know the rest."

"Too well. More excitement than I planned on."

"You get a read on the bad guy?"

"Not really. He was all in black and a man of few words."

"Could he have been someone you've interviewed along the way?"

"The only thing I can say with certainty is that he was male. Probably the same person who's been following me like a coyote after a lost calf since day one."

"I need to teach you a few things about busting a tail."

"Not tonight, please. But if the offer is still good to get back into the prison, I want to talk to Lawrence Washington, find out why he kept quiet about Sara all these years, figure out why he won't help himself if he's innocent."

"I'd like to hear those answers myself. We'll go tomorrow. Bring the father, if possible."

"You want that leverage, huh?"

"Yup. We might even have Thaddeus's DNA results by the time we get to Huntsville," Jeff said.

"I know what the test will show, but if we can convince Lawrence he has a son—"

"He'll talk about his relationship with Sara," Jeff finished. "Her story, what happened to her, is key."

"Right. I'll arrange for the handicapped van. See you tomorrow, then?"

"Absolutely. I'm very glad I *will* be seeing you tomorrow," he said quietly.

"Are you upset with me for going into that storage unit without Burl?"

"Not as much as when I first heard what you did. I should have known you'd keep a set of those keys, and don't repeat this to anyone with a badge, but I admire you for working this case every which way you could, even if you've made a few dumb moves."

"Dumb moves? I'm allowed to label them dumb, not you," I said with mock anger.

"Remember that the next time I do something stupid," he said. "I love you, Abby. See you tomorrow."

The arrangements for the van and Jeff's need for a few hours of sleep came in quite handy. I also had a chance to retrieve my car from the storage facility. We didn't pick up Thaddeus until around three p.m.

Monday. The driver took care of getting Thaddeus and his chair into the back passenger area, then designated me to carry the insulated medical bag containing Thaddeus's glucose monitor, snacks and insulin.

The call from the lab came right after we merged onto the freeway heading toward Huntsville. Jeff put the call on speakerphone so Thaddeus could hear.

"Paternal grandparent isn't always the best—we like maternal connections when you skip generations," said the woman on the phone.

"Bottom line?" Jeff asked.

"Seventy percent probability older donor is closely related to young male donor."

"Yes!" I did a Tiger Woods fist pump.

"Thanks, Bev. I owe you," Jeff said.

"You never owe me," she answered, before disconnecting.

My excitement at having this confirmation was overshadowed by a tinge of jealousy. But I kept my lip zipped about it and said, "I knew it, Thaddeus. You have a grandson."

I was sitting next to him, and he reached over and took my hand. His was cold when he squeezed mine. "Something good for once. Praise God, something good."

"Maybe this will help us convince Lawrence to tell us what he knows," I said. "The bullet found inside Verna Mae came from the same gun that put a round in your wall, Thaddeus."

"How's that help my son?"

"That same gun killed Amanda Mason," I said.

Thaddeus took this in, not speaking for several seconds. "That's hard evidence," he finally said. "Think he could get a new trial out of this?"

"I don't know," Jeff said quickly. "But if you can convince him to talk, tell us if he knew who owned that gun, it would sure help."

"That's why we're a traveling road show today, right?" said Thaddeus. He looked at me. "Tell me again, how old is Lawrence's boy?"

"Nineteen."

"I've missed nineteen years. Got plenty to make up for."

"You ever watch college basketball?" I asked.

"Nope. After Lawrence was taken from us, it hurt to watch kids doing what he should have been doing—using his talent. We'd gone to every one of his high school baseball games, stood behind him when he signed his letter of intent. Nope. I got to hate sports, all of them."

"You'll have to learn to at least like basketball again. Your grandson is a star athlete," I said.

Thaddeus smiled. "Won't be hard to like it. Won't be hard at all."

We talked about Will all the way to Huntsville, and I told him all I knew about his newfound grandson. When we arrived at the prison barricade, however, Thaddeus's good spirits faded quickly.

"He'll be upset at me coming," he said as the driver lowered the automatic ramp and then maneuvered Thaddeus and his chair onto the parking lot asphalt.

"He loves you. He'll get over it," I answered.

Jeff said, "We'll take it from here" to the driver.

After we went through the security checks, Jeff arranged for us to meet with Lawrence in an interview room rather than the visitors' area. Guess he has more pull than DeShay.

"I get a bad feeling every time I come here," Thaddeus said as Jeff wheeled him down a corridor, one of Goree's gray shadow guards leading the way. "But it's worse today. They say hell is hot, but I think it's as cold as this place."

"You need my jacket?" Jeff asked.

"Nah. This kind of cold comes from inside. No jacket gonna help that."

We were taken to a small room, bigger than the chaplain's closet, but still a tight squeeze for a wheelchair. This place had been built long before wheelchairs were common.

We waited in tense silence as the guard left to get

Lawrence. When they finally brought him in, the tension grew a thousandfold.

Lawrence looked at his father for a brief second then turned angry eyes on me. "What the hell do you think you're doing?"

"Sit," Jeff said, his voice hard as granite.

"I wanted to come," said Thaddeus. "I got something big to tell you, son."

Lawrence looked down, rubbing his white-clad thighs up and down. "You don't need to see me like this. It's not good for you, Pops."

"Don't you want to know why they brought me?" Thaddeus's voice was soft, and when I looked his way, I saw his eyes were brimming with tears.

Lawrence had noticed this, too. "See what you all have done? He doesn't need this kind of stress."

"He needs his family," I said. "And that's you."

"What do you know about it?" Lawrence raised his chin defiantly.

"She knows more than I did a few hours ago," Thaddeus said. "You have a son, Lawrence. I have a grandson."

"What the hell are you talking about?" Even though his father had spoken, Lawrence directed the question at me.

"Time to tell us about Sara Rankin," I said.

Lawrence shook his head, looked down again. "I don't know what you're talking about. You've been filling my father's head." He glared at me. "What are you, some kind of sadist?"

Jeff said, "We have DNA proving that your father and Will Knight are related. If we could get your DNA, the picture would be complete."

Lawrence suddenly rose, still shaking his head. "You're lying. All of you. Why, Pops? Why do this to me?"

"Son, have I ever lied to you?"

Lawrence had gone white around the lips, and I could see he was trembling. He turned to the guard. "I want to go back to the cellblock. I'm done here."

He looked confused and lost, and at that moment I was certain Lawrence did not know or yet believe his baby, the child he conceived with Sara Rankin, was alive.

Suddenly, Lawrence bolted, the guard hot on his tail.

Jeff was already on his feet, headed for the door. "I want him back here."

"Maybe we should leave him be?" Thaddeus said. "It hasn't sunk in."

"Wait, Jeff," I said. "I've got an idea. Before we drag him back unwillingly, I know someone who might make this easier."

Ten minutes later, after Chaplain Jim Kelly had arrived and we filled him in, he said, "Do you think that what you're on to will free Lawrence?"

"I can't promise anything," Jeff said.

Thaddeus's shoulders slumped, and I rested a hand over his. "But if you can help get Lawrence to tell us about his relationship with Sara Rankin, we'd be a lot closer to the truth about Verna Mae Olsen's murder."

"In good conscience, I must have Lawrence's permission to speak about what I know," Kelly said quietly.

"Will he come back here with you?" I asked.

"He might. I'll try," the chaplain said.

Once Kelly was gone, I noticed dabs of sweat bordered Thaddeus's hairline, and he, too, looked pale around the mouth.

"Could you get me my bag, Abby?" he asked.

I handed it to him, but he was shaking too badly to unzip it. He asked for the glucose monitor, and Jeff was the one who ended up pricking Thaddeus's finger. After the blood was applied to the little strip, the number that appeared seconds later was 530.

"That's bad, right?" I said.

"I've seen better," Thaddeus replied, his voice weak.

"I'm taking him to the clinic," Jeff said. "You handle this, Abby. You've talked to Lawrence before and the less people staring at him, demanding answers, the better. Learn what you can."

As Jeff wheeled him out, Thaddeus raised a hand and brushed my arm. "Make my boy help himself. Please."

I was concerned about Thaddeus, and when Kelly arrived with a now handcuffed prisoner, Lawrence must have read my anxiety.

"Where's Pops? Is something wrong with him?" he asked.

"He wasn't feeling well. Sergeant Kline took him out for some air," I answered. Sometimes the whole truth is not beneficial.

"You made an old man sicker than he already was. You happy now?" Lawrence said.

Kelly put a hand on Lawrence's shoulder. "I believe this woman wants to help you and your father. You need to tell her the truth. Tell her what you told me."

Lawrence looked sideways at Kelly. "I don't know. She comes here with her stories, brings my father out of a sickbed and—"

"Sit down and start talking," Kelly said. "That's what you do with me."

Lawrence closed his eyes, let out a heavy sigh. And then he sat.

Kelly took Jeff's abandoned chair.

"You haven't tricked my father into thinking I have a son, right?" asked Lawrence.

"No, I haven't. You do have a son, and though I've known it since I first saw Will Knight's resemblance to you, we now have scientific proof."

"I don't get it," Lawrence said, shaking his head. "How could this be true? And how did you find out about Sara?"

"That's a very long story. Jessica Roman convinced me that that you and Sara were lovers. You conceived a child."

"Yes," Lawrence said, his gaze beyond my shoulder, as if he were looking back in time. "God, we were happy."

"I'm here to help you." I leaned forward, hands between my knees.

"But Sara fell. She died. I thought our baby died with her. Died because of me." Lawrence's voice was strained, his expression again confused.

Kelly said, "We've worked on this, Lawrence. It wasn't your fault. You were in the Harris County jail when the accident happened."

"But she ran away because she was pregnant," Lawrence said. "Ran from her parents. If she hadn't, then she'd be alive."

"There was no mission trip?" I asked.

"That's what the pastor and his wife told everyone when she disappeared. She'd left them a note—we wrote it together—saying she had to leave home to take care of someone in need. It was the truth, in a way."

"That's how it became a *mission trip* to them, I guess. Did she even plan on telling them about the baby?" My guess was no.

"We talked about what to do, who to tell. Sara was underage and we were sure her parents would make us give the baby away, so we couldn't go to them. And if you knew Sara—" He stopped, closed his eyes.

"Sara knew what she wanted, right? She wanted you and the baby?"

"Yes. And I wanted what she did."

"You did some shopping before she left town, though. Bought some baby things?" I asked.

Lawrence looked at me. "How *did* you find out about the blanket?"

"Not important. She ordered it, you picked it up, right?"

He nodded. "She'd seen that blanket when she was shopping with her mother in this British store. She said she had to have one nice thing for our kid."

"She was already gone on the so-called mission trip by the time you picked up the blanket, though. You two must have been in touch, right?" I asked.

"We were afraid to. Thought someone might find

out, give us up to her parents. We'd planned ahead for Sara to sneak back to Houston after I'd had time to pull together some money."

"She left town, then came back?"

He nodded. "She'd taken a bus to Dallas, stayed in some shelter. It seemed like a good thing—they don't tell the cops anything about runaways—so she stayed in one when she came back to Houston, too. I'd asked a few uncles for some cash, worked extra shifts sacking groceries. I had a couple hundred bucks to give her."

"Plus, you needed to see each other, right?" I said, thinking how even two days away from Jeff made me crazy.

He sighed. "It was hard being apart. Keeping secrets from everyone."

"These people you asked for money assumed you needed it for your family's medical expenses? Your mother's cancer treatment?"

Lawrence cocked his head. "You've been doing a lot of reading about me."

"You better believe it. Go on and answer the question," I said.

"The cop who arrested me? Dugan? That was *his* theory—that I was trying to get money for Mom. I *never* said that. Anyway, the night they arrested me was the night Sara and I met." He paused, took a deep breath. "I gave her the money and the keys to my car. I kissed her good-bye and never saw her again."

I smiled inwardly, one tiny puzzle piece falling into place. "The police didn't find your car, but not because you dumped it to hide evidence or sold it for cash. Sara drove it away."

He nodded.

"Okay. I have to ask this next question, mostly so I can tell Sergeant Kline I left no stone unturned. Some of that money you pulled together? Did it come from Amanda Mason?"

Lawrence hung his head, his fists clenched in his

lap. It seemed forever before he looked up and said, "I never killed anyone."

"And those unaccounted-for ninety minutes? You kept quiet because you were with Sara and wanted to protect her?"

He nodded, and I noticed Kelly was nodding right along with him.

"You're sure Sara never contacted her parents, told them about the pregnancy?"

"I don't think so. I mean, she knew they'd never accept our child. I'm *black*, if you haven't noticed."

I felt embarrassed then, embarrassed for my own race. "I know this is hard, but let's keep it flowing, okay? The pastor came to visit you when you went to jail. What did he say?"

"First time, he said what they'd been saying since Sara ran off, that she was on a mission trip. Then the last visit was to tell me she'd died. I remember him saying that since she and I had been friends in the youth group, he wanted me to hear the news from him. He was so torn up, and meanwhile I had to hide everything . . . keep it all stuffed down while he sat there across the glass crying for her." Lawrence's lips tightened and he slowly shook his head from side to side.

Kelly gripped Lawrence's shoulder. "Hey. You've worked hard on accepting she's gone, on living here where you don't belong."

I was fighting my own emotions, knowing that my anger might eradicate logic. The pastor said he came to visit Lawrence to offer solace to a prisoner. Instead, he'd brought Lawrence unbelievable pain.

"Once you learned Sara was dead, did you ever consider telling people about your relationship? Tell them you were with her the night Amanda Mason was murdered?" I said.

"What good would that have done?" he asked. "I'd already been tried and convicted when her father came and told me she was dead. She was my alibi and she was gone. Who would believe me if all of a sudden I said I was with Sara when Amanda Mason was being murdered? Besides, no one needed to know about us—especially not her parents. I'd lost Sara, my mother was dying and I didn't care about anything. I—"

The chaplain broke in. "Lawrence went from being a happy, successful young man who'd found the love of his life to a convicted felon, all in less than a year's time. He wasn't thinking clearly, and to be honest, I'm not sure he got the best legal help, either. When Lawrence refused a plea bargain—"

"You see what I'm talking about? Even my lawyer thought I was guilty." Lawrence's eyes flashed with anger.

"Okay, so who set you up? Because I think someone made sure you got arrested that night. Maybe someone who knew you were with Sara."

Lawrence looked at me. "I have no idea. It doesn't matter anyway. No one believed me then and they won't believe me now."

"I believe you," I said.

Kelly cleared his throat. "Lawrence and I have discussed this more than once. It had to have been a friend, an acquaintance, someone who knew where he lived and could plant the evidence. Since he was pretty well-known for his athletic skills, it might have been a jealous kid on his ball team who thought *he* should have had that letter of intent to A&M. Or maybe someone who held a grudge Lawrence knew nothing about. He could have just been someone's scapegoat."

I remembered Frank Simpson's notes. That's what he thought, too. "You're saying you never told your lawyers about meeting with Sara that night?" I asked.

"No," Lawrence said. "Just the chaplain. And now you."

"Were you punishing yourself? Or did you just not care about your own freedom after Sara was gone?"

"I promised her I wouldn't tell her parents about

the baby," said Lawrence quietly. "If I gave her up to save myself—well, I couldn't do that to her."

"But you were arrested in April, put in jail and stayed there until trial. She never came forward, Lawrence," I said.

"That's because she was dead," he said through tight lips. "That's the only reason she wouldn't come back to help me. Besides, nothing mattered with her gone."

"You *assumed* she was dead," I said. "But don't you understand? She lived long enough to give birth. She could have come forward and—"

Lawrence lifted his cuffed hands and pointed intertwined fingers at me. His voice had gone hard again when he said, "If she was out there, she would have come back, she would have told the cops we were together when Amanda Mason was murdered."

"That's why you needed to believe there was no baby, right? But there may be another explanation, Lawrence. There may—"

"I'm done here," he said, his face and voice devoid of emotion. "Take my father home. He doesn't belong here."

23

I would have liked to take Thaddeus home, but the nurse in the prison clinic said he should go straight to a hospital because of his soaring blood sugar. Jeff and I tried to convince him the hospital in Huntsville would be best—it was close—but he insisted he wanted to see his own doctor at the Medical Center in Houston.

By the time we reached downtown, I could tell the insulin shots I'd helped Thaddeus give himself weren't doing much good. He was sleepy, thirsty and a little confused when I wheeled him into the emergency room.

Meanwhile, DeShay had called Jeff to tell him they'd drawn a case and he was waiting in their unmarked car at the hospital. At least I'd had time to tell Jeff what I'd learned from Lawrence before he left with his partner.

When I was allowed into the emergency room cubicle to see Thaddeus, he had an oxygen mask over his nose and mouth. Scary to watch. And did I feel guilty. The stress must have been too much. I asked him if I could call Joelle to help him out, and he said that would be good. Thaddeus wanted her to check on his house while he was hospitalized. During my cab ride home, I ordered the biggest bunch of yellow roses my florist could pull together and had them delivered to the room I'd been told he would be admitted to.

It was nearly eight p.m. when I arrived at my house,

and Diva played pitiful this time, rubbing around my still sore ankles seeking attention. Bet she knew it hurt.

After stuffing down a cheese sandwich, I took a glass of wine into my office and sat behind my computer. Diva tried the keyboard trick—her *I sit on this thing, you'll give me all your love* approach. I lifted her off and onto my lap, then booted up.

After typing up notes of my interview with Lawrence, I sat back in my chair thinking about Sara Rankin's disappearance. Would she have come back to save Lawrence with an alibi if she could have? My gut said yes. She'd already committed to abandoning her life as a preacher's daughter, and that made me think she wanted to be with Lawrence more than anything.

What would make her *not* come back to save him, then? She had to have been hurt or sick.

If I put the events in chronological order, Sara first ran off in March, not long after finding out she was pregnant. But Lawrence and Sara didn't make up the mission trip story to explain her disappearance—the Rankins did. Then, come May, they spread the word she'd fallen from a cliff and her body wasn't found. They told one lie to begin with. Did they change to another in May? Or were they telling the truth after finding the daughter who'd been missing for several months, maybe found her suffering from a head injury and on life support?

Important questions. It all came back to the Rankins. What did they know that they weren't telling me? And who was following my every move, destroying any link that might exist between Verna Mae and the person who placed that baby in her care so many years ago?

Jeff always says the higher the stakes, the bigger the crime, and in this case the biggest crime had not been an abandoned child. It had been Verna Mae's death. What happened after Will and I left her the day we visited her home? What went through her mind? What tipped her world so much that she fell off? She knew about Sara. I'd learned that much before the storage unit went up in flames.

Yes. She knew Sara, so why not her parents? Parents with money who could have been paying Verna Mae's bills all these years. What if she went to see the Rankins the day she was killed? What if for some reason she'd decided to tell everyone she knew about a dead girl and an abandoned baby? Clear her conscience after years of stalking and obsession? Seeing Will in the flesh, talking to him, touching him—were those the things that tipped her world? Could be. Her wishing was over. He'd come home.

I could picture Andrew Rankin's emotional face and his wife's smile. Saw them as wearing masks. If I stripped the masks off, what would I find beneath? Grieving parents who took their grandson and gave him away—and in doing so broke the law? Maybe. I didn't know. I wasn't sure they even *knew* about a grandchild. Mrs. Rankin was too slick to give me much of anything, and the pastor was too close to insanity. And I'd been a little slow on the draw about asking the right questions.

I sipped on my wine, stroked my purring Diva. She was content, but I sure wasn't. Could the Rankins have found their daughter? Tracked her by guessing she had Lawrence's car? Learned she was pregnant? She could have even been in Mexico, exactly where they claimed she'd gone. It's a great place to hide and was an even easier escape destination back then. The story about her fall from the mountain could be true, she was injured and, yes, add half-truths to lies by omission and some of this scenario made sense.

But why the huge cover-up? Why were the stakes so high for these people? These were the questions that reminded me Verna Mae hadn't been the only one murdered. This had to do with Amanda Mason, too. Was that why Simpson's notes were stolen? Why I'd been followed and nearly killed. Yes. This had to do with *her*.

I picked up the phone and called Jeff, grateful to hear his voice and not a machine. "This is about Amanda Mason as much as it is about Verna Mae's murder," I said, so eager to get this out, my words ran together.

"Slow down. Have you learned anything new?"

"No, I'm just certain Lawrence was set up. It's the only thing that makes sense."

"Talking to him today convinced you he's truly innocent, huh?"

"You don't think so?"

"I have a little different take on this. From what you told me, Washington had even more reason to be looking for money than a sick mother," Jeff said. "He had a kid on the way. He saw Amanda Mason with cash in her hands and he wanted it."

"Could you trust me on this? He didn't do it, Jeff."

"I take it there's more you want to tell me?"

"I think the Rankins are the money machine, the ones who paid off Verna Mae. But I haven't quite figured all that out yet."

"That's the problem. Before we go into that church with badges blazing, we *have* to figure it out. We need evidence. You understand that?"

"Oh, I get it. I just want you to believe me about Lawrence, okay?"

"With the gun still out there, I do tend to believe you. It's time for me to step in tomorrow, interview the pastor and his wife, especially if Rankin's the man who left you to fry in that storage unit."

"He's too puny, but he has this man working for him. I only know him by B.J. He could have been the one."

"You have more than initials?"

"He's the pastor's assistant or something."

"Can you do some computer magic, find out his name? Then I can check him out, see if he has a rap sheet. I'd do it myself, but I'm kind of tied up here with a DB."

"You take care of your dead body. I'm on B.J. like a bird dog on a duck." We said good-bye and I disconnected.

I got busy on the B.J. task and found the church website easily—reverentlife.org. I was at first struck by the glitzy presentation—Flash media, color photos of all the pastors and assistant pastors, not to mention scrolling Bible verses. But I felt the hairs raise on the nape of my neck when I read the words above the picture of "Pastor-Teacher Andrew Rankin." It said, "Our church is a safe harbor for those in chaos, a place of forgiveness for the guilty, and a haven of hope for the hopeless."

A place of forgiveness for the guilty, huh? From the way he acted both times we met, I was beginning to think he might be more guilty than grieving.

I searched every inch of that website looking for B.J.'s picture or even a name that began with B. No one but the pastors rated names and pictures on the site, and the "contact us" e-mail box offered only a generic address to their church mail.

I checked my watch then refocused on the monitor. The site calendar said the church library was open until eleven p.m., and I saw that the choir was meeting from eight to ten as well. There'd be plenty of people leaving about the time I got there if I left right now. I could ask around, see if I could get B.J.'s name or maybe find it in the library. Those bound leather volumes had helped me once already.

This was simple. Just a few little questions. No badges blazing, I told myself, as I stood and placed Diva in the warm chair I was abandoning.

Late evening traffic was light on the freeways and I reached the church in less than thirty minutes. Sure enough, streams of cars were pouring from the lot. *Some colossal choir*, I thought, searching for a parking spot close to the sanctuary. I was reviewing my opening line, considering something like, "Have you seen B.J.? And by the way, does the guy have an entire name?" when that handicapped-equipped van once again nearly took me out. Olive, the nurse's aide, was at the wheel.

That woman's dangerous, I thought, not smiling as I stared her in the eye. She maneuvered around my stopped car with another apologetic wave.

That's when it hit me like a plank to the skull.

She's the one in the picture at the storage unit. The person I thought might be Verna Mae's friend or sister. The one I'd seen before someone burned the place to the ground.

Okay. I could go find out about B.J. or I could talk to her. I liked the idea of talking to her a whole lot better, considering B.J. had muscles and maybe owned a gun that killed a few people.

My turn to play follow the leader, and she was easy to follow—seemingly as clueless to my pursuit of her as she was to minor details like double yellow lines.

We were heading toward the NASA area, but turned off at Pearwood, a small town with acreage lots where home owners could walk out the front door and feed their horses. A woman had been abducted and murdered in these parts about five years ago. I shivered a little, remembering all the publicity, the face of her devastated husband, who, in the end, turned out to be the one who killed her.

This was ranchland with dirt roads, plenty of fields and lots of trees. An easy place to hide a body. Better check in with Jeff, I decided, keeping a reasonable distance from the van on the narrow two-lane road.

But it was DeShay who took my call. "Jeff's got his hands dirty right now. You don't want the details. Can I give him a message?"

"Tell him I'm in Pearwood. I'm following a woman who works for the church. I plan to ask her a few questions when she stops, presumably at her home."

I heard DeShay relay this information and then I heard Jeff in the background say, "Shit."

"Does that response adequately convey his feelings?" DeShay said.

"Tell him it's just some ditsy lady," I said. "I want

to ask her about—wait. She's pulling into a driveway. We turned off FM 2005 onto Bluebonnet Road. The house is about a half mile on the right. Tell him I have now checked in with the courtesy call he always seems to want when I'm out late on a case."

"I'll relay the first part, but not the last. He's holding one big-ass bloody knife right now. You take care out there, Abby." DeShay disconnected.

I folded my phone shut, slowed to a near crawl and waited for the van lights in the driveway up ahead to go out. I then sped up and a few seconds later pulled into the driveway. I started to get out, but another car came barreling down the road toward the house. I got back into the Camry and locked my doors, realizing I'd been concentrating so hard on tailing the van, I again hadn't paid much attention to anyone following *me*. Stupid idiot. When the car sped on down the road into the blackness beyond without even slowing down, I breathed a sigh of relief.

This little scare, however, reminded me to take my .38 from the glove compartment. I was in a strange place about to meet with someone who probably wouldn't be too happy to know I'd followed her home.

The house was a one-story log cabin—though not really a cabin. It was big, at least a couple thousand square feet. Could a nurse's aide afford a place like this? Then it dawned on me that this might be a shut-in parishioner's home. Awkward to knock on the door and say, "Hi. I'm a PI who's been hanging around the church asking annoying questions. You want to talk to me?"

The house had a porch along the front with a wheelchair ramp, so I figured I was right, this wasn't Olive's house. Now what?

Light flowed from a side window, illuminating a small garden. No drapes pulled yet. Maybe I could take a peek inside before I knocked on the door.

I slipped from behind the wheel and eased my door shut so as not to alert anyone in the house. Gun at my side, I quietly made my way toward the garden.

The little plot was bordered by stones and I had to step over them. My feet sank into newly laid pine-bark mulch and the smell wafted up around me. I nearly sneezed but held it in. Flattening against the logs, I looked in the window.

It was a living room, but very open, sparsely furnished, with wood floors. I moved closer to get a better look after I spotted Olive talking to a woman standing with the aid of a walker—one of those kind with a basket and wheels. The woman was tall and thin, with dishwater blond hair drawn back in a ponytail. She was looking down. I spied a wheelchair in a corner.

Olive *was* visiting a handicapped parishioner after all. Maybe I should wait until—

But then Olive walked away, out of my sight, and that's when the woman with the walker looked straight at the window.

I gasped. Not a quiet gasp, either.

24

Still blinking in disbelief, I heard a sound behind me—heard too late. Someone grabbed my wrist and twisted the gun from my hand. It fell with a thud near my right foot.

I felt steel against my temple.

"Very bad move coming here," the man whispered. I recognized the voice from the storage unit. "You say one word and you're dead."

I nodded my agreement, my thoughts leaving the woman I'd just recognized as I shifted into survival mode. I wasn't sure I'd be spared again, but this guy didn't want the women in the house to hear, so I at least had a few minutes left. If he was going to kill me, it wouldn't happen near the house.

This time he snapped regular cuffs on my wrists and said, "Where are your car keys?"

"In the ignition," I said.

"Perfect. Now move."

But he didn't shove or push, just laid a hand on my shoulder to steer me around the garden. When I stumbled once on the stones, he caught me before I fell. I looked at the man.

B.J.

He said, "Keep going," his hand resting on my back as we moved forward into the woods. We weren't going to my car as I expected.

His touch on my back reminded me of the caress when he'd left me in that storage unit, the way he stared at me in the church. His obvious attraction made me sick right now, but it had served me well to this point and I'd use it if I had to.

I thought about running—for about a tenth of a second. Unfortunately for me, he obviously knew this place. I didn't. Added to that, my heart was thumping and I was wearing bracelets. Escape would be about as easy as digging a ditch in the ocean.

I risked a glance back at the house after intentionally tripping to get that look.

B.J. said, "You're a klutz, just like her."

Her? Sara Rankin? The woman with the walker? The woman I'd recognized?

"Yeah, that's me. Klutzy kidnap victim," I said as he helped me up.

"Real funny," he mumbled.

Would Sara help me? *Could* she help me? Not a promising prospect.

Turned out, the road leading to the cabin looped around after it passed the house. A short trek through the woods on a well-worn path and we reached B.J.'s car parked on a curve. This was the car that had sped by after I came along behind the van. Oh, yeah. I'd been followed again. Jeez. I could probably screw up a two-car funeral.

Funeral. Don't think about that, Abby.

He'd chosen black for his newest Lexus—and it *was* brand-new, paper still on the floorboards and thin plastic covering the leather seats. After he'd cuffed me to the seat belt and activated the child safety locks, he took out his cell phone.

After a few seconds he said, "Olive? There's a car in your driveway. The keys are in the ignition. You need to put that car in the garage. Now."

A short pause, then he said, "Because Pastor Rankin would—"

Olive interrupted, speaking loudly—though I couldn't catch the words, just her frantic tone.

"Olive, shut up. Give her some pills or one of those shots. Anything. Then hide that car."

He didn't wait for a reply, just snapped the phone shut and started the engine.

B.J.'s gun was in his shoulder holster now, far from my very encumbered hands. He pressed his foot on the accelerator and we took off.

This had all happened so fast and I was still stunned to have seen Sara Rankin in that log cabin. I kept silent for a minute or two, thinking things through. I felt calmer then, as calm as a girl could get, handcuffed next to a murderer. Still, B.J. could have gotten rid of me and he hadn't. He needed me alive for some reason.

He made his next phone call when we reached the church parking lot. He'd pulled behind the main buildings near a row of garages. Not well lit. And deserted. He speed-dialed a number and said, "She went to the cabin. I nabbed her before she got inside. Get everyone out, janitors included, and call me back. Then I'll bring her in."

I heard another agitated voice. Female, too.

B.J. said, "If you don't do this, I'll splatter her blood all over your church. See how well you fix *that* problem, Noreen."

My gut tightened. So much for my belief he had some odd attraction to me and would spare my life again. I was no more than a tool. And if Noreen didn't cooperate . . .

But when I heard B.J. say, "Good thinking," I knew I was safe for a few more precious minutes.

I quietly released my breath.

He took the gun out, held it across his lap, but said nothing. Just stared straight ahead.

I had a little time, and knowing words were my only weapon, I said, "What's wrong with Sara?"

He didn't respond, just kept looking straight ahead.

"Her face, her mouth, the way they sag on one side. Did she have a stroke?" I asked.

Again nothing.

"Has she been in that house all these years? With no one but Olive?"

The rise and fall of his chest picked up speed, his lips tightened. He wanted me to be quiet. But he still needed me, so I could keep hammering at him. Keep picking away. He might make a mistake.

"This Olive, she was Verna Mae's friend, right? Did the Rankins use Olive to sign Verna Mae up for motherhood?"

"Shut up," he snapped. This time he looked at me, but then quickly turned away.

"What I don't understand is why the Rankins have been keeping their daughter a prisoner. She can hardly walk, but she's still young, she's—"

He pressed the gun barrel against my forehead. "Amanda, shut your trap!"

I swallowed hard. *Amanda?* And then I flashed back to my conversation with Kate, when we examined that grainy ATM photo. *"You look just like her,"* Kate had said.

I closed my eyes, tried to remember all the names from Frank Simpson's notes—Amanda's ex-boyfriends who'd been supposedly cleared of her murder. Anyone whose name began with a B? Barry? No. Bob? No. An odd name. An old name. And then I just blurted it out. "Byron."

B.J. turned sharply, glared for a long, cold second.

"Amanda dump you, Byron? Is that why you killed her?"

"She got religion, thought she was better than me. You look like her, you know. Even act like her. Wonder how she'd feel today if she knew I worked for the pastor."

"Did she really deserve a bullet in the head?" I wanted to add. "Or do I?"

B.J.'s strange smile nearly made my fingernails sweat. "She wanted to be with God more than with me. So I helped her out."

The cell phone chirped, and we both flinched. A sound you hear every day and everywhere now made me want to throw up.

B.J., eyes on me, answered, saying, "You ready?"

A short pause followed, then he said, "We're coming in."

If I didn't do something, I might be going *out* feet first. He came around to the passenger side, opened the door, and when he bent to free my hands, I head-butted him in the jaw.

He staggered, wiped at the blood dripping from his mouth.

Not knocked out. Not what I'd hoped for. *Shit.*

"Yeah. You're just like her." He finished uncuffing me, being far more careful, and pulled me out of the car.

Before I could blink, his gun grip came crashing down on my skull.

I must have been unconscious for only a minute, because the next thing I knew, I was being carried over B.J.'s shoulder like a sack of flour. We were walking through the church kitchen, and I smelled buttermilk biscuits. Would I ever eat another one? God, I hoped so. He took me into Pastor Rankin's office and tossed me into one of the chairs surrounding the glass coffee table. By then, my senses had cleared—and I was mad as hell.

"Thanks, *Byron*," I said, the throbbing in my head just background noise compared to my rage. These people were going down tonight. I didn't know how, but I'd make it happen.

"Did she say 'Byron'?" Mrs. Rankin asked as she came into the room.

"She knows. You see the problem?" B.J. answered.

Both she and her weirdo husband had arrived right behind us.

Noreen Rankin, her makeup as perfect as ever and her expensive coral suit fitting every curve, began to pace, acting like I wasn't even in the room. "You had no problem with the Olsen woman, no issue plugging that hole, B.J. I don't understand what you want from us? You could have taken care of this without bringing her here."

"I'm not killing anyone else to protect your secrets," he said. "Not without a better deal. If you won't fix me up, then I kill her in the sanctuary. That ought to bring a few unwelcome questions your way."

Rankin had sat at his desk and was giving me that stare I was beginning to know well and dislike intensely. I glared at him, and he covered his face with his hands and began mumbling. I heard "Jesus" and "Lord" a few times. Must be praying.

Noreen walked over and rested a hand on her husband's shoulder. "That seems reasonable, doesn't it, Andrew? We have the money."

Rankin didn't look up.

These people were plotting my murder right in front of me and I couldn't do anything. Hell, maybe I couldn't even walk right now. Still, the only imminent threat was B.J. and his gun, which now hung down at his side.

Noreen said, "How much?"

"A hundred grand right away and a steady income in my new home somewhere in the Caribbean. You don't have to pay the Olsen woman anymore, so it won't hurt your budget."

"That's acceptable. What will you do with her?" she said, glancing my way for the first time.

"Good question. She has friends in HPD. Close friends. I'll have to take her out of town. Tonight."

Pastor Rankin was rocking back and forth, his hands clasped together, head still bent. But when he started this little high-pitched moan, both Noreen and B.J. turned his way.

That was my opening. The only chance I might get.

I dove over that coffee table and rammed into B.J., hitting him low, on the side of his leg at the knee— the closest weak point.

The gun went flying.

Noreen screamed.

B.J. and I crashed into the heavy oak lectern holding the Bible. When we fell, a corner caught him in the temple. Blood poured from the wound as he thudded to the floor, out cold.

I fell on my butt next to him and looked around. *The gun. Where was the gun?*

I saw it on the floor by the pastor's feet. He was staring at it, smiling, then slowly bent and picked it up.

He took the weapon in both hands, held it out in front of him, his hands shaking.

Noreen smiled, cocked her head. "Andrew? Give me the gun, sweetheart."

He shook his head. "God has spoken. I have received His word. This ends now."

She stepped toward him.

Their eyes locked.

While they were occupied with their trust issues, I did what I'd been wanting to do for the last hour. I slipped my hands into B.J.'s shirt pocket for the hand-cuff key. Nothing like a good marital disagreement to provide distraction.

I quickly freed my hands and stood. "I think this long, sad story should come to an end, too, Pastor. Give me the gun."

Noreen looked at me, then back at her husband. "Try to clear your mind, Andrew. You give in to her, and everyone will know what you did. How you made a deal with the devil." She pointed at B.J. "That devil. The one who walked into this church nineteen years ago. *You* made a pact with *him*, not me."

I noticed B.J.'s phone clipped to his waist. I bent and retrieved it, ready to dial my favorite three numbers.

Pastor Rankin said, "Get out of here to make your call, Abby Rose," he said. "May God be with you."

But before I could even decide whether to leave or punch in the numbers immediately, Noreen Rankin came at me like a bull out of the chute.

And that's when the pastor shot his wife in the back.

25

Noreen Rankin splatted face-first, missing the glass coffee table by inches. The wound under her left shoulder blade was creating a widening round stain on her lovely, expensive suit. Keeping my eyes on Rankin, I bent and checked her pulse at the neck. Dead. I shook my head to indicate this.

"Praise God. Her spirit has left us," Rankin said, dropping the gun.

I walked over and picked it up. *Easy as breathing,* I thought. And boy, could I breathe again. But though Noreen was definitely dead, B.J. wasn't, so I put the cuffs on him before I called 9-1-1. Meanwhile, Pastor Rankin went over, knelt by his wife's body and prayed, that little high-pitched moan that had offered me a split-second diversion earlier again assaulting my ears.

I sat on the coffee table, rested a hand on the pastor's shoulder. "Why?" I said. "Why did you keep your own daughter a prisoner for nearly twenty years?"

Rankin was rocking, but he wasn't crying as I would have expected. His face was as empty as a clear sky. He used his pulpit voice and said, "Deuteronomy tells us this, Abby Rose: 'But if the thing is true, that the tokens of virginity were not found in the young woman, then they shall bring out the young woman to the door of her father's house, and the men of her city shall stone her to death with stones, because she has wrought folly in Israel by playing the harlot in her father's house; so you shall purge the evil from the midst of you.' "

"You're telling me you purged your evil daughter from your life by hiding her away, leaving her sick and alone and—"

He covered his ears, rocked faster. "No. I saved her from being stoned to death—stoned as we do so today. With sideway looks and whispers. I *saved* her, Abby Rose. It was the black boy and the baby who were evil, not Sara. They were the ones who had to be purged, who deserved to be stoned."

I nodded, understanding his ridiculous logic and feeling sick to my stomach. "Okay. I get it."

He looked at me and smiled. "I knew you would."

The man truly didn't have a clue that *he* was the evil one.

While Rankin resumed his prayers over his wife's body, I called Jeff on B.J.'s phone—and offered him another odd caller ID to wonder about, the third since the case started. "Who is this?" he said sharply.

"Me."

"Abby, where are you?"

"At the church."

"We're at this log cabin, found your car in the garage and—"

"Would you come? I need you."

"You're in trouble?" He was sounding a little panicked—unusual for Jeff. "I'll have dispatch send a squad car."

"I'm okay. Police and ambulance are already on the way. Just get here."

"DeShay," I heard him call away from the phone. "I got her on the line. Let's go."

What I liked most about this last call to him on a strange phone was that he never hung up, even when he could hear the chaos around me as police and paramedics crashed into the office. He just said he needed to keep the connection open.

Yeah. Me too, I thought.

Thirty minutes later, I was sitting in the soft chair with B.J.'s phone still pressed to one ear when a paramedic came over and started parting my hair, examining my head.

"What are you doing?" I asked.

"It's about the dried blood on your neck, ma'am. Looks like it came from a—"

"Ouch!" I cried as he fingered the spot where I'd been hit with the gun grip.

"You might need a few stitches. What happened?"

"Yeah, what happened?" came Jeff's voice over the line.

"Just a little smack on the head. Didn't even know I was bleeding until now."

"You sure you're okay?" Jeff asked.

"It's nothing," I answered.

"I'll decide for myself. We just pulled in."

When Jeff strode into the office, he tried to use that damn little cut to make me leave and get stitched up. But if Rankin was talking and making any sense at all, I wanted to hear what he had to say and I told Jeff as much.

"Okay, where's the suspect?" Jeff asked one of the patrol officers who'd responded to the 9-1-1 call.

"Library. Thought you'd want to transport him. Ms. Rose says this is your case. Couple uniforms on him, but he just keeps crying. You might consider a suicide watch when you get to the jail."

"Thanks," Jeff said. "DeShay, Abby. Let's do it."

With only starlight coming in through the stained-glass ceiling, the library seemed far less welcoming. Not that anything about this church was all that welcoming anymore.

The pastor was seated in the study area, hands cuffed behind him. He was motionless for the first time all night, staring into space, his cheeks wet with tears—which I liked a whole lot better than what I'd seen on his face after he gunned down his wife.

The two officers flanking him nodded at Jeff and DeShay.

Jeff read the pastor his Miranda rights, then said, "Are you willing to tell us everything, Pastor?"

"Yes."

"Do you want a lawyer with you?"

He shook his head no.

"Then we'll take you downtown so we can record our conversation. Again, do you understand your rights, sir?"

Rankin stared at Jeff with red-rimmed eyes. "I understand God's will, that this is His plan for me. But I want her there." He nodded at me.

I blinked in surprise.

"You got your wish," Jeff said.

The interview room at HPD was bigger than the one in Huntsville Prison, but still pretty bare-bones. Taping and videoing had been set up, the pastor waived his Miranda rights again and Jeff, the pastor and I sat around a table that I wished had been bigger. Though I wanted to be here, I didn't want to be too close to this guy.

Jeff stated for the record the date, time and who was present, then said, "Pastor, do you wish to give a statement at this time?"

"Can I begin with when I first met B.J.?" he asked. "That's what started everything."

"Begin wherever you want. But can we have full names, please?" Jeff leaned back, arms folded, a wad of gum already going.

The pastor looked at me. "B.J. is Byron James Thompson. He came to me in need many years ago, not knowing I had great trouble in my own heart that night. I believed his arrival at such a dark moment was a sign that God had sent him."

"The night he murdered Amanda Mason?" I said, unsure whether I was supposed to ask questions. Jeff said nothing, didn't shake his head or anything, so I assumed I was okay.

"That's right. Remember how you brought the light with you when you came to question us last week?"

He smiled. "I knew then you would find out. You see, I was wrong about B.J. But you? You were on a mission. God is with you, Abby Rose."

I shifted uneasily. "Okay. Back to the night B.J. showed up after he shot Amanda Mason and asked for your guidance."

"He came in off the street," Rankin said, beginning to rock.

Uh-oh. I hoped he could hold it together, stay halfway coherent.

"You didn't know him?" Jeff asked.

"He was a complete stranger. So upset, so angry with himself and seeking God's forgiveness. I was very troubled about Sara, and it seemed we had much to offer each other in the way of comfort."

"Troubled because you knew she loved Lawrence?" I asked.

"You see why I wanted you here, Abby Rose? There are things you don't understand. She *thought* she loved the black boy." His cuffs had been removed and he placed his palms on his balding head. "Noreen was so upset. Sara had called her right before B.J. wandered in off the street and told her mother that she and Lawrence were planning a life together with their baby. Said she had the black boy's car and was leaving town. Can you fathom what that phone call did to us?"

She'd told them the truth. What a huge mistake. I said, "You must have been devastated . . . desperate," pretending to sympathize to keep him talking.

"Yes. And it is in our desperation that Satan finds a way inside us. B.J.'s arrival was the answer to a prayer—or so we thought. We were wrong. I know that now. Abby Rose, you came and showed me the way."

This guy was slap-assed crazy. I might be persistent about my cases and adamant that justice be served, but I wasn't God's messenger. If you asked me, Rankin just needed an excuse to end the major guilt trip he'd been on for a couple of decades.

Jeff said, "You gave B.J. Lawrence's address, maybe told him to return to the dead girl, grab some evidence and plant it at Lawrence's house. That about right?"

"I left those details to Noreen. She is so much better at those things."

"*Was* so much better," said Jeff. "You shot her, remember?"

Rankin straightened, squared his shoulders. "At God's urging. I prayed for guidance while Noreen and B.J. spoke of death and murder in my office tonight, and His voice came to me, told me to rid my life of Satan. Cleanse my soul."

"Did God tell you to rid the world of Verna Mae Olsen? Was she part of Satan's brigade, too?" Jeff's voice was hard, his eyes cold.

"I knew nothing of that until after she was gone. Mrs. Olsen was my sister's best friend, and I would have had serious questions about their methods."

"Whose methods?" Jeff asked.

"Noreen and B.J.'s decision," said Rankin. "It was only later I learned how Mrs. Olsen had come to Noreen, said she had met our daughter's child. That foolish Olsen woman thought she needed to tell this tarnished young man the truth—tell a bastard born of sin the truth. Stupid woman. B.J. was supposed to convince Mrs. Olsen she was wrong. From what I understand, he was unable to do so, and she had to die."

Jeff leaned forward. "*From what you understand? Do you have any idea what he did to that woman?*"

Rankin shrank back in his chair. "Noreen kept the details from me. I didn't want to know, anyway. The images of death and sin might have tarnished my next sermon."

"Yeah, you wouldn't want that, would you?" Jeff leaned back again, chewing hard on his gum.

"Tell me about Sara," I said. "How did you find her after she ran away?"

"We hired detectives. We were certain that once she knew Lawrence had killed someone she would accept our plan. We could place her in a home for . . . for girls in her condition and then she would return to us afterward."

"Where and when did you find Sara?" I asked.

"If I recall, Noreen found her right after the black boy had been sent to jail."

Right after Lawrence, the first evil, had been purged, I thought.

He went on, "She was in a shelter in Dallas, living like a street person with other harlots."

"You picked her up?" asked Jeff. He kept his tone even, but a muscle in his jaw was tight with tension.

"Noreen and Olive went."

"Your sister's name is Olive Rankin?" I asked.

"Yes. Have you met her?" He smiled the smarmy smile he seemed to have reserved for me. He simply had no clue how serious this all was and probably thought God had another plan to get him out of this mess.

"Remember? I was introduced in the library," I said.

"That's right. Olive is an absolute saint. Helped Noreen take Sara to a . . . place of confinement."

"A home for unwed mothers?" I asked.

"No. Sara wouldn't agree to that. She wasn't right in the head after being touched by so much evil. She kept saying she was going to marry the black boy, and we kept telling her he was in jail, that God had protected her by sending him away. She wouldn't believe it."

"You said she wasn't right in her head. Did they take her to a psychiatric hospital?"

"No, no, no. They keep records. We chose a wilderness camp, one I'd heard about from a parishioner. With their counseling, we thought she'd have time to reflect on her mistakes."

"You sent a pregnant sixteen-year-old to *wilderness camp*? Did her counseling include prenatal care?" I asked.

Rankin looked down at the table. "Olive had to go

get her in September. That's when we learned she was sick, might be lost to us forever. Her sins had caught up to her."

"What was wrong?" Jeff asked.

"A blood pressure problem. After the bastard child was born, Noreen and I were certain we'd done the right thing, put the black boy father in the right place. It was his fault Sara became ill. And God made sure that through us, he was punished. You must understand, that after our arrangement with B.J., the help we'd given him to elude the police, we couldn't tell the truth about exactly how we lost Sara, couldn't tell anyone."

"But . . . she's alive," I said. "I saw her."

Jeff looked at me, confused. "You did?"

"At the cabin. You didn't?"

"There was the nurse's aide and a lady with a walker—looked like she had a stroke. Couldn't seem to talk. That's *her*?"

"That's Sara." I looked Rankin in the eye. "Not totally *lost*, huh, Pastor?"

He hung his head.

Instead of saying, "You make me sick," like I wanted to, I opted for, "I need some aspirin."

As I left I heard Jeff move on to questions about Noreen's death. I didn't need to relive those events right now, so I was glad to be gone.

DeShay, who'd been watching through the two-way mirror, had water and aspirin waiting when I came out. "I thought you might need this. You took a good crack to the head tonight, I hear."

"Thanks, DeShay." I gulped down the pills and water. "Now can someone take me home?"

26

Once I was sitting on my couch with Diva in my lap, I ate my way through a pint of Cherry Garcia ice cream while reflecting on all that had happened in so short a time. The truth Will and I sought when he and his family came to me for answers turned out to be far messier than we could have ever imagined. Although I wanted to say mission accomplished, I decided the word "mission" might be forever banned from my vocabulary. Besides, two innocent people were still imprisoned. Sara Rankin was in jail just like Lawrence, a prison without bars, but no less horrible.

I checked my watch. Past midnight. Will wasn't due back from camp until the day after tomorrow, and I didn't want to wake his parents. But Burl? He was a cop, used to late calls. He'd want to know what had gone down tonight, and I was too wired to sleep. I spent the first fifteen minutes of the call summarizing tonight's drama.

"Verna Mae did this to herself," Burl said when I was done. " 'Course if she went and got another kid like she tried to do, we'd never know they got the wrong guy up in Huntsville."

"I didn't know she tried to get another baby," I said.

"Neither did I until today. I've been asking questions around town since the day you and I met, trying to figure out what I missed back then. Found a woman who once worked with Jasper, and she told me he got pissed off royal because they paid some huge private adoption fee a year after the kid was left on their doorstep and Verna Mae backed out of the deal at the last minute."

"Maybe she originally took money from the Rankins so she could get another baby. Then, when she got cold feet, she fixated on Will."

"Makes sense. I sure hope Lawrence Washington will be freed."

"What do you mean? We know what happened that night. He's innocent."

"You got the preacher's confession, but you better hope Byron Thompson pulls through and tells the truth."

"We have his gun, Burl. We know the same weapon was used to kill both Amanda Mason and Verna Mae."

"Pray the gun B.J. used tonight was the *right* gun. Then your friend Jeff will have something to take to a judge. Tough to get out of jail in Texas, Abby. Even if you're as innocent as a fresh-laid egg."

"They *have* to let him out," I said. But I knew he was right. I could recall more than one case where the courts dragged their feet for nearly a year, even after DNA proved the men weren't rapists.

"That's why hard evidence, carefully collected and preserved, is so important," he said.

"You've taught me a lot about evidence on this case. Frustrated the hell out of me a few times, though. I can tell you this, when Lawrence walks out of jail, I want to give him that blanket. Think you could hand it over then?"

He laughed. "Sure."

We chatted a few more minutes about Lucinda and his boys before I hung up. I was almost tired, until I saw what I looked like after I faced the bathroom mirror. What a wake-up call. I had streaks of dried blood down my neck that had stained my collar, and my lip was still swollen from the storage unit fire. I looked like I'd been in a bar fight.

I began to carefully separate strands of hair looking for the cut, but the blood had clumped and hardened, and I was afraid to probe more for fear of making my head bleed again. This was a job for Kate. In the morning.

Jeff called me early, seven a.m. to be exact, and gave me an update. Olive had been taken into custody for questioning, and after an evaluation by a Health and Human Services caseworker, Sara had been sent to the hospital. If Olive cooperated, she might not be charged as an accessory to murder. Ironically, all three hospitalized people—Thaddeus, Sara and B.J.—were in the same place, though Jeff told me B.J. would be moved to the jail infirmary when his condition improved. If he'd confessed to anything, Jeff hadn't heard. He advised me to call Mark Whitley, a defense lawyer, as soon as Whitley's office opened. Lawrence would need counsel to help get him out of prison.

Even before Kate arrived, I'd decided I needed her assistance with more than just my head wound. I wanted her to go with me to visit Sara Rankin. When Kate arrived with salves and ointments in a little makeup bag, I put in my request. She made some calls and rearranged her schedule to make time this morning.

While my sister carefully washed blood out of my hair, I provided a more detailed, but still modified, version of what happened last night. She didn't need to know how close I'd come to getting myself killed. By the time I was finished with my summary, I discovered I liked the version I told her, the one where I was in complete control from the minute I was taken from that log cabin—playing B.J. for the fool he was.

If Kate didn't believe me, she never let on. She carefully treated the cut once she was done with shampooing and said I'd have a scar, but she didn't think I needed stitches. No problem. One more scar for my collection.

I dressed in lightweight jeans and a yellow camp

shirt, not as attractive as Kate's pale blue linen shirt and matching slacks, but comfortable. I was a little sore after the head butting and tackling I'd done last night, but surprisingly not tired.

We left for the hospital with Kate at the wheel. She had to drive, since my car was in police impound. Kate's office is in the Medical Center, and she was the better choice to find the ever-elusive parking place anyway.

We got lucky and found a space on the third floor of the hospital garage, then made our way through throngs of visitors and medical personnel and took the elevator to the neurology floor, where Sara Rankin had been admitted for evaluation. When we arrived at her doorway, a slew of white coats surrounded her bed—doctors' rounds going on, I assumed. We couldn't even see Sara, there were so many of them.

An older black woman with mottled gray hair looked down at a clipboard and said, "This patient is unusual, suffered a toxemia of pregnancy neurological event, most certainly a stroke, nearly twenty years ago. What's rare is that she may have never had an evaluation or follow-up care. From what her longtime caretaker reported to the police, the patient was in a coma for several months postdelivery, has been aphasic and was never rehabbed. We'll be transferring her to a rehabilitation facility after our evaluation is complete. Moving on, ladies and gentlemen . . ."

The woman looked up from her clipboard as the interns and residents began to file past us. "You family?" she asked.

"Um, no. But I was hired by family to find this woman." My eyes were on Sara. She wore one of those awful, hang-off-your-shoulders gowns, and though she was now thirty-five years old, she looked like a terrified child. Her walker was in a corner, far from her reach.

Sara stared at me. Her slack jaw and weakened facial muscles couldn't hide the perceptiveness I saw in those eyes.

"Oh," the doctor said. "You're the detective. A police sergeant called and told me you'd be coming. She may not be able to communicate well, but she understands everything you say. Talk to her. She could use some friends."

The woman then hustled after her pack of interns.

Kate was already at the bedside. She picked up one of Sara's hands and said, "I'm Dr. Rose, a clinical psychologist. Can my sister and I talk to you, tell you why you've been brought here?"

Sara looked at Kate with questioning eyes, then at me.

"Remember me? You saw me through the window last night. I'm Abby."

Sara nodded slowly. A yes.

Kate, still holding onto Sara's hand, dragged over a nearby chair using her foot. She sat down. "Things have happened over the years, Sara. Things you probably know nothing about. My sister knows all of it, though, and we want to tell you what she's learned. Some of what you hear may be very difficult. I'm here to support you through that. If you're not ready, let us know somehow."

She made a sound then, a combination groan-grunt, almost like she was in pain. She lifted her free hand with effort. Though her hand was limp, I knew she was pointing at me. And then came her first words, slurred but understandable. "You. Tell."

"That's why I came," I said with a smile, pulling over a plastic chair to sit next to Kate. "Do you remember Lawrence?"

Sara rolled her head left away from us, squeezed her eyes shut for a second. Then she used her hand to make an L and rested the fingers against her heart.

Unexpected tears sprung to my eyes. Kate's tears were already slipping down her cheeks.

"You know he's in prison?" I said.

She nodded.

"And that he's innocent?"

Another nod, stronger this time.

"We'll get him out. We have proof now, but it may take time," I said.

She closed her eyes, hit her finger-made L against her chest several times.

"There's more," I said. "Do you remember your baby?"

She looked at me again. It was Sara's turn for tears now. As they ran down her thin, tired face, she worked hard to speak and finally said, "Dead."

"No," I replied, way too loud for hospital pros to like. "He's *not* dead."

She stared at me, eyes wide, while Kate grabbed a tissue and wiped Sara's cheeks.

"He's not. He wants to meet you," I said.

Sara began to shake her head, and Kate clutched her hand tighter, saying, "It's true. It's real."

Sara struggled again to speak, each word, it seemed, like climbing a mountain. "Look . . . at . . . me."

Kate said, "Are you saying you don't want him to see you like this?"

Sara nodded.

"He's a special young man," I said. "And he's the reason we found you. I promise, he wouldn't care if your head was screwed on backwards."

One side of Sara's mouth turned up in a smile. This time she answered by making a fist, and with effort turned her thumb to the ceiling.

Kate had already advised me not to mention Noreen's death or Pastor Rankin's arrest, so we were grateful when an aide interrupted us to take Sara for a CAT scan. We told her we would be back and left.

Next stop was Thaddeus, and I was relieved to find him in far better shape than when I'd last seen him.

He was sitting in his wheelchair by the window, the roses I'd sent on the bedside stand. "Going home soon, Abby," he said. "Few more stable days is all I need. But you got my heart racing bringing in a woman as good-looking as your friend here."

"Thaddeus Washington, my sister, Kate Rose," I said.

"Figures you two would be related," he said with a smile.

Kate went over and shook his hand. "I've heard wonderful things about you, Mr. Washington."

"Everybody calls me Thaddeus." He looked at me, his expression now serious. "Lawrence ever gonna speak to me again, Abby?"

"How about on the outside? I'm hoping we have what we need to set him free," I said with a grin.

"Did I hear right?" came a voice from the door. It was Joelle, carrying a big bottle of Evian and a box of sugar-free chocolate-chip cookies.

"You heard right," I answered. "I'm meeting with a defense lawyer when I leave here. He'll get things rolling. The sooner we're on this, the sooner he'll be out."

After I introduced Kate and Joelle, Thaddeus said, "Was it something Lawrence told you that helped him?"

"He told me about Will's mother and headed me in the right direction." I didn't want to be too specific. Thaddeus may act strong, but I'd learned my lesson about stress and his blood sugar fluctuations.

"About time that son of mine came to his senses," Thaddeus said.

"Joelle helped, too," I said, looking at her. "One of those wrongs Frank worried so much about will soon be righted."

She placed the cookies and water on Thaddeus's bed, walked over and wrapped her arms around me. "Thank you, Abby. Thank you so much."

We visited a little longer, and after we left the hospital, Kate drove me to police impound to pick up my car. She had afternoon patients to see, so we said good-bye and I headed for Mark Whitley's law office on Houston's southwest side. Mark had helped me on another case a few months ago, but this was far more complicated.

Defense attorneys as successful as Mark make big bucks, and he'd poured plenty of that money into his office, a stand-alone redbrick building off the Southwest Freeway. I noticed his Porsche parked in his marked spot, and when he came out to greet me, he could have been walking on some fashion runway in Paris.

"Nice," I said, nodding appreciatively at his navy suit with wide lapels and pinstripes.

He smiled. "Like it? Neil Barrett."

"I should have known," I said, pretending I knew who Neil Barrett was. Dark-haired, young and very good-looking, Mark seemed to have it all, including brains.

Once we were settled in his office, me with my Diet Coke and Mark with his Perrier, I spent the next half hour explaining the case and how I needed his help getting Lawrence Washington out of jail ASAP.

Mark leaned back in his black leather chair. "Last time all I had to do was intimidate a small-town police force for you, but this, Abby? Texans take their guilty convictions very seriously."

"But he's innocent," I said.

"You think that matters?" he said, eyebrows raised.

"Wait a minute. We have evidence and—"

"I'm not saying I can't get him out. I will. But we're talking three months at the least. More likely a year."

"He has to stay there a *year*? I don't get it. Can we try for a pardon from the governor or—"

"Innocence pardons are considered only on unanimous recommendation of an applicant's three trial officials—the sentencing judge, the district attorney and the police involved in the arrest. Then we'll need unanimous agreement from the Board of Pardon and Paroles. Can you see there might be a lengthy delay?"

I sighed and leaned back against the cushioned client chair. Damn. After my last meeting with Lawrence, I was pretty sure he'd be thrilled to know Sara was alive, happy to know I'd told the truth about his son. But he'd never let them inside that prison to visit. He wouldn't want them to see him in that place.

I looked at Mark. "Is there anything you can do to

speed this up? Because the one surviving arresting officer, Randall Dugan, will never cooperate. You'll have a major barrier right off the bat."

"I don't know, Abby. This will require some intense effort starting the minute you walk out the door. I got some favors out there, a couple D.A.'s who might listen. Maybe I can work a miracle, get him out in less than three months."

"Do whatever you have to. Spare no expense. This is on my personal tab, not my client's," I said.

"We'll talk money another day," he said.

A few minutes later, I was back in the Camry. Funny how I'd never paid much attention to how long it had taken innocent men to get out of Huntsville after the Houston crime lab debacle in 2004. But it was all very real now. On my way home, I was feeling down and trying to hide it when I called Will's house and his mother answered.

"This is Abby," I said.

"Abby. How are you?"

"Pretty good," I said.

"Any news?"

"Big news. I've found Will's mother and his father. I don't know how to get in touch with Will, though."

"He'll be home the day after tomorrow—but this is *wonderful*. You found them in less than two weeks. What about the poor lady who died? Was her murder connected to your search for Will's birth parents?"

"I'm afraid so."

"Is that why you don't sound very happy?" she asked.

"Things are just . . . complicated. Let me begin at the beginning."

Again I had to tell a long story, which only reinforced what Mark had made clear. The happy ending might not be so happy after all. A year or more could pass before Lawrence walked out of Huntsville Prison to see his son, his father and the woman who, even though he thought she was dead, he had protected for nineteen years.

27

Jeff came home close to eight that evening, tired but in a great mood. Wish mine could have matched. He'd brought French dip sandwiches and herb pasta salad from La Madeleine, and we ate at the counter. Despite the great food, I was still glum when I told him about my visit with Mark.

"I needed Mark's reality check about as much as Aunt Caroline needs a face-lift," I said.

"Yeah, I've talked to Mark today," Jeff said. "He wanted to know exactly how much evidence HPD has to exonerate Lawrence. He's on this. He'll get it done."

"In about a year. But no use whining," I said. "Guess we both did our jobs. I only wish they'd hand me a key to his cell and I could let him out myself."

"You should be proud. I know I'm proud of you," Jeff said.

"I couldn't have done it without your help. Daddy always said success is the result of backbone, not wishbone, and you're the one with the backbone."

"You're the strongest woman I've ever met, Abby. Now put away the wishbone for Lawrence. You've done all you can." He took out a fresh pack of Big Red and stared at it for a second. "We got any beer? I could use one while I tell you what Olive had to say."

"Sure. I'm well stocked with staples. Beer, wine, Diet Coke and frozen pizza."

He smiled and returned the gum to his pocket.

I grabbed a couple Shiner Bocks from the fridge, saying, "I nearly forgot about Olive. I'm anxious to hear that lady's excuse for keeping Sara a virtual prisoner."

We went to the living room—or as I like to call it, the loving room—and sat on either end of the couch. Jeff took off his shoes and we faced each other, assuming our favorite position, legs outstretched and intertwined.

"Olive is actually a nice lady," he said. "Clueless, but nice. I'm guessing her IQ hovers around 80 to 85. She and Verna Mae went back a long time, and she knew her friend wanted a baby."

"I figured that's how Will ended up where he did."

"What you don't know is that Verna Mae visited Sara Rankin every week. Those scrapbooks, pictures and news stories about his athletic accomplishments? She took them with her, told Sara that Will was her own child." Jeff took a pull on his longneck.

"You're kidding me. Sara was told stories about her own baby thinking he belonged to Verna Mae? That's crazy, Jeff."

"Are you really surprised?"

"I guess not. But it seems so cruel."

"It might explain why, after meeting Will in the flesh and knowing Sara as well as she did, she decided to set things straight. She had no idea those wonderful people who had been filling her bank account for years would turn on her after she told them she'd been collecting information about Will and sharing it with their invalid daughter."

"No wonder B.J. was on a search-and-destroy mission when Verna Mae wouldn't tell him where she'd saved all the Will mementos," I said.

"He tried to beat information out of her. Guess she was just as tough as she was crazy. Too bad."

"Has Olive cared for Sara all these years?" I asked.

"Yes. She told us the Rankins had her take some

quickie nurse's aide course after they brought a very sick, very pregnant Sara home from the wilderness camp. Olive took care of her, even delivered Will."

"No way," I said. "Guess the Rankins thought everything would be okay, that Sara would return from her fake mission trip after she'd recovered from delivery and they could brainwash her into thinking Lawrence was a killer. Everything would be back to normal. She must not have told her parents she was Lawrence's alibi."

"Probably not. According to Olive, Sara had the stroke right after delivery, went into a coma and couldn't even speak when she finally woke up—all this without a doctor ever setting foot in that cabin."

"She knows Lawrence is in prison, though. How'd she find out?" I asked.

"She can talk?"

"A little. She's not brain-dead, Jeff."

He nodded and drank more beer. "Olive told us that Verna Mae told Sara about Lawrence's arrest and conviction. It wasn't like Sara could run to a judge and offer the alibi Lawrence needed—not in her condition."

"Rankin and B.J. better get everything they deserve and more," I said, anger firing my face. "B.J. *will* live to meet a tough judge, right?"

"Oh, yeah. He lost a lot of blood, but he's fine. I expect he'll join your ex on death row within the year. Maybe Rankin will, too, though his attorney will probably claim he was protecting you when he shot his wife. I think they'll leave out the 'ridding the earth of Satan' defense. No insanity option there, thank you. He knew right from wrong."

I finished my beer, thinking about the reunion I was planning, probably in Sara's room at the hospital. Will wanted to meet the woman who'd given him life, meet Thaddeus, but it would be a little hollow without Lawrence there.

Jeff set his empty bottle on the floor and took off his already loosened tie. "You ready to call it a night?"

I checked my watch. "It's early."

"Yeah. I know." He grinned.

Two days later, I picked up Will so we could head to the hospital for the much-anticipated reunion with the family he'd hired me to find. He wore a T-shirt imprinted with the words UT BASKETBALL and had on a pair of pressed jeans. I swear he'd grown another inch since the last time I saw him. He and I had talked yesterday, but his mother had pretty much filled him in on all that had happened.

When he ducked into the passenger seat, he immediately moved the seat back all the way to fit his legs under the dash. It was still a tight squeeze.

"Where are your parents?" I asked. "I thought they were coming, too."

"Mom and Dad want to wait. They say I need to meet Sara and Mr. Washington by myself first. They do want to have them over to the house, if Sara—is 'Sara' what I should call her?"

"I think Sara is perfect."

"Anyway, when Sara and Mr. Washington are both well enough, Mom wants to have a party."

I smiled. "You have great parents, Will, but having known you even for such a short time, I wouldn't expect anything less."

"I don't know what will go down today, Abby. I just know I'm lucky. One day, I'll have enough money to make sure Sara gets all the help she needs. My grandfather, too."

"You already have money, remember?" I said, turning the key in the ignition.

"I don't know. That money Mrs. Olsen left me in her will creeps me out. It came from . . . I don't know. What's a good word?"

"Evil?"

"Yeah. That's it."

I pulled out of the Knight driveway. "The Rankins seemed to have turned good into evil, so the reverse should work, right?"

"Okay. You got any ideas?"

"Indeed I do," I replied with a smile as we pulled away. "I know some folks who could sure use handicapped-equipped transportation."

Kate had spent several hours with Sara yesterday, preparing her for this reunion. When Will and I walked into Thaddeus's room, she was there with both him and Sara, who were side-by-side in wheelchairs. I had no idea psychotherapy extended to makeup and clothes, but Sara looked even more like the picture from so long ago. Her hair was curled and hung softly to her shoulders and she wore a peach cotton sweater, tank and pants. Even her athletic shoes were new.

Kate and Thaddeus had been talking, but went silent the minute we appeared. Sara's blue eyes were all over Will. I didn't think she even knew I was there—as it should be. It was the most emotion-filled silence I'd ever experienced aside from when they'd lowered my daddy into the ground.

Kate was holding Sara's hand but let go. Sara slowly raised her arm to Will and said, "You. You."

He slid past me, knelt and took his mother's face in his huge hands. "Yes. It's me." Then he planted a kiss on her forehead.

Tears slid down her cheeks, Kate's makeup job disintegrating. But it didn't matter.

Then Will turned to Thaddeus and extended his hand. "Pleased to meet you, sir."

Thaddeus shared one of his wonderful smiles, and they shook hands. "See you been raised proper. But 'sir' don't do for today. 'Sir' is for when you're in trouble. It's Thaddeus, and maybe soon you'll try out 'Granddad.' "

" 'Granddad' works for me."

Kate came over to me as Will gripped Sara's shoulder and held onto Thaddeus's hand.

"I think they have a lot to catch up on. Want to get some coffee?" I asked.

"Coffee never sounded so good. Let's go," she said.

But when we turned, I cracked a smile so big I was thinking the San Andreas Fault might just have a rival.

Jeff stood in the door. We were blocking Thaddeus and Sara's view, and besides, they were busy, so they were unaware that Lawrence was with Jeff. He was holding the blanket.

Lawrence, who had waited far too long for anything good to happen, pushed past me, but stopped in the center of the room. "Sara," he whispered. "God, it's true."

She looked up, blinked and then both her arms came up, even though she had to lift her bad arm with her good hand. She gave the biggest lopsided smile she could manage, let go of her useless left arm and made her finger L. She thumped it against her heart.

He strode to the wheelchair, put the blanket around her shoulders and kissed her lips. Then he rested his forehead against hers for a long moment.

A smiling Will was holding Thaddeus's hand, towering above all of them.

Lawrence pulled back and looked into Sara's clear, blue eyes. "We'll get you better. I promise." He rose and stared at the young man whose features so resembled his.

Will extended his hand. "I don't think we've met. I'm Will."

I was grinning like a jackass eating cockleburs as Jeff, Kate and I retreated to the coffee shop. We were soon sitting at a small table sipping on brew so strong you could chew it.

"Now this is a cop's drink," Jeff said.

My coffee turnoff might just resurface. The stuff tasted like motor oil. "How'd you get Lawrence here?" I asked.

"We took I-45 south to—"

"Shut up," I said while Kate laughed. "How?"

"Mark's coup. He filed habeas corpus on Will's behalf yesterday and—"

"I'm not up on my legalese," I said. "What's habeas corpus?"

"Basically habeas corpus is an appeal when all appeals have been exhausted, as in Lawrence's case," Jeff said. "It's a filing for a court order to bring him before the judge to determine whether his imprisonment is illegal, the only way to get our new evidence presented and free Lawrence for good."

"Ah. Go on," I said.

"Anyway, Mark presented all we had and asked for an immediate hearing. Usually the D.A. asks for time—time that almost always turns into months—but Mark pulled the right assistant D.A., which might not have been a coincidence. She waived her right for time to prepare, basically threw in the towel. She told the judge it was in the interest of justice that Lawrence be released, and the judge agreed. End of story."

"So he *is* free for good?" Kate asked.

Jeff nodded. "Mark may also file for a full pardon based on innocence. Since the prosecutors traded two bad guys for Lawrence, I don't see anyone having a problem with that. A full pardon, however, *will* take a long time."

I rested my hands on my chin, stared into Jeff's eyes. "This is great. Thanks for picking up Lawrence."

He tucked a stray hair behind my ear. "For you? Anything."

Kate stood. "I'm going back upstairs. You two? Get a room, okay?" She left us alone.

Jeff grinned, and I think I probably was blushing.

I said, "How'd you get the blanket?"

"Burl overnighted it. He knows this case is finally closed."

"Do me one more favor," I said. "Call upstairs and tell Lawrence and Will we won't leave them without a ride, but we'll be gone for about thirty minutes."

Jeff raised his eyebrows. "Where are we going? Someplace kinky, like a janitor's closet or a deserted X-ray room?"

I took his hand as we stood. "No. We're going to get a decent cup of coffee."

Read on for a preview of Leann Sweeney's
next Yellow Rose Mystery

REALITY CHECK

Coming from Signet in December 2006

My daddy always used to tell me the biggest trouble-maker I'd ever meet watches me brush my teeth in the mirror every day. If the people I'd let into my house that hot September morning had an ounce of Daddy's insight, they might not have come calling.

"Don't turn on that camera." Those were my first words once I opened my front door. I delivered the sentence calmly, smiling like a politician in a runoff. But I wasn't saying please, and I was as serious as a snakebite.

I'd seen them through the peephole—the young woman with her three-ring binder and designer sunglasses, the man with the big video camera—and knew better than to ignore them. These were media people, types you better be facing 'cause you sure as hell don't want them behind you.

After my admonition about the camera, the silence that followed seemed to last longer than a week of rain, but finally the petite young woman turned to her older, balding companion. "We'll wait on any footage, Stu."

I searched beyond them, looking for their TV news van, but they must have arrived in the dark Cadillac parked at the curb. "Mind if I ask who you are and why you are here?"

"Shelly was supposed to call," the woman said. "Guess that didn't happen. Can we talk inside? It's, like, *so* hot already."

Since ninety-degree mornings in Houston this time of year were the norm and I heard no familiar twang in her voice, I suspected they weren't locals. "Not before you tell me who you are."

She whipped out a business card and shoved it in my hand. "Chelsea Burch. Venture Productions. And this is Stu." She turned to him. He still had the video camera balanced on his shoulder. "Stu . . . what *is* your last name?"

"Crowell," he said gruffly.

She removed her sunglasses and arched her penciled brows. "Like Simon Crowell from *American Idol*? Are you kidding me?"

"Crowell, not *Cowell*," Stu said.

"Oh." She turned back to me, apparently unbothered by not knowing Stu's last name, something that obviously had pissed him off. "Anyway, we know who you are—Abby Rose. We've seen pictures and read your bio. We're beginning production here in Houston for a *Reality Check* episode. You've heard of it, right? I'm a producer for Erwin Mayo. He'd like to involve you."

Involve me? I didn't like the sound of that, and neither did my gut. I felt like I'd swallowed a tennis ball. The address on the card bore a Burbank, California, address—meaning Hollywood had come calling. If they had my so-called bio, their arrival could have something to do with what happened more than a year ago—the well-publicized murder investigation that changed my life forever and sent me fleeing my late daddy's mansion to a very downsized, wonderful life as a PI. I sure as heck needed to find out what this was all about—and quickly.

But before I even had a chance to speak, Chelsea said, "Listen, Abby, if you won't let us in, could I please have a paper towel before this sweat dripping down my face ruins my makeup?"

I widened the door. Wouldn't want Chelsea Burch melting like a theatrical witch. "Do me a favor and keep your finger off that 'record' button, Stu," I warned.

He nodded his agreement—air-conditioning is a powerful weapon—and I led them past my office, where I'd been finishing up the paperwork on my last case.

"This is cute," Chelsea said, glancing around my living room.

My living room is far from cute. Messy, eclectic, and coated with cat hair, maybe. Not *cute*. The vanilla candle burning on the table by the sofa used to be cute, but was now just a smoldering puddle of wax. It smelled good, though.

Chelsea moved this morning's *Houston Chronicle* and sat down on the sofa. Her blond hair had gone limp from the humidity and hung around her face in thick product-laden chunks. She wore an embroidered peasant shirt with long sleeves, and denim stretch jeans—not exactly the best wardrobe choice for this time of year. Then I noticed the cowboy boots—baby blue and powder pink.

"You like?" She smiled and held up one foot. "Boots are so hot right now."

"Literally," I said under my breath. Around Houston when it's this warm, you usually only see girls wearing boots in western dance clubs in the evening—and those would be real boots, boots that do *not* look like they were first worn by some gaunt runway model at a Paris fashion show.

Stu had set the camera on the wood floor, but he was perspiring like a polar bear on the equator, so I offered him water.

"Oh, me too," Chelsea said. "What brand do you have?"

"T-A-P," I spelled.

"Funny," she said. "No bottled?"

"I have Dr Pepper in a bottle, Diet Coke and water from the fridge door. Iced tea only comes with our afternoon special. I think it's cowpoke beans and collards today—all served cold. Very cold."

"Just water, *thanks*." Bitchy edge in her voice. Perhaps my Hollywood producer wasn't getting the star treatment she thought she deserved?

I caught Stu's eye-roll as I left to get them both glasses of water. He had her number, too.

This trip to the kitchen gave me time to wrack my brain regarding their program, *Reality Check*. I had heard of it and didn't think I was candidate for what they were producing. I held glasses under the ice-maker as I recalled how the show did home makeovers and cosmetic surgeries, gave scholarships, sent people on luxury vacations. I could hear the commercial's voice-over in my head: Reality Check—the life-style makeover show. Turning American dreams into the real thing.

What the hell did a show like that want with me?

When I returned and handed over their glasses, Stu was sitting cross-legged on the Oriental rug with my cat, Diva, in his lap.

Chelsea had apparently rediscovered her "California Dreamin'" attitude, because her tone was pleasant when she said, "Our research assistant caught on to you through the local media, Abby. She said you arranged this wonderful reunion for a college athlete. He was adopted and you located his birth family, right?"

"That's correct," I answered, taking one of the armchairs. Damn *Good Day Houston*. That's how these people had found me. One of my recent clients, a superstar NBA player in the making, had appeared on the program and, though I had warned him not to mention my name, the Katy Couric wannabe host had tricked him into blurting it out anyway.

Since then, I'd been swamped with calls from folks hoping I could help them with their adoption issues, too. This had forced me to create two flyers: "Tips for Finding the Child You've Given Up" and "So You Want to Find Your Birth Parents? The Beginning Steps." I was stuffing envelopes an hour a day now. Most people with a little computer savvy can locate who they're looking for without a private eye's assistance, and this seemed the best way to let them in on those secrets.

"Anyway, Abby, we'd like you to sign on as a consultant for our program," Chelsea said. "Since we work somewhat like a documentary, I was hoping we could video our interview today—we will edit extensively, so don't worry about running on and on, or—"

"You won't be taping anything," I cut in. "Especially since you've told me next to nothing. What does my job as a private investigator have to do with consulting on a TV show?"

"In the story we're currently producing, plenty. Wait until you meet our makeover candidate and her family. In fact, let me show you." She opened her binder and slipped two photos from a plastic sleeve.

I took them from her. One was a Wal-Mart Special eight-by-ten, the colors faded to blurry siennas and dull pinks. A teenaged girl stood in the center of three younger children. The other was a four-by-six glossy snapshot of the teenager, but in this newer photo she was a dark-haired, hazel-eyed woman in her twenties with flawless nutmeg-colored skin and an expression that puzzled me. Fear? Anger? Sadness? Maybe all three.

Chelsea pointed to the snapshot. "You're looking at a real heroine. She's been raising her brothers and sister since she was sixteen. Isn't she just Penelope Cruz all over again? The camera eats her up."

Stu said, "The family's nice . . . really nice people, deserving bunch of kids."

I looked at him. Here was someone I could relate to—sun weathered skin, laugh lines everywhere and brown eyes that could tell you the truth without accompanying words. Plus the man had been sensible enough to wear shorts and sandals, set his empty water glass on a coaster—unlike his companion—and pet my cat.

"Okay," I said. "Tell me more."

"Anyway, just so you know how it works," Chelsea

said, "*Reality Check* receives referrals for the life makeovers we do on air—thousands and thousands of referrals, by the way—mostly via our Web site. This particular one, however, came in through the mail. Unusual, but what a *riveting* story. That's why we're in Texas now. We have been fortunate to get our hands on a fantastic, heartwarming tale of courage and perseverance. You won't believe all that has happened to Emma in her short life."

"So why do you need me?" I asked.

"Problems, that's why. We had everything set to go, then we mentioned the baby to Emma and whammo! She's backing off all of a sudden. We can't have that. Not now."

"Wait. Baby? Emma? You've lost me."

"This is Emma Lopez, our makeover girl." Chelsea tapped the snapshot with a cherry-colored nail. "Put herself through college and is doing the same for her younger brother, Scott. Anyway, their house, the only thing they own, is set for demolition by the city. They will get money to rebuild, but not nearly enough, and since all the kids are getting to be college age—"

I held up a hand. Jeez. This one could talk the ears off a ceramic elephant. "You're still not telling me what this has to do with adoption. I investigate adoption cases."

Chelsea raised her pointy chin. "Don't you think I know? Anyway, the referral letter? That's how we knew about the missing baby."

"Missing baby? Missing how?"

"We have no clue. That's where you come in."

"You have no clue? What does Emma say?" I asked.

Chelsea gestured as though she was giving a speech, hands palms out to me. "There's the problemo, Abby. She clammed up when we mentioned the missing child."

Stu looked at me. "I told Chelsea that Emma must not have realized we had info about the other kid.

Emma was taken off guard when we mentioned her and might want out."

Chelsea flashed an angry glance at Stu. "She's not getting out of anything. Ever hear of a thing called a contract?" She paused, took a deep breath, then smiled at me. "Production delays. So frustrating. Anyway, Emma will have America in tears. She is *amazing*. *Reality Check* wants to pay her back for all the suffering she's endured in her short life. We plan to make magic for Emma and her family, Abby. Magic for the world to see. That's what we do. That's who we are." Broader smile, tooth veneers really gleaming now.

I looked to Stu, who seemed far more capable of a straight answer than California Girl—and with all respect to the Beach Boys, I'm damn grateful they aren't all California Girls. "Let me get this right. You're telling me Emma had a baby and this child was given up for adoption?"

Stu waved his hands in denial. "No, no, no. She—"

"A sister. That's who we think was given up," Chelsea cut in. "By the way, the kid wouldn't be a baby anymore. She'd be fourteen."

"Okay. You've got me as confused as Jennifer Lopez's ring finger. Could we start over, maybe in chronological order?"

Chelsea laughed—an unattractive snorting laugh that gave me this perverse sense of satisfaction.

"You are so cute, Abby," she said. "Everyone on the set will fall in love with you and that great Texas accent. I do so hope you'll let us get you on tape."

Stu cleared his throat. "From what we were told in the referral letter, Emma's mother had another child."

Thank goodness someone had taken his Ritalin today and knew how to stay on track. "What about Emma's mother? Where's she?" I looked back and forth between them.

"She disappeared in 1997," Chelsea said. "As I said, Emma has been raising this family and has been doing the most fantastic—"

"Ah. *Two* missing people. Did the mother take the baby with her?"

"No," Chelsea said. "According to the letter, the child disappeared the day after she was born—in 1992. Our research people think the mother sold her or gave her up or who knows what. But they hit a roadblock. Did you know Texas just won't let you look at anything that has to do with adoption or foster care? I mean, like, *nothing*. That's where you come in. You know the ropes here." She giggled. "Hey, Stu. Ropes? Texas? Get it?"

He offered a tight smile.

Meanwhile, I sat back and took a deep breath, considering all this. I had to admit I was interested. But the thought of working with Chelsea Burch and her TV crew was about as appealing as sticking my hand in a bucket of leeches. Hell, I *would* be sticking my hand in a bucket of leeches.

"I don't think I can help you, Chelsea," I said.

"But I need you."

"Yeah. I know you do."

Chelsea stared at me, her contact-blue eyes practically spitting anger. "So you're refusing to help me?"

"That's right."

She snatched up her notebook and shoved the pictures inside. Stu stroked Diva one last time and picked up his camera.

"Come on, Stu," Chelsea said, marching past me. "I knew Mayo's idea was a stupid one."

"Where are you going?" I asked.

"Out the way we came in," she said over her shoulder.

"Too bad. Because I need more information," I said.

She turned, her skinny little jaw slack. She stared at me in confusion for a second. "But . . . I thought—"

"I won't help *you*, but I sure as hell want to meet Emma. What happens after that is in her hands."